W9-AGV-635

0 00 30 0352032 1

MAIN

Better Homes

– AND –

Husbands

Better Homes
– AND –
Husbands

Valerie Ann Leff

St. Martin's Press New York

This is a work of fiction. Names, characters, businesses, organizations, places, events, and incidents are either the product of the author's imagination or are used fictitiously.

www.stmartins.com

Portions of this novel have appeared in *The Antioch Review, Chelsea, Green Hills Literary Lantern, Lilith, Northeast Corridor, Other Voices* and *The South Carolina Review.*

Library of Congress Cataloging-in-Publication Data

Leff, Valerie Ann.
    Better homes and husbands / by Valerie Ann Leff.—1st ed.
        p. cm.
    ISBN 0-312-33061-8
    EAN 978-0312-33061-3
    1. Upper East Side (New York, N.Y.)—Fiction. 2. Park Avenue (New York, N.Y.)—Fiction. 3. Discrimination in housing—Fiction. 4. Apartment houses—Fiction. 5. Jewish families—Fiction. 6. Social classes—Fiction. 7. Celebrities—Fiction. 8. Rich people—Fiction. I. Title.

    PS3612.E3494B47 2004
    813'.6—dc22

                                                                    2004040558

First Edition: June 2004

10 9 8 7 6 5 4 3 2 1

F
LEF

AER-1975

To Bar and Par, who raised me in a home where books mattered. To Virginia Redfield, without whom this book would never have been finished. To Joey, Anna, and Eduardo, without whom this book would have been finished five years sooner—but I would have missed so much else.

CONTENTS

ACKNOWLEDGMENTS

I am one of those writers who attended workshops—lots of them. I am grateful to my teachers: Roberta Allen, Rachelle Benveniste, Alice Elliot Dark, Carol Dixon, Connie Josefs, Joan Logghe, Carole Maso, Regina McBride, Reginald Mc-Knight, Rebecca McClanahan, Peggy Millin, Francine Prose, Pat Schneider, Lisa Shea, Carla Stevens and Jessica Treat. I am grateful to my fellow workshop participants, to all of the women who have sat with me in writing circles and to my own students. Passages of this book were first drafted in the company of these dear writer-friends: Anne Marie Cunningham, my sister, Laurie Holz, Lori Horvitz, Bobbe Needham, Linda Solomon and Dorothy Yang. Thanks to the Chenango Valley Writers' Conference for fellowship support.

I live surrounded by a network of family, friends, extended family and friends-of-family, too many to name. Thanks to all of you for your encouragement and love.

There are two writers who have been generous with me beyond reason: Tommy Hays and Virginia Redfield. Tommy, thank you for your insight and guidance, for answers to all my dumb questions, for your wise stewardship of the Great Smokies Writing Program. Virginia, you are the midwife and godmother of this book. Thank you for all those Friday afternoons in your sunny living room, while we discussed Henry James and Carol Shields, Quakers and Nazarenes, homes, husbands, hyphens and semicolons.

I want to thank the editors of the magazines and literary journals, who pulled my manuscripts out of the slush piles and first published my work. Thanks especially to Robert Fogarty of *The Antioch Review,* who offered good advice right when I needed it.

Finally, I am grateful to my agent, Bill Contardi, and my editor, Diane Reverand, who have been kind, insightful, funny and smart. Thanks also to St. Martin's editorial assistant, Regina Scarpa. Every step in the production of this book has been a pleasure.

Better Homes

– AND –

Husbands

The Building

On the Upper East Side of Manhattan, the building is limestone and red brick, a heavy front door of black iron tracery, a gray canvas canopy with its white-lettered address, *Nine-eighty Park Avenue*. Here, wealthy New Yorkers occupy grand apartments with their children, cooks and maids. A super lives in the basement, managing doormen, handymen. Throughout the year, drivers in long shiny cars wait by the curb. Nannies push strollers to Central Park, and delivery boys bring groceries around to the service entrance. There are dinner parties, guests, cocktails. Greetings exchanged in the lobby, gossip whispered in the back elevator.

Over time, the building changes. Children grow up, go off to prep school, college. Or they flee, disappointing their parents. Residents die or sometimes move away. An apartment is vacant, and new families up the ante on multimillion-dollar bids and apply to the co-op board. Many are turned down. Families in the building interact—or they don't. Over time, they watch one another, perceive and misperceive, play out feuds of class and caste with ferocious etiquette. There are quiet revolutions, and the inhabitants of the building adjust—some gladly, some with dismay.

In 980 Park Avenue, during the last three decades of the twentieth century, stories have layered the walls of high-ceilinged apartments like coats of plaster, wallpaper, paint; voices linger like the scent of spices in the kitchen cabinets. A suicide, a strike, a seventeen-year-old girl pregnant. A scandalous arrest in the late 1980s. A lawsuit barely averted by the co-op board. No one knows the whole history, and the truth is understood in pieces by one resident or another, by a daughter, a friend of the family, by a doorman. The truth is told in stories, in voices tinged with opinion, envy, regret. The truth is kept in the building, never completely revealed.

The building is brick, mortar, limestone, lath and plaster. Plumbing and wires run through it. The building is also stories and lives, concurrent and overlapping. On the Upper East Side of Manhattan, the building, 980 Park Avenue, holds these stories within its walls, silent, like a book. . . .

Claudia Bloom: Trader Vic's

— 1970 —

There used to be a hallway in the Plaza that led to Trader Vic's. You walked past creamy white doors with gilded moldings, crystal wall sconces, and turned right, down a flight of red-and-gold-carpeted stairs. Then, suddenly, you found yourself in Polynesia. The carpet became green, a giant canoe hung from the ceiling and the walls were draped with fishing nets. Green, blue and rose-colored lights illuminated starfish and oars. Two tiki statues—blocky, life-size, carved wooden men, dark brown and gleaming—stood guard on either side of the stairway landing. The sound of soft waves and South Seas melodies filled the air.

On a dare, in full view of the coat-check lady, my best friend, Madeline Sapphire, bit the left-hand tiki statue on his chunky rectangular penis. I screeched, "Penicopter!" We held hands and ran, giggling all the way to the maître d's podium. Madeline's parents, Dick and Lauren Sapphire, were waiting for us, together with her little brother, Ritchie. I patted Ritchie on the head and said hello. We didn't mind Ritchie as much as two eight-year-old girls might disdain a younger boy. After all, he had invented the word "penicopter" the summer before at Westhampton Beach. We even gave him Batman's part whenever we played Catwoman, though he usually tired pretty quickly of being tied up.

My mother had followed us into Trader Vic's, and when she caught up with us, she reprimanded us as severely as she could while keeping a straight face. "Claudia! Madeline!" She pulled us aside and, leaning one hand on a large tribal drum, whispered that she could not imagine where this obsession with penises had come from. We solemnly told her that we didn't know. "Well, I don't know, either!" my mother said. For the past four years, since my father died, she had been desperately trying to find a new husband. Maybe that had something to do with the penis thing?

At the big round table, Dick Sapphire sat between my mother and Lauren. We children filled in the other side of the circle. Dick immediately ordered drinks and some appetizers. Within minutes, a small hibachi was lit, and platters of butterfly shrimp and cho-cho beef sticks were slammed down onto our lazy Susan. Madeline, Ritchie and I roasted cho-cho sticks over the blue flames, then dunked them—sizzling and sputtering—into glasses of ice water. We stuck them back in the fire, and they steamed. We nibbled on barbecued beef and sucked the crystal-rock-sugar swizzle sticks that came in the grown-ups' drinks. When we finished our appetizers—the only part of the meal we liked, since the main courses were always gooey, mixed-up messes of unrecognizable meats and strange vegetables—Madeline and I left the table. We ran out past the drums to the powder room, which was not Polynesian but regular Plaza pink-and-green floral, with pink liquid soap. The return from the powder room gave Madeline a crack at the other tiki statue. Just as she bit it, an older couple arrived at the bottom of the stairs from the lobby above. The wife, in a silver fox stole, glared at us, and we fled back into the restaurant, nearly tripping a Chinese busboy who held a huge tray of dirty dishes. Though our families came to Trader Vic's nearly every Sunday night, no one who worked there ever smiled at us.

Since there were six of us, Dick Sapphire had the doorman whistle for a Checker cab, then handed him a tip and sat up front. Madeline and I grabbed the two folding jump seats, sticking Ritchie in the backseat with our mothers. We rode to Madison and Eighty-seventh Street, where my mother and I got out. The others would cross over and head downtown to the Sapphires' duplex at Park and Eighty-third.

The Sapphires were richer than we were, and their apartment was fancier than ours. Their lobby had heavy scrolled ironwork doors, burgundy leather chairs trimmed with brass nail heads and a marble fireplace with an electric log. They had a doorman and an elevator man who knew how to land exactly level at their floor, without adjusting the car up or down. The duplex was enormous, with high ceilings and an

Oriental-carpeted staircase. Madeline and I would have loved to bump down the steps on our bottoms or slide on the thick mahogany banister, except we were never allowed to.

Once I asked my mother how much money the Sapphires had, and she said, "Oh, millions."

"Well, how much do you have?"

"About half a million."

"And me?"

"Your trust is worth a little over two hundred and fifty thousand."

"What about Millie?" Millie was my nurse.

"She probably doesn't have as much."

"Like around one hundred thousand?"

"Something like that."

Millie lived in the third bedroom of our apartment, and on her days off she stayed with her sister in the Bronx. She cleaned our house, fed our Siamese cat, Surpy, and changed the litter box. If my mother went out, Millie cooked dinner and let me watch Lawrence Welk in her room. She could do the Irish jig. When the Shannon Sisters came on and the fiddling started, we jumped off her bed and hopped about on the shag carpet, jigging until we were sweating and thirsty. Millie also sewed her own clothes, and for Christmas that year she sewed me a white silk queen costume with sequined trim and a blue velvet cape.

Madeline Sapphire was jealous of my queen costume and my nurse. In her home, the maids kept quitting, and she and

Ritchie were left in the hands of a series of West Indian baby-sitters, all with humongous breasts and bad tempers. When the Sapphires finally found someone permanent, it was Greta, a Swiss nanny from Grindelwald who made the kids eat calves' liver and red cabbage whenever Dick and Lauren went out. Even when the Sapphires were home, the food wasn't good, because Lauren was always on a diet. The only soda they had was Tab, and one afternoon she told Madeline and me, "If you spread cottage cheese on a piece of toast and sprinkle it with cinnamon sugar, it tastes just like cheesecake."

Our household was a lair of dietary permissiveness, and even though Madeline and I went to different schools, she spent as much time in our apartment as her parents would allow. We ate every junk food invented—Ho Hos, and Twinkies, fluffernutter sandwiches with the crusts trimmed off, Ding Dongs and Pop-Tarts and Funny Bones. My mother knew how to make real ice-cream sodas. She shook up a bottle of club soda and sprayed it into a glass filled with Hershey's syrup, half-and-half and vanilla ice cream. She cooked us Stouffer's macaroni and cheese, Ronzoni wagon wheels with meat sauce, Swanson turkey TV dinners.

Madeline and I baked Betty Crocker cupcakes dyed turquoise with food coloring. We hardened cookies in my Easy-Bake oven over the heat of a hundred-watt lightbulb. We served each other hors d'oeuvres, spreading chocolate frosting from the can onto Triscuits and Wheat Thins. We sat at our kitchen table with three open gallons of Baskin-Robbins ice cream—peppermint, rocky road, pink bubblegum. We dipped our spoons into the cartons, sucked off the ice cream, spit out the bubblegum bits and saved them to chew later.

We laughed about bras, boys and penises. We wrapped our skinny bodies in silk scarves from a trunk of my mother's discarded clothing and then stripped slowly in the living room to the song "Strawberry Fields Forever."

Before she married my father, my mother was a fashion mannequin and the swimsuit fit model for Jantzen. Yet Millie told me that while my mother was surely an attractive woman—with her chestnut-colored flip, full lips and hourglass figure—Lauren Sapphire was a true beauty. Lauren had black bouffant hair, pale skin and blue eyes, and she reminded Millie of the black-Irish lovelies she had known growing up in Sligo. Even if my mother was not a true beauty, she managed to go out on plenty of dates—maybe because she was nicer than Lauren Sapphire. When she came home late, she peeked in on me in bed and kissed me. Sometimes during the winter, she would drape her perfume-scented mink coat over my blanket, and I would sleep the rest of the night under the sweet-smelling, glossy fur.

One of my mother's dates I'd named Baldy. He was a surgeon, very intelligent, my mother said, and she wondered why I'd chosen to pick on him, since Dick Sapphire was bald, too. But Dick's head was round and tan, and his ring of dark gray hair was always combed back neatly, turning up into tiny curls at his neck like a baby duck's. There was a perfect circle of smooth bronzed skin on the top of his head that made you want to smack a big kiss right in the middle of it. Baldy had a tall, shiny, speckled head, slightly pointed, with a lumpy, leathery texture like the dinosaur egg in the Museum of Natural History.

Anyway, Baldy didn't last long. One night he came to dinner, and as we were having cocktails, Surpy—who was such a smart cat that she often brought pipe cleaners or cigarettes over to the couch so we might start a game of fetch—padded into the living room mewling, with a Tampax grasped lightly between her teeth. "She uses those when she bleeds," I told Baldy, and both adults reddened. Somehow my mother recovered the tampon and her poise, but a few minutes later, after Baldy got up to examine the painting that hung over our fireplace, he sat down on the old cane rocker that Surpy always used to sharpen her claws. I guess that was the day Surpy had scratched too much, or maybe Baldy was heavier than he looked, because the rattan gave way and Baldy fell through the seat. He sat stranded, with his butt grazing the floor, like I had the time Ritchie Sapphire left the toilet seat up and I slid through into the water. I laughed so hard I was sent to my room. We didn't see Baldy anymore.

I could tell whether or not my mother liked a date by how nervous she got before he came over. If she really liked him, she stuck Kleenex into the underarms of her dress to keep from staining the fabric with sweat. The evening of her date with Bluebeard—an English professor from Columbia—she sat at her dressing table with her sleeveless dress unzipped,

pieces of tissue tucked into her bra and sticking out the armholes. Bluebeard was coming over for champagne and caviar,
and my mother had instructed Millie to drop me off at the
Sapphires' for a sleepover. I sat on the edge of my mother's
bed, watching her draw black lines around her eyes to make
them pointy, like a cat's. Then she curled her eyelashes. She always kept a few rollers in at the crown of her head until the
very last moment. She stopped before brushing lipstick on her
mouth to say, "Honey, will you ask Millie to open the caviar
and put it in the little crystal bowl on the counter?"

I ran to the kitchen but then called back into my mother's
room, "Millie can't find it."

My mother came in, clip-clopping on her high heels, zip-
ping up her dress, tissue still sticking out from the armholes.
She said, "He'll be here any minute."

"I'm sorry, Rosalind. I don't know what caviar looks like."
Millie and my mother both peered into the refrigerator.

"Well, I put it here right on this top shelf. It was in a flat glass
jar, about so big." My mother made a circle with her fingers.

All at once Millie's face looked strange. Her eyes dropped
and shifted back and forth, as if she were sweeping the white
linoleum floor with her gaze. "Did the jar have a gold metal
top?"

"Yes!" I could see my mother getting impatient. She pulled
the curlers out of her hair, stacking one on each finger of her
left hand.

Millie covered her mouth. "Oh my heavens," she mumbled.
My mother fanned herself with the handful of curlers and

stared at her. Color rose in Millie's cheeks like a juice stain. "I . . . I thought it was for the cat."

"You what!"

"Well, it was in one of those little jars. And . . . and it was all black and smelled so awful . . ."

All three of us looked down the galley of cabinets to the end of the kitchen floor, where, indeed, in Surpy's ceramic bowl, was a dark smear and two or three tiny black eggs. My mother screeched, "That was forty dollars' worth of beluga caviar!" She looked like she might cry.

Millie offered to run down and buy another jar. She would pay for it herself. Gristede's had closed, but the A&P would still be open. She'd run down right now and be back in two seconds.

The buzzer rang. It was the doorman announcing a Dr. Silverman. "Yes, Brian," said my mother. "Please. Tell him to wait in the lobby a minute. I'll buzz you back." She hung up. "Jesus Christ, my hair!"

"Shall I go to the store?"

"They don't sell beluga caviar at the A&P! Forget it. Forget it! Just take Claudia and go!"

Millie was lucky she could even grab her purse before my mother pushed us both out the back door. Millie rang for the service elevator with her head bowed, shaking it again and again. Just as the elevator arrived, we heard through our door that terrible sound a cat makes when it has eaten rich food and too much of it. *"Ulack-ulack-ulack-ulack-ulack!"* I could perfectly imagine Surpy's spasms and the stinky black puddle gushing from her jaws. My mother's high heels clip-clopped back into the kitchen, and then we heard, "Shit!"

Millie whisked me into the elevator and pushed the button for the lobby. At about the halfway point, our eyes met, and we could contain our laughter no more. Doubled over in the elevator car, Millie said between gasps, "I just hope she remembers to take the Kleenex out from under her arms."

My mother didn't go on dates the week Dick Sapphire came to stay with us. The phone rang one school night around nine o'clock, and my mother said, "Yes, of course, come over." As she tucked me into bed, she explained that Dick was going to be with us for a couple of days while he and Lauren were "sorting things out."

He showed up a few minutes later. Out in the foyer, I heard him say, "Thanks so much, Rosalind. I swear, I must have called five hotels—I couldn't get in anywhere. And Lauren was standing over me screaming bloody murder."

"I know," my mother said. "I could hear it on the phone."

Dick slept in my mother's room so he could have a private bathroom, and my mother slept on the living room sofa with an extra blanket and pillow. We didn't have our traditional Sunday-night dinner at Trader Vic's that week, and Madeline didn't come over. Dick went home once or twice to visit her and Ritchie. While he was staying with us, he came into my room sometimes to talk.

"Madeline loves Barbie, too." Squatting down, he balanced on his heels. "I'll bet you and she have all the same dolls."

"My Midge is a redhead—hers is brunette. And Madeline has Skipper with lifelike bendable legs. I have Tressy—you press her stomach and her hair grows."

"Um-huh." I didn't know what this man was doing looking at my dolls. He stood up and went back out into the hall.

The last night Dick stayed with us, he woke up the whole household yelling for my mother. "Rosalind!" I ran, and my mother rushed to her room from the couch. Dick stood on top of the bed, his feet planted in the pillows, one arm clutching my mother's headboard to steady himself. He held a closed umbrella in the other hand, extended straight out, as if he were sword-fighting. He wore only a pair of gray silk pajama bottoms, and his chest was big and sculpted like a Ken doll's, except Dick's had a thick patch of hair. He looked like a hero. At the foot of the bed was Surpy, her back arched, her fur spiky and her tail pointed to the ceiling. She hissed and emitted soft, low growls.

"Jesus Christ, Rosalind! Get that beast out of here!"

My mother grabbed Surpy, handed her to me and told me to lock her in the powder room. As I was walking out, I heard Dick say, "The damned thing hid under the bed till I turned the light out. Then it jumped up here and attacked me."

When I came home from school the next day, my mother's eyes were puffy, and she was sniffling. Lauren had died during the night. "She took too many sleeping pills," my mother said.

"It wasn't really an accident." She packed up Dick's things and gave them to Millie to drop off at the Sapphire's building.

I was sad at first that Lauren had died, because I felt like I was supposed to be sad. But as I lay in bed, I thought about how I'd never liked her that much, and I didn't think I would miss her. I had always liked Dick a lot, and I thought how wonderful it would be if Dick and my mother got married. He could be my father. Madeline and Ritchie could be my sister and brother, Millie could be our nurse, they could fire Greta and we could all live in their duplex on Park. I stayed up late that night, happy, and in my mind I arranged my bedroom furniture into what had been their guest room, sorting my toys and dolls on the built-in shelves.

I had been too young to attend my father's funeral, so Lauren Sapphire's was my first. Frankly, I was disappointed with it. From everything I'd read or seen on television and at the movies, I thought a funeral should be a Gothic affair by the side of a grave on a dark, stormy day. Campbell's Funeral Home on Madison and Eighty-first Street had powder-blue walls, it was clean and there was no coffin in sight. "Honey, Lauren was cremated," my mother whispered. "I'll explain that to you later. Be good, now."

No one was crying in the entrance hall leading to the chapel. Men stood around in groups, in gray or dark blue suits, talking about business or the war in Vietnam. The only way it differed from a cocktail party was that no one held drinks. My mother greeted a few of her friends and chatted with Elsa Arkin. "What a shame to be doing this on such a lovely day," Elsa said. "Well, I guess it would be a shame anytime."

I didn't see Madeline or her father, and I asked my mother where they were.

"They're in a private room just for the family."

"So shouldn't we—"

"No." My mother shook her head. "Not now."

We stood around for what seemed like ages. Finally, a pair of white double doors opened, and we were ushered into the chapel. My mother led me to a pew on the right side, about a third of the way from the front. I looked for the kneeling benches I'd seen at Millie's church, but there were none. When everyone was seated, some music came on, and then, from a door at the front of the chapel, Dick, Madeline and Ritchie walked in, together with their grandmother Ethel and other relatives I'd met at their holiday parties. The Sapphire family filled the first two pews, which had been roped off and left empty for them. As Madeline crossed the front of the room, I noticed her eyes were red and tired-looking.

A man in a suit came out and talked about Lauren. More music played, and then the man spoke again, mentioning the names of Madeline and everyone else in her family. Occasionally, one of the women would pull a tissue from her purse, or a man would retrieve a handkerchief from his pocket and blow his nose. My mother sat still. I could hear her breathing, but she didn't cry. I picked up her wrist and sniffed it. She wasn't wearing her usual perfume. At the end of the service, we all stood. The Sapphires left first, through the door at the front, then everyone else lined up to say hello to them.

When we reached the family, I nodded at Madeline's grandmother. Then I said, "I'm sorry," to Ritchie, as my mother had instructed me to do. Greta stood between Ritchie and Madeline, and I mumbled hello to her. When I came to Madeline, I didn't know what to say, so I just looked at her. Her eyes were glazed, her skin was blotchy and her lips and nostrils looked cracked and raw. I had expected her to be soft and sad, but instead she glared at me, seeming angry. I tried to think of some way to console her. "Maybe you could sleep over this weekend," I said. She clutched Greta's hand and turned her face into her nanny's thick body, away from me.

Dick Sapphire was the last person in the line. Even with dark circles under his eyes, he was still the handsomest man I'd ever seen. He wore a dark-blue double-breasted suit, a crisp white shirt and a navy-and-gold diagonally striped tie. Standing so still in the line, he reminded me of a navy captain, and I wouldn't have been surprised if someone came and pinned a medal to his dark jacket. He stooped to hug me and said, "Hello, Claudia. Thank you for coming today." He straightened and turned to my mother. "Hello, Rosalind." He took her hand and leaned forward to kiss her cheek, as he always had.

My mother let out a soft gasp. She whispered, "Oh my God," and broke into sobs. She shook so hard that Dick couldn't even kiss her. She brought her other hand to his face and caressed his cheek with the back of her trembling hand. She took my hand and pulled me into a hallway. "Stay here," she said and slipped into the ladies' room. I waited for her, listening to the conversation of two women in high heels and short black dresses.

"Yes, dreadful," one said.

"Well," said the other one, "I guess it's time to pay our condolences to the most eligible bachelor in New York," and they both walked away.

My mother didn't cry as we walked home, but she didn't want to talk, either. When we reached our apartment, she shut herself in her room for the rest of the day and night. Millie made me a Swanson frozen Mexican dinner, and we spent the evening in her room watching television and eating chocolate-chip cookies.

It is possible in New York City to live five blocks from someone and never run into them. Or perhaps I did see Madeline again, but by then we had grown the breasts and hips we'd always giggled about, and with our young women's bodies and faces, we failed to recognize each other. In my senior year of high school, it was popular for the kids from the private schools in Manhattan to get together in large groups and drink mai tais in the bar at Trader Vic's. I went several times to get drunk on the sickeningly sweet drinks and smoke Rothmans or Sobranei Filters until late at night. Once, as we passed the tiki statues on the way out, I told a boy from Dalton that I'd had a friend who bit the statue's penis. The boy stumbled, laid his hand on my shoulder and, laughing, he said, "Do you think I could have her number?"

Toy Soldiers

— 1976 —

It's May 1976, the New York City doormen are striking, and everyone is wondering how long this will go on. The Building Managers' Association says there is no way to continue operating during this recession, what with the exorbitant cost of the men's salaries and their benefits. The men of Union Local 32B will not accept a ten-percent wage cut; nor will they agree to a reduction of sick days and vacation time, no matter how deeply the economy is sinking. Mayor Beame has asked everyone to stay calm, to try to approach the matter with a spirit of goodwill and cooperation. Channel Five has advised New Yorkers to brace themselves for what could be the worst labor-management confrontation in years.

The doormen show up to their buildings each morning—the better co-ops on Fifth and Park avenues, Central Park West, West End and Riverside, Sutton Place and Gramercy Park. They stand outside all day in their street clothes with strike placards, hoping to be filmed by a passing news van and hoping that it doesn't rain. By the third day of the strike—a warm spring day with a brisk wind that picks up by mid-afternoon—it has become clear to everyone that there is no threat of violence. Only boredom for the men and inconvenience for building residents trying to settle into new routines. The owners of the co-ops will have to guard their lobbies, drive their own elevators and distribute the mail as long as the standoff continues. In the lobby of 980 Park Avenue, Beverly Coddington tells Peggy Payne she has canceled three bridge dates this week to work her shift at the door. "After all," says Beverly, tucking the crisp edge of her gray-blond pageboy behind an ear and looking straight into Peggy's face with her blue eyes, "I feel it's my duty."

Peggy Payne sits primly, ankles crossed, next to Beverly, just a few feet back from the lobby's heavy glass and ironwork door. Sunlight from the street shines through the scrolled black tracery, illuminating a rectangular patch on the pale green wall opposite. A few dust motes and pollen particles float in the air. Otherwise, the lobby is dim, lit by brass wall sconces and a small crystal chandelier. The two women sit like receptionists behind the antique cherrywood desk that usually occupies a quiet corner near the elevator, topped only by a defunct but charming pen set and a green leather blotter. Now the desk has been cleared off, pulled out by the entrance and put into action. From seven A.M. until eleven at night, two residents at a time serve four-hour shifts at the desk, signing visitors into a guest book, announcing these guests and delivery boys to the apartments where they are expected and checking the provisional identity cards that have been issued to the co-op owners and their employees. "Of course, I know every owner," says Beverly, "but who can keep all the help straight?" Peggy Payne is proud of the proficiency she's gained with the building's intercom system. Standing up and straightening her navy gabardine skirt, she goes to the wall phone by the door and presses the button for apartment 6A. "Good afternoon," she says to the maid who answers, "there's a little Mary Wilcox here to see Rebecca. Shall we send her up?"

Beverly praises her efforts. "Thank heavens for you, Peggy," she says. "You can see the buttons. I'm afraid I've reached that age when I need reading glasses. And I positively refuse to wear them!"

Both women titter, though Peggy is slightly annoyed that during the entire shift, she is the one who has to keep hopping up to make the calls, while Beverly just sits around, chatting with all the visitors like a guest at a party. Peggy's especially annoyed when Mrs. Onassis stops in to call on the baroness in the penthouse and Beverly practically dispatches Peggy off to the intercom, all the while asking after the health of Mrs. Onassis's children, her husband, her sister, as if she's known the woman all her life.

But it's that flair, Peggy supposes, that ability to feel at ease with anyone and know exactly what to say, that makes Beverly Coddington who she is, and that has helped Harold Coddington achieve prominence socially as well as in business. Beverly is the benefit chairman of the Red Cross Ball this year. She serves on the board of the Metropolitan Museum and the Public Library. The Coddingtons are frequent guests at the Ford White House. Harold himself is a director at Chemical Bank, AT&T and Philip Morris. He is currently president of the Knickerbocker Club, while Charles and Peggy are only members. The Coddingtons have always been neighborly with the Paynes, but you couldn't say they count Charles and Peggy among their close friends. Perhaps this strike will change things, Peggy thinks. Though she complains to Charles in the evenings about the nuisance of sitting downstairs all afternoon, secretly she's not quite ready for a labor agreement. Perhaps if Beverly grows fond of Peggy during their time together behind the cherrywood desk, Harold Coddington might ask Charles to serve on the Knickerbocker's nominating committee.

Peggy is anxious to make intelligent remarks to Beverly and strike up lively conversation. After Mrs. Onassis and her two Secret Servicemen disappear into the elevator, Peggy says, "She looks as beautiful as she did at her husband's inauguration."

"Yes, she certainly does."

"And having gone through all that tragedy. First her husband and then her brother-in-law."

"She's an admirable woman." Beverly crosses her legs, showing off her finely developed calves and taupe suede pumps. "Though I don't understand why she's always going about in slacks."

"What a shame, Beverly, to think what happened in that family."

"Yes, of course. On a personal level, for her. But really, Peggy," and here Beverly raises her eyebrows, pulls her shoulders back and fastens one button of her cream cashmere cardigan, "think of where our country would be under a Kennedy dynasty!"

The front door opens again, and Peggy's daughter, Sandra, struggles through, wearing a jean jacket and a long nylon wrap skirt over tan boots. She carries an army-green canvas book bag over one shoulder. The door slams shut behind her, and Sandra whirls around and glares at it. "Christ, that thing is heavy." Her long blond hair is messy, as if it's been whipped by the wind.

"Hello, dear," Peggy says.

"Hi, Mom. Hi, Mrs. Coddington." She approaches the desk and stands with her weight on one leg, her head cocked to the side. "You want to see my I.D.?"

"I think your mother will vouch for you," says Beverly with a twinkle.

Peggy asks if Sandra has much homework tonight.

"Not really, but it's chemistry." Sandra wrinkles her nose.

"Chemistry?" Beverly says. "How dreadful."

"Yeah." Sandra smiles at her. "Dreadful, totally." She leaves them for the elevator. Peggy notices there wasn't a smile for her.

"She's quite a handful, I suppose," Beverly says.

"If we survive these last years of school and get her off to college in one piece, it will be a miracle." Peggy shakes her head. "Although the teachers over at Brearley keep telling us she's doing fine."

"Oh, well, Brearley," Beverly says, commiserating. "Yes, really, they are so intellectual there, I worry about the girls." She whispers the word "intellectual" as if it means "communist." "That's why I sent my daughters down to Madeira. They can play sports and keep their horses. Get the kind of training that makes a woman ready for the real world—our real world, anyway."

How has Beverly managed to twist things around so that Peggy feels badly Sandra is bright rather than some kind of horsey debutante? Somehow Beverly has made Sandra appear inferior, and Peggy, too, feels diminished. She dislikes this woman, truly she does. Still, she hangs around like a lady-in-waiting, and deep down, Peggy admits to herself, she would give anything to be more like Beverly.

The elevator opens, and out comes the Frenchman whom both women recognize as the baroness's butler, wheeling a small cart loaded with a silver tea service and a number of china cups and saucers. The bottom shelf of the cart holds a platter of cream puffs, éclairs and some cookies from William Greenberg. The butler bows to Mrs. Coddington and Mrs. Payne and speaks in his nasal accent: "Madame la Baronne was taking tea upstairs, and she thought you ladies who are working so hard might enjoy refreshment as well."

Though this is not quite an invitation to the penthouse, both Beverly and Peggy are thrilled to be even remotely included in the tea party with the baroness and Mrs. Onassis. The butler pours two steaming cups of tea, adds sugar and cream for Beverly, lemon for Peggy. He sets china plates and linen napkins edged with lace on the cherrywood desk. He serves them pastries with small silver tongs. Peggy thanks him, and Beverly says, *"Merci."* He nods. Then he replaces the pastry platter on its shelf and wheels the cart toward the front door. Beverly watches him, puzzled. "Where on earth are you going?"

"Outside," the butler says. "I have tea for the men outside." He pulls the door open and wheels the cart over the brass threshold onto the sidewalk, then closes the door behind him.

Beverly's cheeks betray a pink flush, which, if asked, she would swear came from the heat of the tea. "Well, I never," she says. She pushes her hair back and forces a shrill little laugh. "I never thought I'd find myself sharing the baroness's tea with Peter the doorman."

Dick Sapphire's plane lands at La Guardia at four o'clock, and he grabs a taxi for the ride into town. When the strike erupted, he was away, working with clients in Cleveland. He was worried about Ritchie and his new wife, Shelley—Shelley who was such a doll, so sweet, so beautiful and free of all those crazy problems Lauren had—what if sentiments turned ugly and something happened to them? At least Madeline was safe in boarding school up at Deerfield. He wanted to fly straight home, but this Cleveland suit was huge—millions to be made in his firm's fees alone. "Dick, relax," Shelley said on the phone. "It's fine, we're fine. It's the same guys who help us every day. They just stand there like poor lost souls, waiting for a contract. This afternoon it was raining, so I had the Madison Deli send them chicken soup. See? I'm becoming Jewish—your mother would be proud. Is it wet there?"

Today it's clear, just windy. As his cab turns south onto Park at Ninety-sixth Street, Dick notices that the tulips are nearly gone from their beds in the middle of the avenue—one really hot day, and the last of their petals will fall off. He can see how it is with the strike. Three or four men milling around in front of each building. They've abandoned their signs, which sit idly against small trees and lampposts. The men seem placid, like cows out to graze. On Dick's own block, he barely recognizes Peter and Vinnie—the usual afternoon shift—talking in a group with the boy from the back elevator and one of the doormen from 990 Park, next door.

They look especially mild—smaller than life, it seems—stripped of their uniforms. Dick thinks of how accustomed he is to seeing them each day in their light gray suits, with the double white stripe running down the side of their pant legs, another double stripe around the edge of each sleeve. Who are these men without their brass buttons, white gloves, stiff, round, flat-topped gray caps with the little plastic visors? In their uniforms, they're like toy soldiers from a country that never went to war—Canada, maybe—sporting their battalion number stitched in white and gold embroidery over their hearts: 980 Park Avenue. Today they are just men—men who are not working and don't know what to do with themselves.

The cab stops in front of the 980 canopy, and Dick unloads his suit bag from the trunk. He nods to Peter, who stands near the curb. Peter is dapper in a herringbone sport jacket over brown trousers. "Good afternoon, Mr. Sapphire," he says, "I'm sorry I can't help you with that." He puts his hands in his pockets as if ashamed of their uselessness. "Please thank Mrs. Sapphire for all the food."

Dick nods again. "I will."

Peter rejoins the other men. Vinnie turns around and smiles at Dick. He is wearing a zippered, hooded navy blue sweatshirt over flared blue jeans. He's in sneakers. He looks like a kid from Brooklyn, which, Dick thinks, is probably what he is.

Dick glances at the doorman from next door, in tight jeans and tan horse-riding boots (Frye, Dick remembers; Madeline drove him crazy last year about getting her a pair of Frye boots). He's got on a slinky patterned top, zigzags in shades of blue, green, aqua and brown; he wears it tight, tucked in. There's a gold chain around his neck, with a cross, and the man swaggers a bit—in his own circle, he must be some kind of ladies' man. What strikes Dick is how different from the others each man looks in his street clothes. Dick has always thought of them as a team: the trusty uniformed men who hailed cabs, drove the elevator, protected his home from intruders. He imagined them loyal to one another, like brothers. Now he sees how unlike they are, thrown together only by employment and shift schedules. Maybe Peter and Vinnie have nothing to say to each other. Maybe for the past three years they've been stuck together on that three-to-eleven shift, bored out of their minds and piqued by an accumulation of small resentments. Dick is a bit disappointed, but he consoles himself that at least the doormen have all the screwballs in the building—including himself—to discuss.

Dick heaves open the lacy ironwork door, surprised by its weight. How strange, he thinks, to have lived in the same building for over fifteen years without ever once opening his own front door. Beverly Coddington and Peggy Payne— whom Dick has privately named White Bread and Mashed Potatoes—sit like charity-ball greeters behind the spindly wooden desk.

"Oh, good afternoon, Richard, how was your day?" asks White Bread with an artificial smile. None of the WASPs in the building move their mouths much when they speak, but White Bread's lockjaw is the worst. She's also the only person on earth, besides his mother, who calls him Richard.

"Hello, ladies," Dick says and walks past them to the elevator. Jesus Christ, he thinks, imagine coming home each night to that.

White Bread's schmucky husband, Harold Coddington, is driving the elevator tonight. His beefy red face breaks into a grin as he opens the brass grate of the elevator's inner door. A glint of light reflects off his gold wire-framed glasses, so his small eyes are barely visible. "Hi, Dick! Welcome back home," he booms in his usual overly friendly manner that Dick has decided is probably a cover-up for Nazi sympathies during World War II. As Dick steps into the elevator cab, he stumbles and nearly trips, because Harold hasn't stopped the elevator even with the lobby floor. "Sorry," says Harold, laughing. "I don't have my license yet."

Harold is holding a martini glass in one hand, and the elevator stinks of gin. He bends forward and pulls the outer wooden elevator door closed. Then he slams the brass grate. That's when Dick notices the rifle. There is a rifle, an old-looking one, leaning against the oiled mahogany elevator wall, next to the driving apparatus. "Going hunting?" Dick asks.

Harold turns to face him. "It's the new security system," he says, chuckling, "now that we've lost our guards." He lowers his voice to a whisper. "Actually, it's not really loaded. Beverly and I were just having a bit of fun, you know, keeping everyone on their toes." Dick forces himself to smile. "Anyway, it seems like the joke's on me. Ever since Beverly got my gun off the wall, she's been talking about replacing it with a Corot she saw over at Sotheby's." Harold takes a gulp from his martini. "I tell you, Dick," he continues, "this strike is going to cost us in ways we haven't yet imagined."

Yes, Harold, Dick wants to say, *being rich is expensive.* But he keeps his thoughts to himself.

"Of course, I understand that a woman likes paintings, but it's too bad about the gun." Harold strokes the barrel end of it. "You know, this rifle belonged to my great-great-grandfather. He carried it in the Civil War."

Dick is wondering how long Harold will hold forth in the closed elevator, which can't be larger than five feet across and four feet deep, before they get off the ground. He studies Harold's round face and his small nose, his barrel of a stomach with the pink oxford-cloth shirt and gray Brooks Brothers suit jacket stretched over it. Who would wear a tie like that—green, white and gold sailing flags against a maroon ground? With a pink shirt? Dick can't believe that he and Harold are nearly the same age. Harold is standing close to Dick, holding up his drink and telling how the gun was lost for years, then rediscovered in the attic of his grandmother's Hudson River country home.

Dick interrupts him. "So show me how you drive this thing," he says, trying to be jovial, but it comes out curt.

"Ha, ha. I'm forgetting my station." Harold takes another gulp of his drink, turns his back to Dick and pulls the brass lever all the way to the left. The elevator lurches up, and Dick's knees buckle. "Whoa!" Harold shouts, gin spilling over the edge of his glass. He pushes the lever to the right, and the elevator halts. Dick's stomach jumps. Turbulence over La Guardia was tame compared to this. Harold is laughing. "Okay . . . easy, horsey." He pulls the lever left again, this time more gently, and the elevator rises at a reasonable speed. He faces Dick. "Sorry, old boy. I had the hang of it before. It's not as simple as it looks." Dick is watching the floors go by, uneasy, wondering if Harold is paying attention or if they'll just crash the penthouse.

"Harold, we've gone past the twelfth floor." Dick doesn't want to betray any urgency in his voice.

Harold whirls back to his lever. "Oh, we have, we have." He throws on the brake again, and Dick bites his tongue. Then Harold lowers the elevator—drops two feet below the twelfth-floor landing, then jerks up three feet over it, then down below it by a foot, then up—"Tch, tch," he says, wagging his blond head back and forth. Looking at him, Dick thinks—no, it couldn't be—yes, goddammit, he's doing it on purpose! He's intentionally not driving the elevator right. And maybe he does it all on purpose: the bluster, the buffoonery, the ridiculous clothes. Not that he isn't a natural asshole—Dick has never seen him break character—but there's something sinister here, something smug, provocative, something that says, *I am an asshole, and I can afford to be an asshole, because I come from a line of assholes who have been running this country for so long we're a part of the landscape, like purple mountain majesties and fruited plains. And anyway, ha ha, aren't jolly assholes like us basically harmless?*

The elevator goes up, down, up, down. Dick clenches his teeth, grips his suit bag and briefcase with sweating palms. These weights keep him from swearing at his neighbor, keep him still and patient and breathing until Harold finally lands close to the twelfth floor, close enough—within six inches. Harold opens the brass grate that has imprisoned Dick in the tiny space and grins once more. "Dick, I believe you can climb from here. My goodness, perhaps those boys outside do deserve a raise!" Harold gives a big, tipsy chuckle inherited from robber barons generations before him. Dick thanks him, says good evening and flees to the comfort of apartment 12A.

According to Vincent Ferretti, striking is even more boring than work. Plus he's off his regular schedule, so he's tired all the time. Usually, he works from three P.M. to eleven—meets his friends late to party, bullshit around. He never goes to bed until three or four in the morning, never wakes up before eleven. It's different from how most people live, but Vinnie's used to it. Now, for the strike, all the shifts are on the same schedule, with men rotating their days off. Vinnie has to be there at nine, and he leaves at six. The hour lunch break doesn't count. "We need maximum exposure for the press," says Peter, who's a kiss-ass whether he's working or striking. A news van rolled by on Monday, but there hasn't been a reporter on their block since.

Peter got on Vinnie's case for coming in at nine-thirty this morning. "It's like jet lag," Vinnie said, trying to make a joke, but Peter didn't laugh. Vinnie couldn't tell if Peter didn't get it or didn't want to. Peter is always watching Vinnie, making him nervous, making him feel like he's not "white glove" enough. Vinnie remembers how he started on the job five years ago, the summer after he graduated from St. Eugene's School. He started on the back elevator—everyone begins there. Then, if you don't bomb out with the maids and delivery boys, they give you one of the fancy uniforms, and you actually get to work with the owners. Vinnie can still hear the super's lecture: "It's your mission to make them feel like they live in the safest, cleanest, most gracious building in New York."

It was funny to hear the word "gracious" coming from Mr. Ulofski's fat lips. Vinnie had stared at his wide nostrils, the black hair coming out of his ears, his bald head with its fringe

of gray frizz that stuck straight out sideways like that of a
clown, a cranky old Polish clown. The only person Vinnie
knew who said things like "gracious" was his grandmother,
and she always said it in Italian—*grazioso*. She said it about
things like lace tablecloths, or hemlines, like when Vinnie's sister, Lisa, had wanted to wear miniskirts. "Oh, no, longer,
longer. That's more . . . *grazioso*," their grandmother insisted
and made a little sweep with her hands. Finally, Lisa learned
how to sew and did her own hemlines. Vinnie laughs now,
thinking about those first short skirts Lisa wore—uneven,
lumpy with bunched fabric, up to her tush. He remembers his
sister's defiant face as she huffed out of the house, passing their
mother and grandmother in the living room, deaf to their
protests.

It was always the same. As soon as his sister went out, their
grandmother would turn to their mother, with a look on her
face like Lisa was dying. Grandma would tip her head back,
roll her eyes to the heavens and say, "What can become of a girl
like that?"

In a way, their grandmother was right. Lisa was three
months pregnant at the altar by that winter. But she looked
beautiful on her wedding day—radiant, everyone said. And
now she has two great kids, and her husband, Don, is a construction supervisor out on the Island with a firm that will
probably make him a partner one day.

Part of what's so annoying about this strike is that Vinnie
gets home early enough to eat dinner with his parents and his
grandmother. Then his girlfriend, Anna, expects to see him,

when normally, he has to take her out only on weekends. If he complains to Anna about how his family is driving him crazy, she says, "Well, we should get our own place. There's nice apartments in Park Slope—we could get a nice starter apartment near Prospect Park." Translation: *It's time for you to hurry up and marry me.*

Vinnie doesn't want to marry Anna ever, but he can't tell her that, so he says, "Forget it. Park Slope is a middle-class slum. You know how there are black ghettos? Well, there's also working-class ghettos, and I'm not ending up there. I'm not moving till I can get a place in Manhattan, on the Upper East Side."

Each day at work, Vinnie sees the girls come in and out of the building. Gorgeous girls, they all go to private school and dress in clothes from stores like Saks Fifth Avenue and Bloomingdale's. Vinnie helps them out of taxis with their piles of shopping bags. The Coddington sisters are the prettiest, both with silky, straight blond hair, ice-blue eyes and long, long legs. Robin Horowitz from 7B has that same silky hair, but jet black, like an Indian's. Robin's always nice to him—she laughs and smiles, almost makes him feel like she thinks he's good-looking. But he'll never forget that time he was taking Robin and one of her friends upstairs in the elevator.

"It was outrageous," Robin's friend said. "This guy kept talking to me yesterday in the park. I mean, he was cute, but he spoke with this borough accent—like the word 'dog' had two syllables: 'doo-wog.' He was totally bridge-and-tunnel!"

"Oh my God, forget it," Robin said. Vinnie stopped the elevator at the seventh floor and opened the door. "Thanks, Vinnie," Robin added and smiled at him as they left.

Vinnie felt as if he'd been stabbed in the stomach. *Bridge-and-tunnel.* It was like some kind of animal. To girls like that, if you weren't from Manhattan, you might as well be dead. It wouldn't ever matter how smart he was, what he looked like or how much money he made. He'd always have his Brooklyn accent, his Italian-speaking grandmother. Vinnie hates the girls in the building because they make him hate himself. Still, he has dreams about them, their long legs and soft hair, and when they're around, he can't help looking at them, smiling at them, treating them like they're princesses. Which they are. Anyway, it's his job to treat them like that.

The door of the building opens, and Sandra Payne pushes her way out with the weight of the door on her butt, just as clumsily as she heaved her way into the building when she came home from school an hour ago. Vinnie thinks it's funny that none of the residents seems able to open the front door, but he can't laugh, not even with Peter, because Peter scolds him for saying things that could cost them their jobs. Sandra has changed into a thick South American–looking sweater, pulled her hair back in a ponytail. She's a pretty girl, too, but there's a sharpness about her face. She's a wild child, always running around with boys, or just alone. That's something unusual about her, how much she comes and goes—alone. And then, out of nowhere, she'll be super-friendly, like she and Vinnie are old friends. A couple of times they've lit up a joint together in the service hallway.

Today Sandra comes straight over to Vinnie, touches his arm. Vinnie freezes up. Not only is Peter ten feet away, but Sandra's mother is sitting at the desk right inside the lobby.

"Hey, I like your sneaks," Sandra says. "You look like a normal person when you're not in that uniform." She has this strange smile like she's being sarcastic, and Vinnie never knows how to take what she says. "You should grow your hair out. Why don't you grow your hair a little longer?"

Vinnie is embarrassed, awkward, flattered. "Well, for one, I couldn't keep my job."

"Oh, God, fuck the job!" Sandra pulls a pack of Marlboros from her sweater pocket, flips open the box to show Vinnie it's filled with joints, about ten of them. She picks one out. "Here. Take this. It'll help you through the rest of the day." She puts the joint in his hand.

Jesus, Vinnie thinks. Right out on the street, right in front of everyone. This crazy girl will do worse than lose him his job, she'll get him arrested, too. Vinnie's heart pounds, and he tries to look casual as he slips the joint into his sweatshirt pocket.

"I'm going to the bandshell. See you tomorrow," Sandra says. "And keep on striking, don't give in. Those shits in there," she points her thumb back toward her building, "they've got more money than God. Take 'em for all you can!" She smiles her weird smile again, then turns away.

Vinnie watches her run to the corner and hail a taxi. He wonders why these rich kids hate their parents so much. It's not like he's been a model son—he gets high, stays out late. He's done plenty of stuff his mother wouldn't exactly approve of. But he doesn't hate her. He doesn't hate anyone in his family. It's strange—his parents have given him a lot less than these Park Avenue kids have, yet he loves his parents, even his irritating grandmother. At least I respect them, he thinks. They work hard, I work hard. I see where they've come from, where they've gotten. I see what they want for me, and they want good things. If I play the game right, my kids will go to college. It's like we're all part of a plan. He fingers the joint in his pocket, wishing it weren't there. These people, Vinnie thinks, perplexed, his lips slightly apart, these people are on top of the world. But they haven't got a plan.

Sandra Payne:
The Next Four Thousand Years

— 1977 —

Nobody in my family was supposed to be born, and the tiny brown baby in my stomach was no exception.

My aunt Eleanor told me the family story when I was thirteen. We were in Wisconsin, for my grandmother Annie Miller's funeral. Eleanor got drunk and said she once saw her mother throw herself off the top of her icebox, trying to induce a miscarriage. Annie was "with child" again, and there were already five girls in the house. At four-foot-eight, my grandmother stood a good chance of breaking her own neck when she jumped, yet she and the fetus were not harmed. She sat on the floor of her farmhouse kitchen and said, "Goddammit, I'll bet it's another girl!" That baby turned out to be my mother.

Eleanor also said I was lucky to have made it out of my

mother's womb alive. "She had two abortions, you know," my aunt whispered. "They would've been your older brothers." It seemed that my mom kept getting knocked up while my father was studying at the university down in Madison. "Charles had ambitions," Eleanor explained, "and there was no way he could afford college and a family at the same time. Of course, those midnight appointments at the doctor's office weren't cheap for him, either!"

When I asked my mother about this, she said, "Sandra, your aunt has always been unbalanced, and now that Mother is gone, I'm not ever coming back to Wisconsin."

So we stayed in Manhattan, where my father was a bond trader and my mother played bridge. We lived on Park Avenue and Eighty-third Street. Our apartment smelled like my father's cigar smoke and old leather chairs, and my life was as boring as a Brearley School history class. I often thought about my unborn brothers, and I missed them. I promised myself I'd never have an abortion, unless I was raped at knifepoint or accidentally slept with a mongoloid.

But nothing like that had happened, so here it was, Monday morning, and my stomach was on the spin cycle. I knew I couldn't get away with skipping school again—the Brearley headmistress had called our house last Friday and said if I took more than two additional absences this year, I wouldn't graduate—and it was only the beginning of April. My eyes burned like crazy, and my head ached as I lay in bed dreading the day like a root canal. The whole day: my school, those stupid smart girls and their constant yakking about where they would be accepted to college. "Oh, you'll get into Wesleyan," Baa Willoughby had assured me the week before. "You're real bright, and no one else applied there." Everyone from the class of '77 had applied to Radcliffe, Yale, Princeton, then someplace like Duke or U. of P. as a safety. The dumber girls would get shipped off to Smith. Wanting to go to a school like Wesleyan was considered adventurous.

I dreaded another afternoon at Michael Wallach's house, getting high with the guys from Collegiate. Listening to Brubeck and Charlie Parker albums, all of us hanging out smoking and nodding to the complicated beat, being cool. Why couldn't I have been a teenager in the sixties, when you got to run around in fields at be-ins and dance like flailing willow branches? Instead of sitting there stoned, mired in the white shag carpeting.

I'd eat dinner with my parents later—my father would blab on forever about some new bond issue or rising interest rates. My mother would smile and nod like an idiot, pretending to understand and care about what he was saying, when really it all floated over her well-coiffed head.

The door opened, and I pulled the covers over my face. Sofia, our semi-alive maid from Argentina, brought in a can of Mott's AM with a flexi-straw and put it on my night table. "Miss Sandra, you up!" she commanded. In the kitchen, she gave me my usual breakfast of bacon and cinnamon toast. I choked it down. I didn't know why I was doing all this. I wasn't going to college, anyway.

At school, I left AP calculus early, because I thought I might throw up. In the girls' room, Malabar Merrill and Diana Bottomsly were standing at the sinks. I said hi and shut myself in a toilet stall, trying to keep my breakfast down.

"Yeah, I *do* like him," Diana confessed.

"So you should have sex with him!"

"Well, I don't know, Mal. Bonnie had sex with Kip Rogers this weekend, but she said she didn't like it."

I tried to tune them out. When would I have to tell someone? How much did I show—would somebody figure it out? When do you have to start going to the doctor? I peed so Malabar and Di would hear me do something normal. I rubbed my belly, hoping my baby was having a better day than I was.

"God, I have the worst cramps," I lied when I joined them at the sinks. Diana tried to give me aspirin, but I refused.

"Christ, Sandra, how do you stay so skinny?" Malabar asked. "Even with your period, you look like a rail!"

"Thank you." I blinked and looked into her eyes, maybe for the first time in my twelve years at that school. Amazing. No one was going to notice. I could get by for a while, as long as I gave up tight sweaters and managed to keep from puking into my second derivatives. I had some time to figure out a plan.

I skipped going over to Wallach's place to see the guys. Instead, I spent the afternoon sitting on the green velvet sofas in the main hall of the Frick Collection, gazing into the Turners and reading and rereading a section about the female reproductive system in my biology textbook. Every so often I'd wander down to the Bronzino portrait of the young nobleman at the end of the left wall. Now, there was a guy I could love—

intense and brilliant, the Jim Morrison of the sixteenth century. I stared at him and wondered at what point you have to tell a guy that he's having a kid.

Dinner was fucked. We sat in our usual places, my father on his throne at the head of the table, and my mother and I halfway down either side. My parents were discussing a hand from a bridge tournament they'd played the night before. After the vinegary salad, Sofia passed around lamb chops and then came back with a silver tray of spinach and mashed potatoes. I watched the meat bleed into my potatoes, turning them pink. I told myself to eat and even asked Sofia to bring me some milk, which she served in a tall glass with an iced-tea spoon. I figured I should drink milk. I stirred it around like a zombie and then faced my father.

"Dad? Can I go downtown with you in the car tomorrow morning? I have a breakfast interview with an alumnus from U. of P."

He turned toward me like the Austrian emperor asked to spare a prisoner. "You don't want to go to Penn."

"It's my safety school," I explained.

"Sandra, you'll have to take a cab. I have no chauffeur now, and I'm going to the Carlyle in the morning." He reached into his pocket and pulled out a wad of carefully folded bills, clipped with his gold monogram. He handed me ten dollars.

I caught my breath. "What do you mean, you have no chauffeur?"

My mother laughed and dabbed her napkin at the corners of her lips. "You wouldn't imagine! The other night Simon took some girlfriend of his to a rock concert on Long Island. In our Mercedes, no less."

I started to get very nervous. "And so?"

"Well, the car must've impressed the young lady. Simon didn't show up at the office until three-thirty the next afternoon. And poor Charles flew in early from Washington and was stranded out at Teterboro for nearly an hour."

I put down my shaking milk glass. "So what happened to Simon?" I tried to sound merely curious. It was a reasonable question, right?

"Well, I fired him," my father said.

"How could you do that?" I blurted out. "He's worked for us for, like, seven or eight years! He's like—like family!" I told myself to calm down and lowered my voice. "What'll happen to him?"

"Actually, I think he's gone back to Jamaica already. You know, Sandra, people like that can't expect to get ahead in this country. I'm sure we're better off without him, and him without us."

"You fascist!"

I ran from the room. I wanted to burst into tears, to explode in a great sobbing lament, but all I could do was pace in my bedroom, from the desk to the window to the desk, with the muscles of my chest all tight and hard. I picked up the telephone receiver a few times in outrage, but who was I going to call—the police? The Jamaican ambassador? Impossible.

I sank into the pink-and-green-flowered armchair in the corner. It wasn't comfortable, even after all the money my mother had spent on the decorator. I stared at the poster of Raphael's *Madonna* that I'd hung over my headboard.

I should've told him last week at the Bob Marley show but I just hadn't known what to say. I mean, after "Simon, I'm pregnant." What comes next? You can't tell a guy that you're having his baby and then drop the subject. What if he'd wanted to marry me? I loved Simon, I supposed; he'd been my friend for most of my life. But marry him? And live in the Jamaican section of Brooklyn—wherever the hell that was—while he worked as somebody's chauffeur until I got my trust fund? I didn't think Simon was exactly looking to settle down with someone like me, either. I mean, he was like *thirty*, and I didn't have a clue what he was planning to do with the rest of his life. We never talked about stuff like that. I couldn't remember ever telling him anything that didn't make him laugh. Really, we hardly talked at all—just laughed, listened to music and relaxed together.

That's how it always was with us, fun and easy. That's how it'd been when I was a kid and he drove me to the orthodontist on Friday mornings. When my father got out of the car at the office, I'd move up to the front seat, and Simon would toss off his chauffeur's cap. We'd pull Perry Como out of the eight-track, pop in the Rolling Stones and break up in hysterical laughter. Of course, in those days we were in a Cadillac. And back then we weren't having sex.

I thought of our last night together. I had stood in front of Simon at the concert and wrapped his smooth brown arms around me. He leaned his head forward, chin on my shoulder, and pressed a high-boned warm cheek against the side of my face as we sang along with the band. Afterward, we drove out to the beach, where we smoked a joint by the water and walked giggling to a silent reggae beat. "Come over here, my little trapped princess," Simon said in his funny Jamaican accent. "Come over here and give some affection to this crazy Rasta man!"

We made love in a sand dune, kissing and laughing. We went to sleep in the back of the Mercedes, nestled close together, quietly dreaming, and waking up every so often to kiss again. We dozed until one in the afternoon—it was okay, we thought, my father was out of town. We picked up coffee and tuna sandwiches, and Simon drove me back into the city and headed downtown to the office. Then he got fired. Shit. The last memory I have of my baby's dad is Simon laughing because his long legs were cramped from sleeping squished in the car all night. And now he was gone. "Now what?" I asked the Madonna.

The next day during milk lunch—our late-morning break when the old Irish woman stood outside the Upper School library to give us chocolate-chip cookies and miniature cartons of milk—I slipped downstairs to the pay phone by the alumnae office and called Planned Parenthood.

"I need to see a doctor," I said.

"For family planning?" The lady at the other end of the line had this high singsong voice, the kind they use for radio jingles.

I didn't know what that was.

"Our ob-gyn will acquaint you with a variety of methods

for preventing unwanted pregnancy, ranging from abstinence to the Pill." She might have been offering a free trial of the *Encyclopedia Britannica*.

"I think I'll need something more advanced than that," I said. "I'm already pregnant."

"Oh." She had to switch product lines. "Then you'll want a urinalysis. I can schedule one for you tomorrow morning at eleven-thirty."

Why did I want to shoot this woman in the head? "Look. I don't need a test. I'm pregnant. My boobs hurt, my bras don't fit, I barf my guts out every morning and I haven't had my period since the end of January." I was practically in tears. "I need to see a doctor!"

"I'm sorry, dear, but we don't make prenatal appointments without laboratory confirmation. Now, would you like to come in tomorrow, or shall I release the time?"

I took the appointment.

Thursday, on the way to school, this group of black guys followed me across Lexington, heckling me. "Yo, mama! You got no ass! How come white girls don't got no ass?" I pressed my fingernails into my palms and kept on walking. I wanted to scream back at them: *How come it's always the black guys who talk to you on the street about your pussy and your ass? How am I supposed to fucking not be prejudiced when you're always doing this shit? How will I explain this to my baby? Do you do this to black girls or just white ones? What about half-black girls? How's my kid supposed to have any kind of a normal life? How's she gonna fit in anywhere?*

Actually, I didn't fit in anywhere, either. Maybe things would get easier when my daughter and I were a team.

The minute I got to Brearley, the Upper School dean nabbed me and made me follow her to her office. This was bad; it had to be something serious, and I mean *awful.* Fuck! They knew about me—somehow they'd figured it out. This was it, they'd expel me and then tell my parents. Shit, shit, shit, shit, *shit!*

Mrs. Oliver was smiling. That bitch.

"Sandra, we had quite a surprise yesterday."

I'll bet they did.

"The admissions director from Wesleyan called us. You've been accepted."

"Oh." My notebook almost slipped out of my hand. "Already?" We weren't supposed to hear from colleges for two more weeks.

"Yes. It's highly unusual, quite an honor. She said you were such a strong and interesting applicant that they wanted to tell you right away, in the hope that you'll choose to go there. Isn't that wonderful?"

I nodded and tried to smile.

"Now you won't have to worry about anything!"

Right.

My classes were a disaster. Madame Girard carried on for a full minute in front of everyone about what was wrong with Mademoiselle Sandra, who couldn't seem to remember the subjunctive mood. My history teacher gave a pop quiz on the material from the day before when I was downtown peeing for

Planned Parenthood. And in the cafeteria, they had run out of napoleons and éclairs—the only things that got me through a stupid Brearley day.

In my last class, phys ed, I tripped over my own feet playing badminton. I fell hard on the gym floor. Both knees were bleeding, and for a moment I went shocky, like I would faint. Tammy Ansteth got hysterical. "Oh my God, she's all white! C'mon, you guys, help me take her to the nurse!" Tammy had gotten into Dartmouth early-decision and was going premed.

I sat up blinking. There were ten Brearley girls in my face. "Look, I'm fine. I don't need to go to the nurse." I took a few deep breaths.

"You don't look fine." Fucking Tammy, always ready to turn to the authorities.

Baa Willoughby, who agreed with me that Tammy was the biggest asshole in our class, helped me stand up and walked me down the hall to the girls' room, past bulletin boards that kept going in and out of focus. Because Baa was there, I washed off my knees first. Then I went into one of the stalls. "Do me a favor and guard the door?" I asked her. Even though in principle I didn't like anyone at Brearley, Baa was the one I didn't like the least.

I sat on the toilet and prayed not to have a miscarriage. I remembered that my aunt Eleanor had said no boys were ever born alive in our family. If my baby was a boy, I'd have a miscarriage right now—that was the way it went. I kept looking between my legs to see if any blood or guts were coming out; then I folded my arms on my thighs and leaned my head over, resting. Oh please, God, I thought, please, please don't take this away—it's the one thing that matters! Please let me keep my baby, *please*! I promise I'll quit smoking dope. I promise I won't screw the next chauffeur. I'll even name the baby Margaret, after my mother. I tried to bargain with Him, but I didn't have much to offer.

I felt something cramp in my belly, and my head started to sweat. I crumpled up a piece of toilet paper and wiped myself. A small dab of red blood stared at me from the white tissue, like a stop sign in the distance. "Oh no," I moaned as I collapsed over my legs, and my mind went to black-and-white dots, like the UHF channel.

When I came to, they were all banging on the metal door, screaming about getting the janitor to take off the hinges. I heard the voices of Miss Danby and Miss Greene, our PE teachers who lived together, and the school nurse, Mrs. Klingenhoffer. I opened my eyes and saw Baa lying on the bathroom floor looking up at me. It took a moment to remember.

"What the . . . ?" I said.

"Sandra, I *had* to," she whispered. "You were out cold." Then she yelled, "She's conscious now!" Baa whispered again, "Hey, are you all right?"

"I'm not sure." I lifted my head and pulled my gym tunic down over my thighs. "Keep them out of here for a second, will you?" I was begging.

Baa slid out from the stall and started explaining that I could see and was speaking. "She just pulled up her bloomers," I heard. "I think she's okay."

I was so fucking far from okay it wasn't funny. I had a bloody dead baby floating under me. *My* baby. Dead in the toilet at Brearley.

I could've flushed the toilet right then. I could've flushed it away and never, ever had to see. Would it look like a baby? Could I tell what it was? Or would it just be a bunch of blood clots?

"SANDRA, CAN YOU HEAR US?" Mrs. Klingenhoffer screamed. How could I not? "OPEN THE DOOR! TURN THE LITTLE LATCH ON THE RIGHT HAND SIDE—"

"Yeah, I'm just getting up."

I had to see my baby once. Even if it was a gory mess. I stood up and turned around to say good-bye.

The bowl was clear. I mean, it was clear and blue, from the SaniFlush. My mouth dropped open. My baby was still here, inside of me. I cradled my abdomen with my arms. It was a girl. And the blood was a spot, a spot like they had in that pamphlet from Planned Parenthood. The pamplet had said a little spotting wasn't usually serious in the early months, but if it occurred, an expectant mother should see her doctor. So, fine. I had an appointment with their doctor for Monday afternoon.

"Sandra!" They were all waiting, Florence Nightingale and her rescue squad. I opened the door and stepped out.

"You're coming with me!" Mrs. Klingenhoffer grabbed my arm and dragged me off to the infirmary.

A half hour later, I was out of there, my condition still undiscovered. But Mrs. Klingenhoffer had called my mother and insisted I be checked by an internist. Shit, everybody was going to find out about me, and soon! I hailed a cab to the Met. It felt like the only place I could stand to be.

I turned past the membership desk in the entrance hall and rode the escalator down into the catacombs of the Egyptian collection, which were always empty. I slumped onto a wooden bench in front of a huge blocky Pharaoh and burst into tears. I cried about the impending fights with my parents, and because for a long time it was going to be uphill from here. I cried about Simon, about how he was really my only friend. I cried about Wesleyan, my "college career" that would never exist. I cried about Madame Girard, who was a completely mean person, and I cried about how my knees were killing me and how difficult it would be to walk the three blocks home. I cried until my head was totally empty and sitting there sobbing with tears running down started to feel good, like taking a hot shower. I took comfort in the cool presence of the statues—people who had lived and died four thousand years ago. How could they worry about problems like mine?

"My dear, would you like a tissue?" It was a foreign accent.

I hadn't heard her come in, but now there was this regal woman in front of me: tall, with coppery brown skin, a high rounded forehead and slanty green eyes. She reminded me of someone I'd seen just recently—Queen Nefertiti, in fact—and I got a shivery feeling. Her tissue smelled good.

"Where did you come from?"

Fortunately, she misunderstood me. "Oh, well, I come from Ethiopia, but now I am living in Paris."

I stared at her in wonderment—in love, really. She was so beautiful. "You know, I am going to have a daughter who is exactly like you, and I am going to take her to Africa and Paris."

She smiled at me playfully, like I'd given her a crazy story and a big compliment at the same time. "You are? Well, that will be interesting for you." She patted my shoulder and walked off toward New Kingdom Sculpture.

I was going to have this amazing daughter! Her skin would be light coffee brown, her eyes like antique tourmalines, and she'd have long, thick brown hair. I fingered my own fine blond strands. We'll be so different, I thought, but we'll love each other so much. And no one will come between us.

I looked up at the pharaoh, trying to see into his eyes, but he had no pupils. His cool limestone face was unlined, and his lips curved slightly in a gentle smile. This massive god-king gazed serenely out over my head, off into a distance of miles and centuries. He sat there, fixed and heavy as he'd always been, wise and calm, ready for the next four thousand years.

Lucia Sanchez: Angelita *y* Rafael

− 1980–1981 −

Let me tell you about Angelita Somoza. First of all, she was so guilty about having a dictator for a grandfather that she ruined ten years of her life by marrying her sociology professor at Harvard. Some Mickey Mouse guy with a beard, he kept her trapped in a one-bedroom apartment in Cambridge, even though she surely had the money for a place on Beacon Hill. They associated with Marxists and hippies.

Carlos and I had met her before all this, while she was still a student and came down to New York on weekends. She was a lively and elegant girl—we immediately became friends—and she was popular among the whole European and Latin American crowd. Naturally, everyone was sad when she made such a horrible marriage, and we missed her visits, although I can't imagine what we would have done with the husband. Anyway, none of us really knows what happened between the two of them, but fortunately—and thank God it was before they had any children—when she turned thirty, she came to her senses and moved to Manhattan.

She wasn't the ideal age for a single woman—I've always thought the perfect time for a girl to marry is between twenty-six and twenty-nine years old. Still, she was a decent catch. Angelita isn't beautiful. Her eyes are a little crooked: They can both look all the way over to the left, but when she looks to the right, one eye gets stuck in the middle and the other keeps going. She is tall and slim, however, with long, shiny black hair, and she has that kind of hard, bony, chic look that she knows how to make into an advantage—like Paloma Picasso, although Angelita isn't nearly as weird-looking as Paloma.

The Spanish ambassador to the UN managed to connect her to the board of a very fine co-op building on Park Avenue at Eighty-third Street, a board that had, by the way, rejected Diane von Furstenberg on the grounds of her excessive notoriety. Angelita was able to buy a lovely prewar apartment, and she found one of those sadomasochistic-type homosexual interior decorators who did her place in the high-technology style popular then—black leather couches, gray walls, metal bookcases and that thin gray carpeting used for offices. Casey Eisenhower had been Angelita's roommate at Harvard, and they remained close over the years. I think it was important for each of them to have a friend whose grandfather was head of state as well as a general—they could talk about certain things that no one else understood. Casey was working as an editor for *Harper's Bazaar* when Angelita moved into her new building, so *Bazaar* did a spread about Angelita and her apartment in the September 1980 issue. The story included a very attractive photograph of Angelita sitting on her black leather couch, wearing a black leather skirt and a gorgeous Gianfranco Ferré white silk blouse that perfectly matched a white phalaenopsis orchid on her coffee table. Rafael Echevarrí, our dear friend from Medellín, took one look at the picture and decided Angelita was exactly the sort of wife he needed to establish himself in New York society. One night while Carlos and I were out with him at Le Cirque, Rafael asked me if I would introduce him to her.

"Certainly." I speared a snail from its shell and swabbed it in garlic butter.

"And do you think I have a chance?"

"My love, she has just spent ten years living in exile with some smelly gringo in blue jeans. She'll fall into your arms."

Rafael smiled.

"Anyway, I know how to make a man look better than he is, and I will do that for you."

Rafael ordered a bottle of champagne. We toasted his betrothal, drank and laughed a lot, and of course Carlos and I were very happy when Rafael picked up the check, because we were not rich. Carlos worked as a consultant to Occidental Petroleum, on their Colombian operations. With the stupid guerrillas kidnapping people and blowing things up all over the place, he could hardly keep Occidental interested in our country, and we were barely managing to pay the bills at our apartment on Fifty-seventh Street. Rafael, thank God, helped by introducing us to some of the Colombian cabinet ministers, so we were able to get permits for oil exploration in areas that were officially off limits to foreign corporations. And I did a little business of my own—shopping in New York for the wives of those ministers, who weren't able to get out of Bogotá as much as they would have liked.

Physically, Rafael is nothing special. He is medium height with a medium build. His nose is rather large and formed like a beak, and his skin has faint scars left over from teenage acne. Still, his eyes are intelligent, he dresses in English suits and Italian shoes, and his smile is charming. He comes from a modest background but projects a marvelous confidence. By hook or by crook—more crook than hook, I fear—he has made a success of himself in international trading and is enormously wealthy. He has fine manners and a way of focusing his attention on you that gives you the feeling you are the most fascinating person on earth: something everyone likes to believe, no? Listen, I admit I found him seductive one night while he was staying in our apartment, as he always did when he came up to New York, before he bought his condo in the Olympic Tower. Carlos was away, meeting with the Occidental people in Los Angeles. Rafael had taken me to the theater, then we stopped for dinner at Mr. Chow's. As we walked back home, Rafael pulled my hand through his arm. "How light you feel," he said.

"Ah yes, I am small, like a chicken."

"Like a dove," he answered.

In the foyer, I felt sort of funny, the way I'd felt as a girl at the end of a date. "Well, you know where your room is," I said. "Lucia." Rafael stood with his hands on my shoulders, looking down into my eyes. "If Carlos weren't such a good friend, I'd beg you to sleep with me." In other words, he was interested, and it was up to me whether or not to start the affair.

I did go to my room alone that night, but believe me, I did not sleep soundly. Several times I sat up in bed, looked out of the window and thought about what it might be like to leave Carlos and become Rafael Echevarrí's lover. I thought of traveling with him, of not having to struggle anymore, of the sexual pleasure of someone new. But after the initial fantasy of delight, I always came to the same conclusion. Life would be complicated with Rafael. He would eventually move on to someone more glamorous, and afterward, where would I be?

Angelita was in a different position. She had some money, the Somoza name, and she was ten years younger than I. She looked stunning the night we introduced her to Rafael, almost radiant. Carlos and I had brought him to a cocktail party at the Spanish Institute. Just as we walked in, a photographer was taking Angelita's picture, together with Nina von Hohenlohe and the president of the Venezuelan Trade Commission. Angelita wore a red silk cocktail dress, emerald drop earrings and had her hair pulled up in a French twist. When the photographer's bulbs stopped flashing, Angelita came over and kissed us hello. "Lucia, Carlos, *ciao!*"

I pulled her aside. "Tell me you are here alone."

"No." She pointed across the room with one and a half of her eyes. "That Swedish one over there." A tall blond man—very handsome—stood talking with Jaime and Monica Hernandez.

"My dear, he is gorgeous." I worried for Rafael. "So, is this some kind of new love?"

"No, not yet." Angelita giggled. "But I would like him to be. It's only our third time out. We haven't even slept together."

"Hmmph," I said. "Probably homosexual."

"Lucia!"

"I'm sorry, my love. It's just that a close friend of ours from Colombia is here. He is new to town, and I was hoping you were free to have dinner with us after the party."

"Well, no, I can't," she said, "but I would love to meet your friend."

I presented her to Rafael. He took her hand and raised it to his lips. He gazed into Angelita's crooked eyes. "Enchanted."

She smiled, but I could tell she wasn't paying much attention. "Come," she said, "I'll introduce you around," and she walked him over to the group with the handsome Swede.

I promised Rafael I would investigate the Swede. It turned out he was a childhood friend of Bjorn Borg. He had been a second-rate tennis player who now handled some public relations for the International Tennis Federation. His name was Boris Something-or-other, and he never woke up until noon. He lunched lavishly each day with a different sportswriter on his ITF expense account, and he passed his evenings crashing parties, getting by on his looks, his toothpaste-commercial grin and the fact that he spoke a few languages. He hung around clubs like Studio 54 and Doubles until three or four in the morning. He'd had affairs with Bianca Jagger, the princess of Savoia and some runway model turned singer named Annie Lennox. The previous spring he had broken the heart of Margaretha of Bavaria's youngest daughter, and all summer long, at Margaretha's villa on Ibiza, the poor girl hid in her bedroom weeping. Clearly, he was Mickey Mouse all around.

Angelita did get more involved with him, and I told her she was making a big mistake. She denied it was anything serious. "Come on, Lucia," she said on the phone one morning, "I'm only having some fun."

"Angelita, you are softhearted, and you fall in love no matter what. The last time you ran around with a man of this caliber, you ended up on his collective with his comrades for ten whole years."

"Party pooper!" She changed the subject to the dress she had bought for the Boys' Town of Mexico Ball.

I wasn't that worried about it. Angelita would fall in love with Boris the Swede, but it didn't sound like he was sitting still with one woman for too long. I told Rafael to keep coming with us to all the parties—to keep coming alone. Sooner or later, I would point, and he could shoot his fox.

———

The Boys' Town of Mexico Ball is one of the truly fun parties of the year. So many of these formal events are boring to die. Insipid American bands play two-steps and waltzes. There's pale chicken for dinner, with a few boiled potatoes and three pieces of mushy asparagus. Finally, someone gets up to the microphone and begins hours of speeches about whatever charity we're supporting.

Boys' Town of Mexico always starts with a benefit concert at Carnegie Hall. Then we go to the Waldorf for a late supper and dancing in the ballroom. The committee keeps a Latin theme every year—the food has some flavor, and when we dance, it's rumba and cumbia, salsa and merengue. Even the gringos like Casey Eisenhower's friends loosen up and have a good time. And although Boys' Town of Mexico is an association of orphanages, no one ever ruins the gay mood of the evening by stopping the music to talk about lonely children.

This year the party was going to be really special. The committee had booked Julio Iglesias for the concert, and he agreed to come over and join the ball afterward. Carlos and I were invited to sit with Angelita at one of Casey's tables, together with Emilio Lisboa—the richest man in Madeira—and his American mistress. The president of the Banco Santander was seated with us, too, but because his mother-in-law was sick and his wife had decided to fly back to Spain, I was able to get Rafael the empty place. Carlos and I took him downtown to Barneys to help him choose a new tuxedo for the occasion.

Rafael was complaining in the taxi. "My other tuxedo is only four years old. I'm sure it would be fine."

"Listen," I told him, "there's nothing we can do improve your face, so please, let's acquire all the advantages that money can buy."

"My God, Carlos, how do you live with this beast?"

"I wear falconer's gloves, a helmet of steel, a bulletproof vest, and you should see what I use for underwear."

I appreciate Carlos because he makes me laugh, and because he has adored me since the day we met at the university cafeteria in Bogotá. He was neither the handsomest man who courted me nor the richest, but I chose him because I have always thought it important that a woman have a husband who loves her more than she loves him. In the same way, I wasn't sorry that Angelita was carrying on with the Swede and that Rafael needed to fight a little to get her. He would value her more, and she would start off the relationship from a better position.

We had an excellent table at the ball, close to the stage and highly visible. Angelita was superb that night, dressed in a straight strapless navy blue sheath with a matching navy scarf draped over her shoulder and pinned to her dress with a diamond brooch. She wore sapphire and diamond clips on her ears, her hair was pulled back in a thick braid in the typical Latin American countryside tradition. She was gracious and friendly with Rafael, but her eyes darted around the room, keeping track of her Swede as he kissed every woman and shook the hand of every important man. The rich guy from

Funchal arrived late with his twenty-two-year-old girl-friend—perhaps because they needed to screw between the concert and dinner, or maybe his wooden teeth fell out in the limousine and he had to run home for another set. The girl was a knockout—blond and pink with boobs and hips all over the place, dripping with the kind of jewelry displayed in the Tower of London. She was seated next to Rafael, and the two of them immediately became engrossed in a deep conversation about the beaches of Australia. I pinched Rafael's earlobe.

"Ouch!" He turned around to face me.

"For Christ's sake, show some discipline," I whispered. "Even *you* can't afford that girl. And it's not good for your future if Angelita remembers you fawning all over a stupid blond whore."

"Isn't that what I have to tolerate from her?" Just at that moment Angelita was stroking the Swede's shoulder while he twisted around to chat with the Ecuadorian consul general.

"Yes, but never mind. You are the one trying to marry her, so you need to behave."

The dinner plates were cleared, and Casey Eisenhower took the stage. She was a pretty girl, in that strong East Coast nautical sort of way. Her light hair was short, cut in layers. Her arms had muscles in them, probably from playing games like tennis and croquet. She thanked everyone for coming, for supporting Boys' Town of Mexico. Then she said the perfect thing: "Tonight every woman in this room will fall for a Latin lover. My dear friends, please welcome Julio Iglesias."

Julio was wonderful, and so incredibly sexy. He did a couple of traditional Spanish love songs and "The Girl from Ipanema." Then he stopped to introduce a surprise guest. "I am proud to share this stage with a singer much, much greater than I." Modesty was cute on him. "Ladies and gentlemen, my friend and idol, Placido Domingo."

Everyone went crazy applauding. The two men sang a duet—Julio's voice sensual and smooth, Placido's tenor astounding. I reached for Carlos's hand and caressed it. If you didn't feel romantic with these two serenading, then your heart was poured from concrete. Angelita was swaying to the music, but the Swede watched the entrance to the ballroom. In the middle of the song, he left the table, and when it was over, with everyone clapping and cheering, Angelita was all alone with an empty seat beside her. The band started playing, and the lights came on. I kicked Rafael in the ankle, and he got up and invited Angelita to dance.

Let me tell you, Rafael is an excellent dancer. When he takes you in his arms, you sense right away that he is absolutely in control, yet he holds you and moves you in a tender way. Dancing with him is as good as making love with most men. I couldn't see much of him and Angelita in the crowd—Carlos and I were on the other side of the dance floor—but when they came back to the table, I could tell from Angelita's face that something had happened. Her skin was quite rosy—not just her cheeks but also her décolletage. She had this look in her eyes, dizzy and childish, like she had gone to the fair and ridden the carousel too many times. She was distracted. When she sat down near me, I said, "Look at Maria Beatriz in that dress."

"Oh yes," Angelita said in a voice that sounded as if she'd been taken away in a spaceship, "lovely."

Maria Beatriz de Segovia was nothing that could ever be described as lovely, and in the dress she had on, she was even worse. A little bit fat, she had squeezed herself into about a thousand horizontal layers of pearl-colored silk that wound around and around her. Her hair was dyed a caramel color, and she wore it piled up in a big mess that looked like chewed English toffee. She had dusted her face with some kind of bronze powder, and her crepe-y bosom, which oozed up from the top of her dress, was dusted with more of the same stuff. She looked like a fat brown caterpillar trying desperately to burst out of its cocoon.

The Swede returned with some Italian prince from Le Marche who didn't have a pot to pee in and now worked in the fashion business. Probably they had been sniffing cocaine in the men's room. They sat down on either side of Angelita, talking quickly right across her, but she didn't seem to notice them. She was staring straight ahead, gazing into the red and white carnations of the centerpiece like this was the first time she had ever seen a flower. I understood that Rafael had lodged his dart in her, and its toxin now flowed in her bloodstream.

At the end of November, Angelita broke up with the Swede. The final straw was when he had promised to attend a Thanksgiving dinner in her home and didn't show up. Carlos and I didn't witness the scene—we were down in Bogotá, kissing the rear end of the trade minister—but Monica Hernandez told me it was dreadful. Angelita was fretting all evening, looking at the clock every five minutes, saying in a silly, hopeful voice, "Oh dear, I wonder what's making Boris so late?" She kept slipping out of the room, obviously trying to call him but getting no answer. A couple of times her maid, Elvira, came out to the living room to ask if she could serve the dinner, but Angelita shooed her away. It was ten o'clock and everyone was starving. After yet another of Angelita's disappearances, Elvira tapped Monica's shoulder and said that Señora Somoza would like her to come to the bedroom.

Monica said Angelita was undone. She sat on the edge of her bed, tears dripping from her cheeks, mascara running everywhere. She was sobbing so hard that Monica could barely make out her words, but it seemed that Angelita had at last reached the Italian rinky-dink prince friend, and he told her that Boris had left that morning on a private jet together with Vitas Gerulaitis, bound for somebody's estate in Santa Barbara.

Monica did everything she could. She brought tissues, cool washcloths, a bowl of ice from the kitchen. She cleaned Angelita's face, tried to help her reapply some makeup. But Angelita kept breaking down. Finally, Monica found a silk nightgown in the bathroom, helped Angelita undress and tucked her into bed. Back in the living room, Monica said, "Boris has a terrible flu, and now it seems Angelita caught it from him." She stepped hard on Jaime's toe to make sure he wouldn't question her absurd explanation. "She has gone to bed, but she asked everyone to please excuse her and enjoy dinner as if this were our own home." Two place settings were taken off the table, and the meal was served. Naturally, the food was horrible from sitting around for so many hours. All the guests were on pins and needles, avoiding the current subject of interest. It was deadly quiet, the silence broken every so often by an inane comment about the weather or one person politely asking another where he or she planned to spend Christmas—something everyone already knew. As soon as dessert was finished, everyone fled the table and went home, and Monica phoned me in Bogotá to tell me what had happened.

The morning after we returned to New York, I called Angelita and went to see her. She was looking pale, even thinner than usual, and her eyes were a puffy mess. I embraced her. "My love, you are not eating!" She was not going out, either; in fact, she had missed several important parties, even the committee luncheon for the Casa de los Niños Ball.

"Oh, Lucia, I have made an idiot of myself. Not only am I devastated, but I'm embarrassed to show my face around town." She blew her nose in a tissue. "Even you," she said, "you were the one who tried to warn me against him."

I had too many real struggles in my life to feel patient in the face of this sort of melodrama. But I thought of Rafael, how he was all coiled like a snake and now had his chance to strike, so I held my tongue. "My dear, no one judges you." I tried not to think of the burning-hot phone wires crisscrossing New York the morning after Thanksgiving. "You need fresh air, and today it's not very cold. Come, put on some dark glasses and a pair of comfortable shoes. Let's take a walk down Madison and look in the windows of the shops."

Angelita nodded. She searched around for a jacket and a purse and put in a call to her pharmacist. "You don't mind if we pop into Madison Chemists? I need a refill of my sleeping pills."

Going down in the elevator, Angelita said good morning to a rough-looking blond girl in blue jeans, holding the hand of a small Negro boy.

"Who the hell are they?" I asked when we were out on the sidewalk.

She told me the girl was the daughter of one of her neighbors. "The boy is her son."

"How is that even possible?"

"Elvira knows their maid," Angelita said. "Supposedly, something went on between the girl and their former chauffeur—a very dark-skinned guy from Jamaica."

"Ay, my God, how disgusting! In this building?" I couldn't believe it. "What a scandal, no?"

Angelita just shrugged. Clearly, she was too involved with her own tragedy to worry about another one.

We had a nice stroll, and we stopped at Rive Gauche to peruse the newly arrived resort-wear collection. I walked her back to her building. When we said good-bye, I made her promise to come over for dinner on Friday night. "Something casual—empanadas, a salad, menudo. Just us. Family." The doorman hailed me a cab.

The minute I was home, I called Rafael and invited him, too.

Angelita was a little surprised when she arrived at our house and Rafael opened the door. "Forgive me for intruding on your evening," he said. "I was in my apartment alone. The only thing I am able to cook is an egg, and when Lucia said you were coming here for supper, I begged to be included." He kissed her on both cheeks.

"No, no." Angelita smiled. "I am happy to see you." She greeted us, too, and followed me into the kitchen to help.

"Ay, Lucia," she whispered. "Had I known there would be another man here, I would have put myself more together." She was wearing a black-and-tan-patterned sweater, black slacks and low-heeled shoes. Her hair was loose, and she wore almost no makeup. She wasn't as striking as usual but looked softer, more vulnerable. I had instructed Rafael to wear a suit, and he had shown up in a beautiful charcoal-gray pinstripe. I liked the idea of matching a dressed man with an undressed woman, sort of like a *Déjeuner sur l'herbe*.

I handed Angelita a tray of empanadas and a bowl of dipping sauce. "Go on," I said. "I am almost finished in here. Why don't you bring this out to the men?"

I had earlier told Rafael that it was important to make Angelita feel sorry for him.

"Why on earth?" The very idea made him bristle.

"She's compassionate," I said. "Idealistic. She likes small animals, wounded souls, Jimmy Carter. So whatever you do tonight, sound a little bit pathetic and don't show off too much."

At the dinner table, Rafael spoke of his boyhood. It was a difficult time, he said. He grew up in a crowded apartment over the family grocery store in Medellín, with his parents, six younger siblings and a sickly grandmother. There was a prestigious private academy at the end of his street, and he had been dying to go to school there, even though he knew he would be teased by the rich boys. Because he was "sort of clever," as he put it, his mother convinced the head of the academy to let him take the qualifying examination. He did so well on the test that the school made an exception and admitted him, waiving the tuition. But at the last minute before the term was to begin, the deputy mayor had a friend who wanted to enroll his son, and Rafael was preempted.

"Oh, how terrible," Angelita said.

"Listen, that's how the world works," Carlos told her.

Angelita was outraged. "But it shouldn't!"

In reality, Rafael's father had been the deputy mayor's grocer, and it was the deputy mayor who arranged for Rafael to attend that school. But there was little chance that Angelita would ever review his early educational records. He told her how he used to study at night in the back of his father's store, since it was too noisy in the apartment, with all his brothers and sisters crying and his deaf grandmother chattering away, unable to listen to anyone else. Because of the diligent work he did beside the sacks of flour and cornmeal that he himself had hauled off the delivery truck that day, Rafael was admitted to the university in Medellín. "My passion was philosophy," he said, "but because of our economic situation, I had to take my degree in business."

Rafael's bullshit was so thick I almost laughed. I coughed into my napkin instead and motioned Carlos to come help me put on the coffee in the kitchen. We could hear Rafael's deep voice from the other room and Angelita's tender cooing. "Jesus Christ," Carlos whispered, "he is going to win an Academy Award!"

"He will win more than that," I whispered back.

Though Rafael Echevarrí surely had his fish on the hook, she was not yet reeled in, flopping and suffocating on the deck of his boat. He did take her to brunch at Tavern on the Green the Sunday after our little dinner party, but on Monday he had to fly off to Geneva for a week and then to Madrid for a friend's wedding. While he was gone, the Swede came back, offering Angelita some sort of apology, and invited her to spend Christmas with him at a friend's villa in Mustique.

"Don't go," I begged her when we met for lunch at La Grenouille. "That man is a refrigerator—all blond and blue-eyed, with a heart of pure ice."

"But Lucia, you should have heard him. He was so kind, so self-deprecating. And you know what else?" Angelita smiled like an idiot, her crooked eyes sparkling. "He said he loved me."

"He did?"

"Well, not word for word . . ."

"What exactly did he say?" I was so annoyed I could barely enjoy my meal, even though La Grenouille grills the best liver in town.

"Oh, he had been speaking about how he was just a big playboy, how he used women and threw them out, how he never thought about their feelings. How he was always off to the next party, the next girl . . . And then he took my hand, and he was staring out the window of my living room like he was looking down the path of a meaningless future. In the saddest voice, almost like the voice of a child, he said, 'But Angie, I do want love in my life.'"

"That is not 'I love you.'"

"I know, but for him it was a breakthrough . . ."

"I would like to break through his head with an ice pick. He is not a refrigerator. He's a freezer!"

Angelita herself was a bit chilly with me as we left the restaurant and kissed good-bye.

"What is wrong with that woman?" Rafael demanded when he returned to New York and I told him the story. We were sitting at Le Relais eating sweetbreads—I love them.

I said she was overly loyal. "Eventually, that will work in your favor."

Rafael cocked his head sideways and stared at me. He resembled an angry parrot. "And what if this big Boris marries her?" He held his knife and fork straight up from the table like weapons. I was glad to see him so jealous. After all, what I wished most for Angelita was a marriage based on love.

"Don't worry. The Swede is married to one thing only: a certain white powder he sniffs up his nose."

"Hummph!" Rafael shook his head, then went back to his plate. I supposed he had become philosophical. I imagined him weighing the economics of the situation. Though Rafael had no personal regard for the drug, he certainly respected the money its industry generated, especially the money that ran through his own businesses and found its way into Swiss bank accounts. People like Boris the Swede were an integral part of Rafael's own well-being. Of course, we never spoke of these things. "You know," he said, "I have become fond of the girl. Really, she is lovely."

I squeezed his hand and smiled. "She is lovely. And stupid enough to fall in love with you.

"I promise you. By the end of January, it is all over with the Swede. So go see your mother for Christmas, get any other trips out of the way, and plan to be back in town next month to break her fall."

"Like a knight in shining armor," he said gleefully, swishing his knife in the air and jabbing it toward the next table. A stiff-backed gringa sat there, looking like she'd been boiled in water for four hours and then wrung out to dry. She glared at him.

"Like a trampoline," I said.

Carlos and I spent a delightful Christmas at home in New York. Most of our friends were out of town, and our business was concluded for the year, so we spent a quiet week that felt like a second honeymoon. We put up a tree with Mexican decorations. We went to *The Nutcracker* at Lincoln Center and Handel's *Messiah* at the Cathedral of St. John the Divine. We shopped together for our presents, having decided in our semi-impoverished state to give each other one fine thing that we really wanted, rather than a bunch of silly surprises. Carlos bought me a mink hat at Saks Fifth Avenue and a pair of red leather gloves with some mink trim around the cuffs. At André Oliver, we found him a beautiful cable-knit cashmere sweater in a shade of mossy green that played up his hazel eyes. We passed a whole day in the Metropolitan Museum, not visiting any special exhibition, just wandering around the halls looking at our favorite things from the permanent collection. We ate lunch in the cafeteria at the end of the classical wing, sitting at a table by the fountain pool. We spoke of how nice it would be if the world stayed out of our way forever, how we could happily spend our lives together quietly, alone on an island, so long as that island was Manhattan.

By New Year's Eve, the city was hopping again. Monica and Jaime were back from Spain, and they gave a party in their Sutton Place penthouse. Angelita and Boris were there, both looking tanned and happy. The Swede was so blond, and Angelita's hair so dark and thick, that together they made a knockout couple. In Jaime's den, I asked Angelita how her trip had gone.

"Oh, Lucia, it was fantastic! The villa was exquisite, and for the last four days, we had it to ourselves. Just us and the sea and the stars . . ."

She was making me sick. As I watched her and Boris throughout the evening, I thought I saw a change in him. He was attentive and affectionate toward her and charming with her friends. I reasoned to myself that of course they'd had a beautiful time together—a week in a tropical villa for free, with nothing to do but swim, eat mangoes and screw—who couldn't fall in love under those conditions? Still, I was concerned. What if Boris did decide to marry her? He had more need of an anchor like Angelita than even Rafael. Maybe he wasn't so stupid and had realized what some money, the apartment on Park Avenue and her family name could do for him.

I was afraid of how Rafael might take defeat. He was a passionate man, not a graceful loser. I knew that in business he had a reputation as a son of a bitch, but up until now Carlos and I had always considered him our son of a bitch, and we counted on him. What would happen if he became furious with us for leading him on, wasting his time and making him look like a fool? Would he tell the Colombian trade department to stop granting us favors? Or would he do something even worse, like set me up to be caught by customs the next time we arrived in Bogotá with eight suitcases crammed full of Calvin Klein jeans for all those bureaucrats' wives?

I decided that something had to be done, but since nothing could happen tonight, I should try to enjoy myself. Fortunately, the party was fun. After a formal sit-down dinner for three tables of twelve, Monica and Jaime gathered us all together in the living room. We counted down the end of the year, and at midnight exactly, every man in the room popped a bottle of champagne. Fireworks went off over the East River, and out of the kitchen emerged a nine-piece mariachi band dressed in the traditional black costume with embroidery, silver trimmings and sombreros, blaring trumpets and strumming guitars. We all drank and danced until the sun rose on the first morning of 1981.

Carlos and I had an argument at our kitchen table on New Year's Day. We were both cranky and had headaches, but we were not seeing eye to eye.

"I will not have that woman in my house!" He pounded his fist on the table and then reached for his brow, regretting the loud noise. "And especially not on my birthday!"

"Carlos, it's our only chance. If not, then you think of another plan."

He swallowed the concoction of raw eggs and Worchestershire sauce that is supposed to be helpful for a hangover. He had offered to mix me one, but even looking at it made me want to vomit. I drank ginger ale and snacked on salted fried ants I had sneaked in from Bogotá. I swear, I am the only person in New York who smuggles from Colombia and is still broke.

Carlos said, "Maybe Angelita just needs to do what she needs to do."

"Ay, bullshit! We need to do what we need to do. And most of all, that means make a living. I'm not going to sit still and watch our lives crumble." I stormed out of the kitchen and down the hall to our bedroom. I slammed the door hard, hoping my husband's skull would crack. I lay on the bed.

A few minutes later, Carlos tiptoed in and lay next to me. "Okay, Lucia. If it means so much to you. Invite the nymphomaniac."

"Thank you."

"Be sure to count the silver and lock up your jewelry. I hear she steals, too."

The nymphomaniac was the wife of a movie star. I won't tell you who, because now they are divorced, and I admire his acting very much. The nymphomaniac was an American girl, but she had been raised in all the finest European schools and resorts. She was sophisticated, she spoke at least six languages fluently and she was beautiful, with long chestnut-colored ringlets, green eyes and a slim, sexy figure. She had every promise of becoming a successful woman at the top of society, except she was absolutely out of her mind. Even though she was married to one of the handsomest men I can think of, she had ended up under the dinner table at more than one Los Angeles party, attending to some film director or, worse yet, a basketball star. It seemed she couldn't resist anyone, so long as he was famous or noble or extremely good-looking. I had heard from Michel de Clovigny, an important homosexual hairdresser, that she was coming into New York this week, to buy a new apartment for her husband and herself.

I called Michel and asked him to bring the nymphomaniac over to supper this weekend. I invited Angelita and Boris and a few other friends who wouldn't be so scandalized by her presence that they would think less of Carlos and me. Jaime and Monica I could always count on. I also asked Richard von Gutburg, a German prince I didn't have to worry about, because he had a good sense of humor and was also quite fat—from him there would be neither judgment nor competition. I invited the former Colombian ambassador to the UN, a distinguished man who was ninety years old, nearly blind and deaf in one ear. His wife, Graciela, was an alcoholic who tended to fall asleep at the dinner table. I figured they wouldn't notice what happened that night. I hired a caterer. I didn't want Lorena, our usual maid, to see what went on.

"I can't believe what you will stoop to," Carlos said.

"Well, look in the mirror," I told him. "You are stooping, too."

The nymphomaniac showed up in a slinky gold-colored dress that looked like a nightgown. She wore no bra, and her pointy nipples slid around against the thin material. Angelita and Boris were jolly when they arrived, she cute in a black-and-white-striped boatneck sweater and a velvet skirt. Boris had on a houndstooth sport jacket and some pleated pants; he looked like the son of an English lord, with better dentistry. The nymphomaniac spotted him instantly, and she followed her bobbing nipples across the room to meet him. "This is Angelita Somoza," I said. "And this is her boyfriend, Boris." I didn't even know his last name. "In Sweden, Boris was a tennis champion." Boris didn't bother to correct me. He put his lips to the nymphomaniac's hand. All through the cocktail hour, she didn't leave his side.

Monica Hernandez cornered me in the dining room as I was lighting the candles on the table. She glanced at Boris's place card next to that of the nymphomaniac. "I see what you are doing," she said.

I turned to face her. "Listen, you and I both love Angelita. The way I look at it, this is like surgery. The doctor cuts you open and tears something out. It's painful for a few days, but then you are cured forever."

"Perhaps you are right. I can't forget what she went through at Thanksgiving. I guess I was just hoping, because she seems so happy now, that maybe he had really reformed."

"There's nothing wrong with testing him, no?"

"No, nothing at all," Monica said. "Better now than later. Let this be his chance to show his mettle."

"Or his ass."

At dinner, the strap of the nymphomaniac's dress had slipped off her shoulder, and her breasts were nearly falling into Boris's plate. Her hand beside him was somewhere below the table. Michel tittered and rolled his eyes. The wife of the ambassador drank her eighth glass of wine and started to doze. At the far end of the table, next to Angelita, the old diplomat was telling a long, pointless story about being stationed in Rome during the Spanish Civil War. Angelita kept stealing looks at Boris, but he pretended not to notice. The nymphomaniac whispered something in his ear, got up and wiggled out of the room. A moment later, Boris looked at his watch and clapped himself on the head as if he were stupid enough to have forgotten something. He asked Carlos if he could use the phone in our bedroom and hurried away. After the two had been absent for about five minutes, I rose and whispered to Angelita, "Darling, I hid a birthday cake for Carlos in my closet. Will you come and help me with the candles?" She already had an alarmed look on her face, and she was all too glad to see what was up.

For all my effort and the expense of the dinner party, I was hoping to witness something outré in our bedroom—someone tied up or a position no one had ever thought of. Instead, it was quite normal: Boris on top, the nymphomaniac's high heels crossed above his tanned behind, which was pumping up and down like oil-drilling machinery. He stopped when he heard us come in, and struggled to get back in his pants. The girl giggled like an idiot. I expected Angelita to faint or begin some sort of hysterical breakdown, and I prepared myself to catch her. I have to say, her composure in that moment will impress me forever.

"Boris, I am not leaving another party because of you!" She spoke in a firm, commanding voice inherited directly from her famous grandfather. "I would suggest that you zip your fly, find your coat and get the hell out of here. If I were you, I'd take a good long vacation and then think twice before showing your face around me or any of my friends." She marched into the room, straight past both of them. "Come, Lucia, let's bring that cake for Carlos."

I was glad I had in fact put a cake in my closet. I never expected her to get that far.

Boris and the nymphomaniac crept out of the bedroom. They were gone from our apartment by the time Angelita and I emerged with blazing candles singing "Happy Birthday to You."

"Angelita," I said at the end of the evening, "you are incredible. To have faced that situation with such character and poise."

"Ay, Lucia," she said, shaking her head with a sadness in her voice that sounded old, "even I knew that things with Boris were too good to be real."

"Well, my dear, if you ever want to return to Nicaragua, you have all the balls necessary to kick those Sandinistas' ass."

Angelita burst out laughing. It was the first time she had ever tolerated someone poking fun at her background.

In the morning I called Rafael. "It is over between Angelita and the Swede. You have her phone number. The rest is up to you."

I was tickled because Rafael sounded nervous. "Does she need some time to recover? Is it too soon to call, do you think?"

I said it wasn't a second too soon.

He took her to the opera one night, and Angelita said she'd had a nice time. I couldn't find out what happened next, because Carlos and I had to travel to Colombia again, and our two-week trip turned into three as we waited to sign a deal. When we finally came home, Angelita and Rafael were both away. It was either a very good sign or a very bad one, and I nearly went crazy not knowing. Carlos teased me. "Do you know what a yenta is, my dear?" Of course I did. "Well, you are a *yenta latina.*"

The third day we were back, Angelita finally called. She was breathless. She had to see me that minute. My hair wasn't done, so I couldn't go out, but I invited her to stop by for a cup of tea. She arrived at the apartment wearing a beautifully cut red suit and, underneath, a silk blouse printed with different-colored flowers on a black background. I kissed her and put on the water to boil, and we sat on my sofa in the living room.

"You look fantastic," I told her. "Ungaro?"

"Yes, of course. Who else does prints like these?" She touched her fingers to her collar, and I was struck practically blind by a diamond the size of Andorra.

"Ay, Angelita!"

"I know!"

I took her long slim hands in mine and looked at her face. We both had tears in our eyes. "I am so happy for you. And for Rafael."

"Rafael? I am marrying Boris. He came back."

"What!" I pulled my hands away quickly. I felt something sharp against my finger, as if I'd severed it on that big rock.

Angelita laughed. "No, no. I am kidding. Of course it's Rafael. Rafael . . ." She said his name like Juliet saying "Romeo" when she was hanging out the window of her parents' house.

"You brat!" I slapped at the sleeve of her suit. "You nearly gave me a heart attack."

She told me the story of how the engagement happened. How he'd arranged for dinner in a suite of the Hôtel Pierre. How he sent the waiters away and served the meal himself. How, when they were finished eating, he bent down on one knee like a prince from the times when princes still had somewhere to rule. How he pulled the ring out of his tuxedo pocket, telling her she was more valuable to him than all the diamonds in the world. How they had been shacked up in that suite for the past week, leaving only once to do some shopping.

"By the way," she interrupted herself, "I have something for you." She picked up her red leather pocketbook, popped open the latch and handed me a thin rectangular box wrapped in silver paper and a gauzy bow. "A gift. From Rafael. Open it." She looked like the birthday girl at a children's party. A kind girl who, although she received many presents, would be happy only if there were favors for all her friends, too.

I tore off the paper and found a hinged leather box from

Piaget. When I flipped it open, I had my second threat of coronary failure that day. Inside was a watch, exquisite and sparkling. On its platinum face, a diamond marked each hour. The bezel was a circle of diamonds. The band was made of pavé diamonds set in platinum links. I had once admired a watch with many fewer stones than this at Cartier, and that one cost over twenty-five thousand dollars.

I am never speechless, but at that moment my tongue felt thick. "What on earth is this?"

"Read the card."

One of Rafael's business cards was enclosed in the box. I saw his name and the three addresses—New York, Miami, Medellín. I turned it over and read his writing. *For you, Lucia, to wear at our wedding and to wear in happiness for the rest of your life.—R.*

"My God, Angelita, this is unbelievable! I am embarrassed." I was shocked by the extravagance of my commission. I had expected, perhaps, air tickets to Paris, a major favor when I needed one. Anyway, it was good that I seemed surprised. "Why has he made me such a gift?"

"Oh, Lucia. Isn't it funny how you can know Rafael so closely for so long, but not know a thing about what he's like when he's in love?

"Lucia, he's the most wonderful man. He gave you that watch to thank you, to express his gratitude for introducing him to me. He says that you are the one who led the way to the greatest happiness in his life. You and Carlos. I have a gift for

Carlos, too." She pulled another box from her purse, the same shape, a little bit bigger.

"Don't you see, Lucia? The generosity. The joyful innocence. That's just how my Rafael is!"

I blinked my eyes and stared at her. Believe me, though it isn't my common practice, that day I let Angelita have the last word. In the kitchen, the teakettle whistled like a rocket taking off for the moon.

Being Someone

— 1981 —

In September 1981, Shelley Sapphire signed up for a women's studies course at the New School. She was reading some books—*The Awakening, The Second Sex, The Female Eunuch.* Dick Sapphire became a little nervous.

"Of course I believe in women's lib," he said, holding open his manicured hand. "It's just that . . . well, sometimes you sound so angry when you read this stuff. You were so angry after synagogue today, going on about the 'oppressive patriarchy.'" It was Yom Kippur, and the Sapphires had just returned home after breaking the fast at Shelley's mother-in-law's apartment. "My mother had no idea what you were talking about. She kept looking at you funny."

They were in the bedroom. Shelley pulled off her gold-and-pearl ear clips and massaged her lobes. "Oh well, Ethel looks at me cross-eyed no matter what I say."

"I thought the service was nice. I don't know where you're getting this idea about oppression. Don't you like our rabbi?"

"Yes, he's fine, the rabbi's fine." She felt irritated. She pulled the bobby pins from her shoulder-length blond hair and shook it loose. "I just don't see much of a role for women in the Jewish tradition. Other than cooking and babies."

"So is Christianity different?"

"No, it's not. That's the problem." She stepped out of her beige-and-ivory leather high heels. Her toes in their panty hose were white from being pinched all day into a triangular shape.

Dick scratched his head, stretched out on the bed and leaned against the upholstered headboard. He hung his feet over the side of the mattress, keeping his shoes off the bed-spread. "C'mon, honey, who cares? We're not so religious—we go to temple twice, maybe three times a year. You didn't have to cook tonight. My mother didn't even have to cook—her maid did it all. Anyway, I thought you liked to cook."

"I *do* like to cook!" She saw Dick shake his head and sigh as she put her shoes in the closet. That wasn't the point, she thought as she undressed, cooking or not cooking, whether or not you liked the stupid rabbi. The point was about being a woman versus being *someone*, but Dick never seemed to get the difference. How could he? He waltzed in and out of his firm, in and out of his clubs—the Harmonie on Sixtieth Street, Old Oaks up in Westchester. Everyone knew who he was: Dick Sapphire, the big contract lawyer, the tennis player with the great serve. He was Madeline and Ritchie's father;

everyone knew them, too. But who was she? Dick Sapphire's second wife. A pretty blonde. No children of her own. A *shiksa*, though she'd converted to Judaism for their wedding. That was about it. She was a pretty, converted-*shiksa*, childless second wife.

Shelley didn't like Yom Kippur. All day in temple with low blood sugar. She was officially there to repent for her sins, but she never found herself doing much repenting. Actually, today had been the opposite. She'd spent the majority of her time in the pew—or whatever it was called in a synagogue—thinking about people who had wronged her. How Ritchie had been so grateful to Dick when he got into Duke, but he hadn't directed one smile her way—and who had edited all those application essays? Her mother-in-law's stinging comments on the way to temple the night before, reminiscing about how beautiful Dick's first wife, Lauren, had been. Of course she was beautiful, Shelley had wanted to scream, she died before she was thirty-five years old. And then Shelley had thought about her first husband, Phillip—Phillip who had left her three months after their son was stillborn. He'd said their personalities "just didn't mesh anymore," but she knew that was French for: *After two miscarriages and now this, it's obvious you aren't going to produce any children, and if you're not producing, I'm not staying.* He'd married a girl ten years her junior the minute their divorce became final. As if she and this new wife were some kind of livestock purchased for breeding.

At least Dick already had his kids, fortunately now both off at college. Shelley hung up her suit and slipped a nightgown over her head. And Dick did seem to truly love her, though she wasn't sure what there was inside of her to love.

She sat on the edge of the bed, close to Dick, and took his hands in hers. "Look, honey, I'm sorry," she said. "The fasting all day and then eating so much. It makes me cranky." Dick looked wonderful this time of year—still tanned from summer, dressed in a natty fall suit. Sometimes Shelley felt sad that she hadn't known him when he was younger. He was so handsome in old photographs, though she couldn't quite picture him talking or moving about with hair on his head.

He leaned forward and kissed her. "Darling, I love you. I love our life together. I don't want you running off to California, burning your bra and becoming a lesbian."

Shelley laughed. "For Christ's sake, Dick, I still wear a bra! I'm just taking a course, reading some books. The ideas are interesting—you can't deny it."

"Mmn." He nodded, noncommittal, then got up to undress and wash for bed.

A week later, Shelley added an acting class to her schedule.

"Acting?" Dick asked in the cab. They were heading down Park Avenue to the 21 Club for dinner with one of his partners from the Boston office. "Why acting?"

"I don't know." The class had met for three hours that afternoon. She and a young man had done an improvisation in which she'd been mugged in the subway and he was the first person to help her. The rest of the class had applauded and said they could tell from the body language that the two characters would become lovers. Later, she'd read a scene from a one-woman play in front of the group. She knew she'd done a fine job, and she'd loved doing it. "There was something I liked about it, Dick. Something I'm good at."

"Honey, you're gorgeous, but no one becomes an actress at forty-two."

"No, I know they don't, but still . . . There's something for me in that class."

"That sounds very vague." Dick checked his watch. They were stuck in bumper-to-bumper traffic, mostly taxis, all honking but going nowhere. He leaned forward to speak to the driver. "Look, I think if you turn right at Seventy-second Street, go across and through the park, we'll make better time."

Shelley understood that what she'd said to Dick was vague, but she also knew it was real. She liked speaking in front of an audience, having something to read or say, a persona to assume. She'd been like that as a girl growing up in Utica. Memories of her high school elocution club were coming back to her. She'd been pretty good then, too, and was always cast in one of the leading roles in the high school plays, although that might have been because she was blond and popular. But she really did have the ability to deliver her lines with clarity, to look straight out into an audience and speak with conviction. When she acted, she felt clearheaded and powerful in a way she never felt in her own life.

Jimmy and Carolyn Deutsch hadn't been waiting long.

They were seated in the Bar Room. A jumble of model cars, transport trucks, football helmets, racing flags and airplanes hung from the ceiling above their table. "God, I remember how Ritchie loved this place when he was a kid," Dick said. "I had to explain to him that I couldn't take him out every week for a sixteen-dollar hamburger." They all laughed. "And to think, now he's at college."

"Where'd he go again?" Jimmy was a trim man with wavy gray hair, sparkling blue eyes and a big nose. "UPenn?"

"No, Duke. He went to Duke," Dick said. "I don't know what a Jewish boy is doing down in North Carolina, but so far he says he likes it."

"Well, Duke's a great school," Jimmy said.

"It's a growing area, Dick." Carolyn was an attractive brunette with thick black eyelashes, a raspy voice and dazzling jewelry. "It's not like they've never seen a Jew in Durham—he's not in *Deliverance* country." Carolyn turned to Shelley and laid a hand on her arm. Carolyn was the kind of person who touched anyone she spoke with, asked questions, had opinions on every subject. "So what are you up to now that both kids have flown the nest? Playing lots of bridge?" Carolyn was a strong bridge player.

"Actually, I've started some classes," Shelley said.

Carolyn cast a meaningful look at her husband. "Classes, you see? My friend Nita Schwartz just started graduate school. She's going to be a social worker. And hasn't Judy Kirbach decided to finish her degree?"

"Education!" Jimmy's voice boomed. "It's the opiate of the missus!" The two men laughed heartily. "Now, who was it who wrote that educating a beautiful woman was like pouring honey into a fine Swiss watch?"

"Good for Judy," Shelley said to Carolyn, who gave her arm another little squeeze.

In late October, Shelley was reading *The Golden Notebook*. She envied Doris Lessing, not bitterly, but she wished that she, too, could find her calling, that place to focus her thoughts, her care, her energy—maybe even have some effect out in the world. It was a beautiful Saturday afternoon, crisp as a McIntosh apple, and she and Dick were up at their new country house in Great Barrington. Madeline, now a sophmore at Amherst, would be driving over the next morning for brunch. Shelley hoped the good weather would hold—perhaps they'd head up to Lenox and take Madeline to see Edith Wharton's home. It was always easier with her stepdaughter if they all had something to do.

Madeline complained so much about college, though she did well in her courses. Shelley attributed the negative attitude to the fact that Lauren had committed suicide when Madeline was only a little girl. Clearly, she was still angry about the fact that her father had moved out right before her mother's death—the same fact, Shelley mused, that made it so much easier for *her* to ignore Lauren's importance in her husband's life. It was hard to feel too threatened by a first wife who was both unloved *and* dead, no matter how many zingers her mother-in-law threw her way.

Shelley supposed she felt sorry for Madeline, though God knew the girl had spent her whole life milking the tragedy for all she could. It was annoying to listen to her snipping and snapping about an opportunity that to Shelley seemed like the greatest gift that could befall a young woman. Four years with no responsibilities: no husband, no children, no one pushing her to find a husband and settle down. Just time to experiment, to find out who you were and who you wanted to become. The permission—God, even the encouragement—to do that.

Shelley had gone to college, but it had been so different for her. Her father had worked in a brewery, and her mother took a secretarial job as soon as Shelley and her sister were old enough to stay alone during the afternoons. Shelley was sent to SUNY Albany with one mission from her parents: to find a husband who would take good care of her. And she'd succeeded, at least on a material plane. She was engaged to Phillip, a law student, by the middle of her sophomore year: It was only incidental that Shelley managed to receive a bachelor's degree along the way. She'd never used it. What might her life have been like if she'd had the same opportunity as Madeline?

Shelley pulled on a thick Irish sweater and slid open the glass door to join Dick on the cedar deck. She lay next to him on a double chaise longue in the sun. He laid down the Sunday magazine section, which now came on Saturdays, and took her hand. "How's my sweetheart?" he said.

"Oh, Dick, everything's fine, but I still don't know what I want to be when I grow up."

"Why do you have to *be* anything? Look, honey, I'm fifty-four. I'm not planning to work forever. Already I don't work Fridays during the summer. In a few years I'll be able to do that year-round—so long as nothing urgent is going on with one of my cases. And I'll take fewer cases. We can spend three-day weekends up here, travel more, go to Aspen, Europe. Our life is fine without your *being* some big thing."

"What makes you think this has anything to do with you?" Shelley felt her face flush. She pictured herself turning pink. Right now—flustered, silly, inarticulate—she was entirely different from how she felt at the New School acting studio.

"Well, of course it has to do with me," Dick said. "You're my wife."

Shelley gritted her teeth. He didn't understand anything. He understood so little that after speaking with him, Shelley began to lose her own understanding. It was the opposite of what conversation was meant to do, as if his lack of understanding unraveled the thoughts in her own mind. Yet still she loved him—this had nothing to do with that.

Shelley played a television reporter during one of her skits at the New School. She interviewed a farmer in his barn, thirty minutes after three of his cows had spontaneously combusted. She reported rumors of an alien invasion from her desk at ZBC studios. She moderated a talk-show discussion among a congressman, an FBI agent, a science-fiction author and a woman physicist from Harvard. Her acting teacher, a Greenwich Village type with a long gray braid and a crystal hanging around her neck, asked Shelley to stay after class to chat for a few minutes.

"I know," Shelley said. "I didn't get the body language right in that barn scene. Where I was supposed to be stepping over all the cow guts, I didn't project the presence of the gore."

The teacher laughed. "Oh, forget about the cow guts!" She swept her arm out in front of her as if to sweep the cow guts, the farmer and his whole barn into the courtyard behind the building. "It was an idiotic scene. What I want to know, Shelley, is this: How did you feel in that role? How did you feel playing the reporter?"

"Well, I felt . . . I don't know." Shelley racked her brain but came up with nothing. "I didn't feel anything special, really. I felt . . . normal. I'm sorry, I wish I could give you a better answer."

"No, no. It's okay. That's the perfect answer."

Shelley was baffled. Her teacher walked across the platform they used as a stage, rearranged a couple of chairs and then came back to where Shelley was standing. She put her hands on Shelley's shoulders and looked into her face with wide hazel eyes.

"Shelley, you *are* a television reporter. Today you *were* a television reporter. You weren't acting, you were one. That's why it didn't feel like acting."

"I'm not sure what you mean. I've never been a reporter."

"No. No, you haven't. Not yet. What I'm saying is, you could be a television reporter. You could be the next Barbara Walters, only you're taller and WASPy."

Shelley stared at her teacher, calculating the woman's credibility. There was the heavy black eyeliner caked up in her crow's feet, the long flowing dress, the crystal. On the other hand, her bio was impressive. She'd studied with Stanislawski, gone on to a successful career in regional theater and a few off-Broadway plays. And there was no questioning her engagement in the classroom, the generosity of her teaching.

The teacher dropped her arms and stepped back. "Listen, dear, I don't know if you're looking for a big high-powered career. You live on the Upper East Side. You've probably got a husband, kids in private school. It's not my goal to interfere with people's lives—all I do is teach what I know to people who want to learn." Shelley had a strong feeling that this woman interfered with other people's lives all the time, but she didn't mind. She felt her life could use a little interference. Her teacher went on. "I'm just saying that if you *are* looking for a career, you've got the best public-speaking ability I've seen in years, intelligence and the kind of no-nonsense look that would appeal to the networks. I'm just saying that if you are considering a serious career—and a lot of women are these days—you might want to look into one of the journalism schools, NYU or even Columbia. You might want to explore that option." She picked up her big woven shoulder bag and stood by the light switch, ready to close up the classroom.

"Thank you," Shelley said, passing her at the doorway. "I'll look into it."

Shelley waited to talk to Dick until she was sure. She had interviewed at NYU, Columbia, even taken the subway out to Brooklyn College. She was surprised when the admissions personnel welcomed her, arranged for her to meet with faculty members from the journalism departments. Her age and lack of work experience didn't bother them at all. Her good grades and her English degree made her a qualified candidate. They said it would be fine if her professors from the New School wrote her recommendations. All she needed to do was take the GRE, send in her applications and her transcripts. Yes, they'd had plenty of students, particularly women, return to school after long absences. They actually liked having mature students, who were often among the most dedicated and best performing.

Shelley knew tonight wasn't a good night to talk to Dick about it—he'd had a frustrating day at the firm—but she had to. The applications were due in four weeks, and she was scheduled to take the GRE this coming Saturday. Anyway, she couldn't stand keeping it from him any longer; she was too excited.

"You what!" He looked like he might faint. He yanked off his tie and collapsed into the leather sofa in the library. "For

God's sake, I'm still putting two kids through college, and now you?"

Shelley hadn't even thought about the money. But she wasn't going to let that get in the way. "Look," she said, "if you don't want to pay for it, I'll work at a magazine or something. I can go to school part-time."

Dick hung his head back, throat exposed, and stretched his arms along the back of the couch. He looked like the crucified Christ. "Of course I'll pay for it," he said. "Don't insult me. Have I ever denied you anything you wanted? Those jade earrings, the raccoon parka for the country, that crazy interior decorator? Honey, I love you. I want you to have whatever you want. Tell me what it costs—I'll write the check." He leaned forward, cradling his skull in his hands. In this position, he looked like a man who had just found out he had prostate cancer.

She poured him a Scotch and water. "Thank you, Dick. Thank you." She was acting then, because something felt odd inside of her, and she didn't feel thankful at all. She knew she should be, but she wasn't. She was angry that she couldn't pay her own tuition. She was angry that the privilege of attending graduate school could be granted or denied by her husband. She was furious that he compared it to some luxurious and silly thing like a fur coat or a piece of jewelry. She could hear his friends consoling him at the Harmonie Club: *Oh well, Dick, we have to keep them happy.* She felt kept, like a fancy hooker, or a pedigreed lap dog with a special diet.

Then she remembered something else, and she felt a spasm

of worry. She put Dick's drink on a cocktail napkin on the table in front of him and sat next to him on the couch. "Listen," she said tentatively. "You know this means we can't go on safari next fall with the Goldmans."

"What!!!"

"I'm sorry." She was nearly whispering now. "I won't be able to go."

Dick groaned.

He would live with it, she told herself. He would live with it, and she would live with it. He wouldn't leave her like Phillip had. Dick loved her—and even more important than that, he was honorable. He was an honorable male-chauvinist pig. He would stay with her. He would live with it, and she would live with it. Sooner or later, they would both get accustomed to the change.

The Second Most Important
Woman in History

— 1982 —

Madeline Sapphire preferred to study at Jones Library, the
public library that served the town of Amherst, Massachusetts.
She was a junior at Amherst and had access to the facilities of
all five colleges in the Pioneer Valley, but Madeline was sick of
what she called "the collegiate scene." She was sick of the smug
fraternity boys, disgusted by their continual parties that
started with bottles and kegs, shouting and dancing. Then a
chair broke, someone vomited. On Sunday morning plastic
cups littered porch steps, and leafy October lawns reeked of
beer and urine. There might be rumors of a date rape. Madeline was also fed up with the boys who either couldn't or
wouldn't join the fraternities—the self-styled intellectuals
who wore berets and sat around student lounges discussing
Doubt in the Eighteenth Century until three in the morning;

the belated hippies who traveled hundreds of miles to Grateful Dead concerts and trafficked in bootleg recordings and Thai sticks; the nerds who never looked up from their textbooks and calculators long enough to notice anyone else. She was sick of the girls who dated these boys, who encouraged their posturing and wrapped their lives around their pretensions. More than anything, she was sick of the girls who didn't, the girls who called themselves "women"—the noisy feminists, the lesbians from Smith, the ones who said "To hell with men!" but were too ugly or damaged or plain insecure to risk stepping into the arena. So all fall Madeline could usually be found studying at a large oak table in the main room of Jones Library, hoping to jump-start her life by sitting near the "real people" who came there.

By midsemester, when she reached Torquato Tasso's *Aminta* in her Italian literature seminar, she had begun to recognize and even greet some of the library's regulars. There was the older woman who walked there to borrow the latest mystery, then took it home and exchanged it a week later for another. And the retired man with the mane of white hair who came in each morning around ten to read *The Boston Globe,* all sections, from cover to cover. And the middle-aged lady with graying blond hair who pulled seven or eight poetry collections from the stacks at a time, sat at a table perusing them and taking notes on a yellow pad, until she finally said, "Yes!" and ran over to the Xerox machine to copy one page fifteen times. She had a warm smile and always nodded to Madeline, who thought she must be some sort of teacher. One man, maybe in his thirties and handsome in a tanned, wiry way, had a severe twitching disease. He read nautical books, batting at the pages like a cat in his attempt to turn them. He was not unpleasant, though Madeline found him distracting when he sat at her table.

Around the corner from the library, on South Prospect Street, Madeline shared a two-bedroom apartment with Lisa Stadtler, one of five girls who had been in Madeline's dormitory suite freshman year. Lisa and Madeline chose to be suitemates for the second year of college, and they dated two boys who were friends. Madeline had broken up with Josh the previous spring on the grounds that he was superficial. "He's premed and wants to be a doctor only to make money," she told Lisa. Lisa broke up with Gordon over the summer when he confessed that he had allowed a girl from the Tri Delt sorority to give him a blow job at a party that Lisa missed because of menstrual cramps. Their unattached status had drawn the two housemates closer at the beginning of the semester, and they spent many evenings sipping chamomile tea or Scotch and sodas, commiserating over what Neolithic morons college guys were. But when Lisa forgave Gordon, dismissing his betrayal with "Oh well, he was drunk, and I was on the rag, and . . . you know how men are," a certain tension developed between the friends. The fact that Gordon, the Neolithic moron, was spending an average of three nights a week at their apartment didn't help. And Lisa didn't seem to understand that Madeline's time at Jones Library felt to her like a revolutionary adventure, the first interesting thing she had done in years. "That place?" Lisa had said. "C'mon, Mad, these are supposed to be the best years of our lives—you're missing them." But Madeline was convinced her time there would yield some crucial and formative experience that campus living could not. All she had to do was continue to put herself into the hands of the library's alchemy and wait.

It turned out that Madeline was right.

She sat at the oak table one Saturday afternoon, trying to plow through *Aminta* but focusing more on the split ends of her light brown hair. She twirled one lock around her finger, thinking she might make an appointment for a trim the following week at the Hampshire Mall and wondering why anyone would care about all the stupid shepherds and nymphs who filled the pages before her. She had loved reading Dante, Boccaccio, Ariosto—Machiavelli was twisted but interesting. But this stuff . . .

"Ma Lei, scusi, Lei parla italiano?" A tall man eyed her book, then her face. He had black hair, layered and thick, heavy eyebrows, dark eyes and the dark gray stubbly growth of an unshaven face. He looked like a hoodlum, but he smelled of cologne.

"Sì." She said it more like a question than an answer.

He continued speaking in his own language. "Ah, thank God!" He flopped down in the seat next to her, unzipped his well-worn leather jacket to expose a green cashmere pullover—four-ply, at least. He set his suede-loafered feet up on the reading table, and Madeline noticed the Gucci *GG*. If he was a hoodlum, she thought, he was an expensive one. "No one here speaks a word of Italian. I've had no conversation in three days other than 'Please, an ambourger' and 'Tank you, check please.'" He put his feet back on the floor, leaned his elbow on the table and turned to face her, grinning. His jaw was bony, his canines pointed like a German shepherd's. "But now I've found you."

Madeline forced a smile.

"*Madonna,* you have those eyes! Pale, clear, celestial blue eyes that I've only seen here, in this country. We don't have eyes like that in Europe. *Dio santo,* how beautiful!" He stared at her as if he'd been hungry, but now dinner was served.

Madeline didn't correct him about the origin of her eyes, which were the same as those of her mother, who had been half Irish and raised in London until she was eighteen. She said only, "Thank you," and reached for her book. This staring man made her uncomfortable, and she wished he would get up and leave. "Really," she said, "I should be studying now."

"God forbid, no!" The man flung his hands about as he spoke. "Tasso's horrible. I read him in high school. It was a torture, long and profound. *Pastoralismo,* what a bore. In painting, at least it's tolerable. You have the country landscape, glowing flesh before you. But in poetry . . .

"You know, I remember reading *L'Aminta,*" he continued. "I remember where I sat, what I wore. But I don't remember what it said, not one word. I would read a line, and before my eye could travel to the next—poof!—it was already forgotten. *Incredibile.* And who cares, really, who gives a shit about all those idiotic shepherds and nymphs?"

Madeline looked up. "I was just thinking the same thing. I thought maybe it was my Italian."

"No, no, your Italian is excellent, my dear. What is your name?" She told him. "Ah! *La Magdalena*." He rolled the name luxuriously in his mouth and pointed one finger. "The second most important woman in history." He pulled off his jacket and pushed up his sleeves. He seemed to have a gesture for every emotion, every sentence. Madeline noticed that his forearms were thick and tanned on the outside, with straight black hairs, paler and smooth-looking on the inside. He had strong, fine hands, the kind people called "artistic." She felt a flicker of attraction that had no rational basis, the way a dog must feel, she thought, when it first picked up the faint scent of a bitch in heat. She made an effort not to smile or laugh as she remarked to herself, This is a man in heat, while he kept on talking. "Tasso's unworthy of you, Madeline. Read Moravia or, if you want poetry, Leopardi. Frankly, I prefer the French writers. Do you know Proust?"

"Just the part about the *'petite madeleine.'*"

"Yes, of course. Because of your name." He shook his head sadly. "Ah, Madeline, you must read all of Proust." He took her hand in both of his and looked her carefully up and down. "Well, anyway, now you will."

His name was Antonio Reggiano. He took Madeline to the China Inn on North Pleasant that night, and she taught him how to use chopsticks. He complained that just as all people from China looked alike, all of the dishes resembled one another: a mixed-up jumble of chopped things, soy sauce, cornstarch and rice. "In *Italia,* each food is allowed its own flavor," he said. He touched his finger to the tip of his tongue. "We know how to taste." Madeline blushed.

Antonio spoke of his life, how it had gone stale. His marriage to the daughter of a wealthy Emilian yarn manufacturer, his position at the news desk of *La Repubblica* in Bologna, Sundays at the country club with his father-in-law, the villa in the countryside where he lived. "*È bellissima,* furnished with antiques. My wife, Enrica, is not ugly. She cooks well and keeps the gardens blooming . . . But for me, ah, Madeline, it is life in the province—the prison of my soul!" He had escaped for a month to attend an international journalism seminar at UMass, and now, two weeks into it, he could hardly bear the thought of returning home. He was ready to change everything—new work, new surroundings, a new woman. He smiled at her. "Maybe the new woman is you."

Madeline felt him evaluate her as if she were some fine collectible, an *objet d'art,* he might wish to purchase. She told him as little as possible about her prep school years at Deerfield, choosing to emphasize the summer she'd spent in Paris and her mother's suicide. "Everyone used to say she was so beautiful," she said with an air of bereavement. "But when she died, my father had already left her. He was living with another woman."

Madeline reflected that this was not exactly the case. She had heard her mother yell at her father one night, demanding that he leave the house that minute. He stayed with Rosalind Bloom the week before her mother's death, and he had told

Madeline when he came home to visit that he'd just found an apartment close by. Of course, he returned immediately when he learned of the tragedy, and when he did start to date again, he never dated Rosalind. Still, Madeline would never get over the rage she felt when she thought about how, on the night her mother had died, her father was sleeping in the home of another little girl—Claudia. "Not only was he living with another woman," she told Antonio, "he was living with the mother of my best friend."

"Divorce is a terrible thing!" Antonio said and then caught himself. "That is, when children are involved."

A waiter cleared their plates, and Antonio requested a fresh pot of tea, "very hot." Madeline translated his fortune cookie, which said, *Travel to new places leads to transformation.* "Aha!" he exclaimed. Then he spoke to her in a low, urgent voice.

"Madeline, you are fresh, intelligent, still unformed. You have such freedom, alone in this Massachusetts, you do whatever you want. It is intoxicating, this freedom. You are a torment to me, *una tortura*, like a butterfly flitting about, dancing before my eyes. I don't know what to do—to trap you in the killing jar," he turned over an empty water tumbler and pressed it into the white tablecloth, "suffocate you, pin you flat under glass, hang my trophy on the library wall . . ." Madeline gasped out loud. Then she laughed at herself, embarrassed. "Or to sprout my own little wings, fly off together with you . . ." He reached across the table, caressed her cheek, pulled her chin up and stared into her eyes. "I desire both things, *mia cara,* intensely."

Madeline pushed his killing jar out of her mind; the flying off together was more appealing. She had trouble thinking clearly with his warm hand on her face. Certainly, she felt aroused, excited in a way she hadn't been since . . . maybe her first kiss in a sixth-grade spin-the-bottle game. If it wasn't the sensation of his fingers stroking her hair, tracing the edge of her earlobe, it was the scent of him—the soap smell rising off the heat of his skin—or maybe the way he held her in his gaze. She felt suddenly elevated to a new level of importance, to a starring role in his life and in her own, which seemed a lot more interesting this evening than it had earlier in the day. She tried to imagine how she might appear to a diner at the next table, someone who watched her as if she were in a movie. She liked her part. The film was beautiful. They spoke Italian in a roomful of New England accents. There would need to be subtitles.

When they left the restaurant, Antonio slipped his arm around her waist. They strolled North Prospect Street, swarming with college students. "Where are they all going?" he asked.

"To parties."

"And you're not going to a party?" He sounded jealous.

"I'm sick of parties."

He guided her into a coffeehouse. "An espresso?"

"I'll have cappuccino."

Antonio laughed, tossing his hands in the air. "Americans! No, no, no, Madeline, no cappuccino. You don't drink cappuccino at night. You have it for breakfast, it's for dunking biscotti." He turned to the barman and spoke in English. "Espresso, please. Two."

Madeline tried to cover her mistake, offering something about how the milk helped her sleep. Antonio pulled her close to him, stroked her nose and bottom lip the way one strokes a baby. "It's okay, *Americana*, I know. Everyone here drinks cappuccino after dinner. Amazing they don't vomit. Tomorrow morning we'll have cappuccino, tomorrow, okay?"

Madeline nodded, then realized what she'd agreed to.

They left the coffeehouse and strolled north, where the street became residential. Antonio guided Madeline down a driveway past a dark-colored saltbox to a converted garage. He said, "This is our little house," and pulled a set of keys from his pocket.

He flipped on a light switch, revealing a living room with a dining table. The couch was upholstered in blue denim; a red, white and blue quilt, star pattern, hung on the wall above it. There was an oval braided rug on the floor, a pine desk facing one window, a bookcase and some American country paintings on wood—a farm scene with a red barn, a large black-and-white hen. There were two neat stacks of books on the wooden coffee table, a three-ring binder on the desk, a silver pen. The walls were wood-paneled, pickled white and trimmed with deep cherry red around the windows and doors. The ceiling was low, and on the far side of the room, Madeline saw the red balusters of a stairway that she supposed led to a bedroom. To the side of the stairway was a small kitchen, its countertop tiled with four-inch blue squares. A white plastic dish drain sat by the sink, holding one plate, one glass, a knife and a fork. Everything was tidy, meticulously clean. Antonio removed Madeline's jean jacket from her shoulders and hung it on a peg by the front door. He hung his own leather jacket on the next peg.

Madeline said, "This is all very patriotic."

"*Sì*, yes. Even in the bathroom, there's a portrait of George Washington on a horse." He told her how he'd first been housed in a graduate-student apartment on the UMass campus. "It was intolerable. Old carpeting—it smelled like feet." He was to share a three-bedroom unit with a Nigerian reporter and a feature writer from Holland. "One bathroom, three men. Clearly, I had to move." He had called home, and Enrica wired more money. Then he rented this guesthouse, belonging to a professor who taught philosophy at Hampshire College. "His wife is a painter. She makes these things." He pointed to the barn scene and the big hen. "Not *La Gioconda*, but cute in an American way."

Madeline laughed. She felt disoriented but hyperaware, the way one feels in a dream where all the details are clear though the story line makes no sense. Her breathing had been shallow all evening, her face tingled. She was going to go to bed with this man. She thought so, anyway, although now, under the bright lights in this overly clean guesthouse, she was starting to wonder. She had slept with three boys since Josh, and this wasn't how it usually went. Normally, one would drink too much, or at least enough to move close to the boy, maybe touch him, without anything looking intentional. Kissing and groping might begin at a party, continue while semi-staggering along the street, and end up on an unmade bed in a room cluttered with books, record albums, beer bottles and laundry. Each time Madeline had awoken with the first grayness in the sky, eased gently off the bed, searched for her clothes on the floor and crept away while the boy was still sleeping. One had called the next afternoon, but she made an excuse about an upcoming exam. The other two knew to leave her alone. Now, with Antonio, she understood she wouldn't be sneaking away in the morning, yet she couldn't imagine how they would get from this wholesome red, white and blue into bed.

Antonio boiled water and served her chamomile tea in a Cape Cod mug. Madeline sat on the couch and watched him as he opened a package that had come in the mail. He pulled out a couple of cans. "Thank God!" he said. It was shaving cream sent from his wife—the only kind he liked, and he couldn't find it anywhere in Amherst. He'd tried some nonsense from Gillette, but it burned his skin. "That's why I have this," he said, rubbing his stubbly beard. "But I can't stand it," he added and said he wanted to go upstairs to shave. Madeline was wondering if she shouldn't go home now; perhaps this wasn't heading in the direction she had thought. But on his way upstairs, Antonio came by the couch, opened a book on his coffee table and shuffled through the pages until he found a certain passage. "*Ecco*, read this," he said and placed the book in her lap. He stroked her hair with one hand and pointed with the other to a paragraph midway down the page. "Starting here."

Madeline obeyed. When Antonio had disappeared upstairs, she sneaked a look at the book's title. It was Proust, *A la Ricerca di Tempi Perduti.* The passage was difficult, its sentence structure complex and convoluted. It was descriptive and full of words she didn't know. There was something about a path and a hedge and then some flowers on the altar of a church. She needed an English-Italian dictionary, and she was sure Antonio had one nearby, but she thought it might be rude to get up and search through the things in his house. Besides, she couldn't concentrate right now. She stared at the paragraph, scanned the words without making sense of them and waited for Antonio to return. She found herself thinking about his wife, Enrica. Madeline pictured her Italian-language professor from the year before—in her mid-thirties, with round tortoiseshell glasses and cropped brown hair with fake blond sun streaks. She was medium height, trim, always wearing one of two knee-length silk dresses. Neither pretty nor ugly, she was the kind of woman one could look at without ever thinking of sex. Enrica might resemble her, running to a drugstore somewhere in Italy to buy her husband's shaving cream, bringing it home to wrap in brown paper, then leaving the house again to take the parcel to the post office. A boring housewife, Madeline concluded, believing that boring housewives deserved unfaithful husbands. Anyway, she thought, Antonio would leave Enrica. He would stay in Amherst with her, because she was younger, prettier, because she was American. She was in a contest, and she would win.

Antonio returned, slightly pink around the jaw and neck, smelling new, citrusy. "*Allora*, how is Proust?" He sat on the couch beside her.

"Difficult." Antonio was handsome. Madeline realized she needed a different aesthetic from the one she used to judge college boys. Antonio was not the blue-eyed, oval-faced pretty type she had always admired most. He had a strong jaw, and his nose curved down slightly. There was the incredible darkness of his hair and eyes. Handsome looked different on a thirty-five-year-old man. "What are *biancospini*?"

"Hay torns."

"What?"

Antonio repeated the words clearly, over and over, but he could not make himself understood. "They are small white flowers." They agreed to make do with that definition. "But the pink ones are more important here. You see, Proust lives the way I do," he said with a burst of energy in his hands. "For example, the eyes of a woman can bring up a sensation from childhood, a sensation far more beautiful and important than the woman herself. You can love a woman because she reminds you of a hedge of flowers you saw one day that transformed your life. She brings you back to an earlier experience, a more formative, essential one. And what is happening in the present doesn't matter, doesn't matter at all . . . You see, the real life—for Proust, for me—is the life of sensation, of memory, the life of the mind."

Madeline wondered if what he was saying were not, perhaps, the slightest bit insulting. Like her being there right then didn't make a difference to him?

"Really," he said as if confessing, "I am not a reporter. That's just what I do because my life has become stupid. Really"—he paused, crossed his legs and shifted on the couch to face her— "really, I am a writer." He stared at her, watching, she knew, to see how his self-revelation would register. She returned his gaze and tried not to blink. When he seemed satisfied, he shook his head, made a snorting noise like a horse and went on, "Instead, I have this job, so I go around banging on doors, asking widows for interviews after their husbands were murdered or crushed to death by a factory machine. It's disgraceful!" His face looked angry, his shoulders tense.

He reached for his tea. "It's gone cold." He set the mug back on its coaster, shook his head again, this time as if shaking himself awake. "Anyway, everything is different now." He looked at Madeline, as if he were speaking to soothe her. His voice was quiet, like a hypnotist's: "Everything in my life changes now."

Abracadabra. Madeline silently repeated his incantation, also wishing that everything in his life would change for him.

"*Carissima.*" He reached his hand to her cheek and stroked it as she bowed her head. "Come. It's bedtime."

A New Man

— 1976–1986 —

Back in the fall of 1976, following the ordeal of the three-week doorman strike, the co-op board of 980 Park Avenue considered modernizing the passenger elevator. They would replace the hand-operated lever with a self-service push-button mechanism. Cyril Cavanaugh, the accountant from 8B, explained that the initial investment required a onetime capital assessment of the residents. One elevator man's shift would be eliminated, however, reducing maintenance costs in the long term. Cyril assured everyone that the doorman on duty through the night could always lock the front door and accompany any resident who might need assistance with the elevator during those quiet hours.

"And at least we won't have to drive the damn thing," said Charles Payne, "if the boys walk out on us again."

"I agree with you gentlemen wholeheartedly." Beverly Coddington laid her unread copy of the proposal on her dining table. It was a building tradition that board meetings were held in the Coddingtons' dining room, with its silver-and-gray-velvet-flocked wallpaper and Venetian blown-glass chandelier. It was convenient, since either Beverly or Harold Coddington always held a seat on the board. "My husband's driving is frightful enough when he's traveling horizontally," Beverly said. "None of us needs him zooming up and down through the floors of this building."

An accident had in fact occurred while Harold was manning the elevator during the strike. He had braked too suddenly, sending Bob Horowitz from 7B lurching forward into the cab's brass grate, bruising his head and blackening one eye. The board members were good-natured enough to chuckle about the mishap, and of course, neither Bob Horowitz nor his wife, Mimi, sat on the board.

When it came time for the vote, six members approved the motion to convert the elevator. Only the baroness from the penthouse dissented. She took off her reading glasses and surveyed everyone with her piercing turquoise-colored eyes. "It seems silly to spend all sorts of money on a new elevator," she said, "when one of our employees will lose his job in a difficult economy."

Beverly Coddington and Charles Payne exchanged a look. In their opinion, the baroness was hopelessly pro-labor. Beverly sometimes regretted nominating the baroness to the board. Despite her title and impeccable social reputation, the first thing the baroness had done as a member was to argue in favor of the Horowitz application to buy 7B. "He can obviously afford to live here," the baroness had said, "and he comes highly recommended by his friends and business associates. I certainly hope no one would think of opposing him on the grounds of religion." Beverly thought the Sapphires up in the twelfth-floor duplex were Jewish representation enough for one building, but under the vigilant eyes of the baroness, how could they turn down the Horowitz application?

Engineering companies submitted bids, the board approved a plan and construction began in June 1977. By September the old mahogany cab had a new door, also mahogany, which matched fairly well. The brass grate was gone, and the old lever was replaced by a brass panel set into the front wall with buttons that lit up when the elevator man pressed. The residents of 980 Park were pleased with their efforts. Vincent Ferretti lost his job.

"Why me?" Vinnie asked the superintendent. "I'm not on the graveyard shift."

"But you were the last one hired," said Mr. Ulofski. He handed Vinnie the envelope from the management company. "I knew that strike would come to no good. Yeah, sure, the older guys got better wages, but you—what are you going to do now?" A typed letter gave Vinnie two weeks' notice at 980 Park but said he should come to an appointment the following morning with their personnel director to discuss a possible transfer to another building.

Vinnie took the train into Manhattan at ten A.M. the next day. A fat lady manager behind a metal desk fanned herself with a manila folder and told him he lacked the seniority to be placed right away in another white-glove building.

"But I was at Nine-eighty for six years."

"Honey," she wiped sweat off her brow, "there's guys worked ten, twelve years getting laid off these days." She said the only thing she had for him was a seven A.M. shift on the freight elevator of an office building at Forty-sixth and Lex.

Vinnie was not a morning person, and the idea of getting up for work at five each day made him miserable. "There's nothing else?" he asked.

The lady shook her head. "Think it over," she said. "Sleep on it. Good jobs are hard to come by, and here you'll keep all your benefits. We can probably get you back into a residential building within a year or two."

A year or two, Vinnie thought as he walked out on the street. He didn't have to be at work until three o'clock. He walked up to Central Park and along the avenue of shady sycamores that led to the bandshell. It was not yet lunchtime. The park was quiet except for a few old men, a couple of hippies tossing a Frisbee and an occasional bicyclist. He crossed the Seventy-second Street transverse, descended the stairs to Bethesda Fountain and sat on a bench overlooking the rowboat lake. A year or two, he thought. He shook his head and ran his fingers through his thick brown hair. "Shit," he said out loud.

He remembered starting out at 980 Park, what it was like being new there. It went the same way in any of those buildings—he knew because he'd asked Bravo, the Yugoslavian who worked at 990 Park next door. You put on the uniform—it was itchy and hot—but soon enough you got used to wearing gloves in the summertime. You smiled, you learned the owners' names, their kids' names, their dogs' names. You jumped to get the door for them, a cab, you carried their bags to the elevator. You wished them a pleasant afternoon, a good night, you agreed that it looked like snow.

The owners thought of you as the new man. They mixed you up with the Puerto Rican guy who collected the trash. Sure, they handed out the perfunctory little envelopes at Christmastime. *Thanks so much, Peter,* they would say to the doorman they'd known for fifteen years, *merry Christmas. And merry Christmas to you.* They'd hand you the little envelope, embarrassed they couldn't recall your name.

After about two years, they'd start to realize that you were the guy who ran out to the curb with the big gray umbrella to shelter them as they stepped from their chauffeured cars on rainy days. The guy who kept track of that bag of fabric swatches dropped off by the interior decorator while the lady of the house was out lunching. After about two years, they'd begin to say *Hello, Vinnie* or *Thank you, Vinnie.* It took two years in any of those buildings before anyone—except the man who shared your shift and maybe the super—before anyone remembered your name.

Vinnie was twenty-four years old. He would be what, he thought, twenty-eight, thirty, before he climbed back to the same level he was at now. Was that what he'd worked for all these years? What he'd graduated from St. Eugene's School to do?

Vinnie had an idea about what he wanted to do, but it had

always seemed like a big fantasy. Over the past few years, whenever he'd sat up late at night blowing a joint at Michael Maiorino's house, the conversation often went the same way. Michael was Vinnie's best friend since childhood and his classmate at St. Eugene's. He worked for an electrical company in Queens. He'd started as an apprentice and learned his trade on the job. Now he was a fully licensed electrician. Since Michael was the youngest on his crew—the only guy who didn't have a beer gut—he was the one who got zipped into the Tyvek suit and crawled under houses pulling wire. Or he was squeezed through tight scuttleholes into boiling-hot attics. "It's fucking disgusting," Michael always said. "I swear, Vinnie, look at how high the dollar is. You know what we should do? Quit our jobs and go into import-export. Think of it, man, I'm good at math, you're good at talking. I swear, there's guys making a fortune bringing stuff in from Italy, and they don't even speak Italian. Shit, Vinnie, we've both got family all the hell over Italy—you think we couldn't find something to bring over here and sell for triple the price?"

Vinnie had never thought that Michael was serious about quitting his job. He talked big, but in practice he was cautious. He'd been like that in high school with girls, always saying he was going to screw this one or another. Meanwhile, on any given Friday evening, you could find him at home in front of the television, afraid to ask anyone out. Thank God Dana Darnopuck had finally called him, and Michael managed to lose his virginity before graduation.

Sitting in the park today, Vinnie wondered if Michael was

really serious about his idea. Was he himself serious about such a leap? Vinnie had saved up money over the years, and just this past summer, he'd finally unloaded Anna, the girl-friend who'd thought he was saving it for their future home. What if . . . ?

Maybe Michael could hold on to his electrician's job a little longer, bringing in some money. In the meantime, Vinnie could go to Italy right away, get the lay of the land. He'd come back and start up the business. Then Michael could quit crawling under houses and jump on board.

Vinnie stretched and walked out on the rocks by the lake's edge. He skipped a couple of stones on the still water. He almost hit a duck. He laughed, because the ruffled duck reminded him of Mrs. Coddington when her chauffeur was late. He smiled, thinking what it would be like never to see her again. Actually, he might not have to see her again. He did some calculating in his head. He'd subbed twice this year, covering two Saturday shifts for the weekend doorman whose wife had a baby. And with the vacation and sick days he had coming to him, hell, he could collect his wages for another two weeks and never wear that damn uniform again.

It was one-thirty. He strolled over to the concession stand at the boathouse and bought himself an ice-cream bar covered in toasted coconut. He walked to the subway station at Lexington Avenue and Sixty-eighth Street. Sitting next to him on the train was a shabbily dressed man marking up the help-wanted page of the *Daily News*. Something in Vinnie's chest felt tight. The train roared and screeched on the tracks. Vinnie checked his watch. There was still time to turn around, go back up to 980 Park before his shift started. He got off the local at Union Square and ran across the platform to the waiting train. He rode the express downtown, away from Eighty-third Street, out to Brooklyn. That was it.

Beverly Coddington discovered a leak under her powder-room sink that afternoon. She buzzed the in-house intercom for Mr. Ulofski, but no one answered. "My goodness, where can he be?" she said out loud in her kitchen. Her cook, Brightie, kept on chopping celery. Eight were expected for dinner.

Beverly found Mr. Ulofski in the elevator wearing a tight-fitting doorman's uniform, the pant legs cuffed. What on earth was he doing in there?

The super shook his head. "That Vinnie Ferretti. We gave him two weeks' notice yesterday. Today he doesn't come to work, doesn't call in sick. Nothing. Just doesn't show up. So here I am on the elevator."

"How utterly unprofessional," Beverly said. Mr. Ulofski looked down at the uniform jacket stretched across his thick torso. "No, not you, Mr. Ulofski. This Vinnie fellow. Who will supply him with references now? You'd think he'd have more concern for his future." Beverly blinked twice. "And more concern for us, too.

"Anyway, I have a small emergency on my hands. Four couples coming to dinner and water on the powder-room floor."

Mr. Ulofski assured her that he'd get to her apartment just after five o'clock, when Luis, who was now driving the service elevator, got off his shift and could take over the front. Thank God, he thought, that Luis agreed to stay on tonight, though he was short and skinny and would look even more ridiculous wearing Vinnie's old uniform. And while Mr. Ulofski was lying under Mrs. Coddington's sink, she'd grill him about the wisdom of putting a Puerto Rican on the passenger elevator. The woman was unbearable, but her husband tipped well.

At the kitchen table that night, Vinnie's grandmother almost had a heart attack when he told her he'd quit. She was even angrier when she found out he was going to Italy. "Italy! Why you go to Italy? You go to Italy, you go vacation—no work." She put on a pair of glasses that seemed to double the size of her eyes, and she glared at him. It was a new maneuver—a scary effect—and Vinnie wondered if she'd been practicing it in front of her dresser mirror. "Vinnie! You spoiled. You never hungry. *Santo Cristo,* you no understand. Your *babbo* and me—we *come* from Italy. We come poor. We come hungry. We work, we work, we work. You never hungry. Now you go to Italy. Vinnie, you ruin the family." She sat still, then raised one finger, like some new idea had just come into her mind. "Why you no marry like your sister? Your sister is a good girl. She marry."

"My sister got pregnant. Remember? You called her *puttana.*"

His grandmother swatted the air in front of her. "You ruin the family!"

"*Nonna,* calm down. I have to live my life. Isn't that what you came here for? For freedom? So your family could live in freedom?"

"Tch!" She shook her head until it looked like it might fly off. "Freedom," she finally said. "Bah! Freedom is no hunger."

After a couple of slow years importing first olive oil and then silk scarves, in the spring of 1980, Vinnie stumbled into his business. On a train from Milan to Como, he shared a compartment with a women's-wear buyer from Nordstroms. She was a curvy woman with chin-length blond curls parted on one side. She became talkative when she noticed Vinnie reading the *International Herald Tribune,* and her blue eyes flashed as she spoke.

Her name was Ann Marie Huey. She had just come from the March fashion week in Milan, where next fall's collections had been unveiled. She'd attended at least twenty runway shows, filled the rest of her days running to appointments at the Armani, Versace and other designer showrooms, spent her evenings at parties sponsored by Italian fashion manufacturers for store representatives and the press. "It's crazy," she said. "They wine and dine you, dazzle you with choreographed shows and exquisite clothing. Then when it's time to ship the orders, they don't deliver. I can't sell fall in October—I need my merchandise by the end of August." She slipped off her high heels and rested her feet on the empty seat across from her. "And no one in these companies speaks a word of English.

You'd think someone would, given that they want to sell to the United States. What's your name, anyway?"

"Vincenzo Ferretti." He never introduced himself as Vinnie anymore.

"No offense, Vincenzo, but the Italians are impossible."

Ann Marie was stopping in Como for a few days, she said, to relax and catch up on her paperwork before the shows started in Paris the following week. She and Vinnie happened to be booked at the same hotel. He invited her to dinner at a tiny trattoria on a charming side street, promising a better meal than she'd find in the hotel or at any of the more touristy restaurants by the lake. After *polenta con ragù* and a bottle of Barolo, Ann Marie sat next to Vinnie on a couch in the hotel lounge, sipping the local grappa and showing him the Polaroids of the outfits she had ordered for her store. "Look at the tailoring," she said. "It's fantastic." Her skin glowed pink, and Vinnie could tell she loved fashion. "And the fabrics are the best—gabardine, wool crepe, silk—never mind the leather. I tell you, if the Italians could ever get their act together, they'd blow Paris away. These are clothes that normal American women can wear. Of course, most American women can't afford this stuff."

"Ann Marie." Vinnie slipped one arm around her shoulders and studied the Polaroid of a black-and-white tweed suit. "What if someone, someone who was, say, both Italian and American, who could communicate well in both languages and who understood how things worked on both sides of the Atlantic—what if that person happened to have a great-uncle who owned a textile factory near Ancona?" Vinnie's great-uncle did not actually own a factory, but it was true that he worked in one as a mechanic, and he was highly valued for keeping the pattern-cutting and sewing machinery in good repair. "What if someone could produce stuff like this, changing the styling or the colors just enough not to piss off your designers, maybe even customizing the clothes more to what an American woman might want to wear? What if he could have the merchandise in your store by the middle of August at two-thirds of the price?" He was winging it here. But he figured that if he cut out the salary for the big designer, the budget for advertising, shows and other hoopla, he could knock the price down by a third and still come out ahead.

"Are you serious?" Ann Marie asked. "Do you think we could even, like, put the Nordstrom label on the clothes?"

Vinnie kissed her forehead. "You could sew on Donald Duck's name for all I care."

Her blue eyes widened. "That would be amazing." She kissed his lips.

She slept in his room that night and for the rest of their nights in Como. During the day Vinnie worked on his scarf order with the silk factories and made some inquiries about fabric suppliers for blouses. He cabled his great-uncle, announcing an immediate visit and the reason for it. Ann Marie sat at a café table by the lake and dreamed up her ideal private-label line, putting together the best and most wearable ideas from the Armani, Versace, Basile and Gianfranco Ferré collections. A local photography studio was able to make reasonably good duplicates of her Polaroids, and she gave the set to Vinnie when they parted.

"Listen," she told him, "we'll start off this season with an order for the flagship store in Portland. If you deliver and the quality is solid, I'll have you in all our branches next spring."

Vinnie took the train down to Ancona and caught a bus out to the industrial neighborhood in the hills above the city, where his uncle Fabrizio lived and worked. His aunt Romana met him in the doorway of their apartment and hugged him tightly. She was a short woman, heavy and solid, wearing a printed cotton apron tied over her skirt and blouse. She had thick gray hair, cut stylishly, and thick ankles that appeared to spill over the edges of her black leather shoes. Fabrizio sat at the kitchen table in soiled gray canvas pants and a sleeveless undershirt. His entire body was rounded, from his fleshy, spherical head and round brown eyes down to his round-toed work boots. His belly in between looked as if he'd swallowed a melon. He extended a meaty hand to his nephew, who clasped the broad palm and short stubby fingers, darkened by tobacco stains and machine oils that never completely washed off. Then Fabrizio pulled Vinnie close to him and smacked each cheek with a kiss. "Welcome, nephew," he said in Italian. "We are so happy to see you again. Come. Sit down. Have a glass of wine while Romana cooks. She's making fried artichokes for you—her specialty—and a green salad and some spaghetti.

"I've waited to take my shower because I didn't want to

miss your arrival. But now I'll go wash, and afterward we'll eat."

Vinnie sat in the kitchen and talked with his aunt about the weather in Ancona, the weather in Como, a murder in the news. He actually found it easier to make small talk in a foreign language. His occasional mispronounced words were sources of amusement and even conversation itself. When his uncle came back with a wet head and clean clothing, they ate dinner, gossiped about the family, watched the evening news and talked some more. Vinnie was anxious to ask if his uncle had made an appointment for him with the factory boss, but he knew that people didn't jump so quickly to business talk here. Only when Romana slipped out to make up the sofa bed in the living room was Vinnie able to mention the matter that had brought him to visit.

"Vinnie," his uncle replied, stubbing out a cigarette. "You are welcome in my house for as long as you want. You can stay with us forever—you are my eldest sister's grandson, though we both know what a ballbreaker she is. But you can't talk to Renzo Terranova. I can't even talk to Renzo Terranova. He is here," Fabrizio gestured above his head with his fat hand, "and we are here." He dropped his hand level with his knees.

It wasn't possible that Fabrizio was refusing to make the appointment. "But I have to see him," Vinnie said. "I have this one opportunity—I need to take it."

His uncle shook his round, flabby head. "Forget it. This isn't America."

It drove Vinnie crazy that, all over Italy, everyone seemed to believe that America had no snobs. Doors were open there—all you had to do was work and you would become a million-aire. Boy, were they wrong.

"Listen," Fabrizio said. "I know you're disappointed. But spend a few days here. Go around the shops—maybe you'll find something to sell in New York. And I have a great idea. Why don't you take your cousin Marina to the movies tomorrow night? Who knows?" He winked. "Maybe you'll import a wife."

Vinnie felt his two platefuls of fried artichokes sink to the bottom of his stomach like rocks in a pond. Why don't I just kill myself now? he thought. He was exasperated with Fabrizio, yet he couldn't show the extent of his feelings. He didn't want to appear ungrateful for his aunt and uncle's hospitality. This was family, he reminded himself, his own flesh and blood. He couldn't offend his family, especially since, at the rate he was going, he'd probably be living off of them for the rest of his life.

Vinnie remembered perfectly the graduation-day picture of the cousin that Fabrizio and Romana had sent with their Christmas letter a few years ago. A big, wide face, just like his aunt's, a torso like a Russian tank, stringy hair pulled back into a high ponytail, ears like Dumbo the elephant's. A dog, he thought, no, worse than a dog—a dog mutant. He took a deep breath. "That would be nice to meet Marina," he told his uncle with as much enthusiasm as he could dredge up.

Vinnie invited his cousin out to dinner. He figured it might be easier to spend the evening with someone closer to his own age rather than sit through another meal with Romana and Fabrizio. Marina had improved slightly since the picture. Her hair was short now and hennaed, and she looked slimmer, though that did not mean she was slim. She was pleasant enough company in a town where Vinnie didn't have to worry about running into anyone he knew. In a bustling seafood restaurant overlooking the Adriatic, she made lively conversation, asking Vinnie all about New York. She seemed impressed by what he told her of his import-export business.

"Oh, Como," she said. "Yes, we get all our silk there for the factory. It's the best in the world."

"You work at the factory, too?"

She laughed. "Everyone here does. It's either that or the port. But I got lucky," she added. "I don't have to sew. Franca, my best friend from school, and I—we both did well in our studies. So I work in the accounting office, and Franca is the director's personal secretary."

For the first time in twenty-four hours, Vinnie felt like blood was running in his veins. "So, this owner—he's Mr. Terranova, right? What's he like?" Even his homely cousin was looking a little attractive.

"Dr. Terranova is charming. Sophisticated. He has an English teacher come to the factory each Thursday afternoon. He is planning to spend his holiday in America this summer. He wants to play golf in California. Of course, Dr. Terranova complains that his teacher comes from Edinburgh, so he's learning the wrong dialect.

"You know, I bet he would love to meet a real American.

You should come by the factory tomorrow morning. Come around noon, before we all go home for lunch."

Click, click, click. It felt like everything Vinnie had been wishing for, waiting for—for years—was all coming to pass in one week. It was all he could do not to grab his cousin and kiss her. Don't go there, he thought and caught himself just in time.

The first few moments with Dr. Terranova were tense, since he immediately asked Vinnie about golf, and Vinnie had never set foot on a golf course. "I live in New York City," Vinnie said. "It's all full of skyscrapers, buildings everywhere. There's no room for golf." Dr. Terranova looked dismissive. But he warmed up as Vinnie began to describe the women in Central Park, roller-skating in bathing-suit tops and spandex shorts, dancing to music that only they could hear through their Walkman headphones.

"My God, I have to see this," Dr. Terranova said. He put his arm around Vinnie's shoulders. "Come. I invite you to lunch at my villa today, and this summer in New York, you will take me to Central Park."

Three days later, Vinnie left Ancona with a signed contract for the Nordstrom order. "I'll be back in July," he said to Dr. Terranova and Bisi, the head of production. "We'll get that order shipped before you close for August vacation, if I have to sit here and sew all summer."

Fabrizio accompanied Vinnie to the station and kissed him good-bye. "My American nephew," he said, beaming, grasping Vinnie's shoulders and jiggling them. "He has balls made of iron!"

When Vinnie landed at JFK, he took a taxi straight over to Michael Maiorino's house and waited for him to come home from work. When Michael walked into his bedroom, he found Vinnie sitting on his bed, listening to a Ramones album and making calculations on a sheet of lined paper. Vinnie turned off the stereo and said, "Jesus Christ, you're finally home. Shut the door, we have to talk."

Michael, exhausted and covered in dust, collapsed into a plaid-upholstered easy chair in the corner.

"I need you to quit your job tomorrow," Vinnie said, "and I need ten thousand dollars." Then he told Michael all about his trip. Though he was jet-lagged and not entirely coherent in his presentation, he was so confident and full of hope, and Michael was so tired, filthy and beaten from the day's job, that he agreed to the plan. "C'mon, get in the shower. I'll ask your mom to make us some coffee. We have to go into the city."

In the men's department at Macy's, Michael stood on a carpeted platform and awkwardly turned right and left in front of a three-way mirror, trying on a new Pierre Cardin suit. Vinnie and a trim salesman stood back with their arms folded, admiring him. Dressed in fine business attire, Michael was suddenly handsome, his wavy dark blond hair crowning a Roman profile and a tall, well-proportioned body. "My goodness, you're a whole new man," the salesman said. "You should come model for us.

"Oh! And I have the perfect tie for that suit. Don't move— I'll be back in two shakes."

Vinnie laughed. "Two shakes of his dick."

"Shut up, you asshole," Michael said.

The next morning the two men leased a tiny office on Seventh Avenue. They met with a lawyer whom Michael's father knew, and by that afternoon Vincenzo Michele Ready-to-Wear, Ltd., was a legally registered business.

"I'm just warning you, Vin." Michael's cheeks were flushed with adventure. "You can go around introducing yourself as Vincenzo or Bozo or President Reagan, but no one's calling me Michele!"

Vincenzo Michele Ready-to-Wear delivered its Nordstrom order in August, as promised. From that time on, Ann Marie and Vinnie met for the five days between the Milan and Paris fashion shows each October and March, sampling different locales like Venice, Cortina and Santa Margherita. They ate splendidly, became connoisseurs of little-known Italian wines, made love and plotted over the season's Polaroids. Three days into their second rendezvous, as Vinnie lay with his head on her bare belly, Ann Marie confessed to the existence of a husband and a young son. "But I want to keep meeting you. It's not like I do this with anyone else. Do you think I'm sick?"

Vinnie looked up at her full breasts. "I think you're beautiful and you're smart and you have a secret lover in Italy."

Ann Marie smiled. Vinnie couldn't believe his good luck.

March 1984, Vinnie returned from the fashion season in Europe with orders totaling over five million dollars. He signed an offer for a three-and-a-half-room condo on the twenty-ninth floor of a sleek high-rise on West Sixty-seventh Street.

"Why you buy one-bedroom apartment?" his grandmother demanded over Sunday-night dinner. "You need two bedroom. Where you gonna put the children?"

"Please. I'm not ready for children. I'm not ready to get married. I'm only thirty-one."

"Thirty-one! Your *babbo* have you kids when he's twenty. What's wrong with you? You work in fashion, you turn *finocchio*?"

"No, I'm not gay, Jesus!" Vinnie laughed. "*Nonna,* you have no idea what Manhattan is like. It's crawling with single women—they swarm the health clubs, bars and restaurants. They're desperate for dates, boyfriends. I've got girls all over me. They call me up, they invite me to parties—hell, I date models."

Vinnie's dad rarely spoke up against his own mother, but today he said, "Mama, leave the boy alone." He winked at his son, a wink that said, *I came to America so my son could date models.*

"Models!" Vinnie's grandmother made a foul face. "Skinny girls. Nobody need skinny girls. Models starve. They starve the children!"

In 1986, Vincenzo Michele Ready-to-Wear moved into a new showroom with white marble floors and a wall of windows looking west over rooftops. Vinnie and Michael sold to Nordstrom, Saks, Nieman Marcus and Marshall Field's. They had also hired a young gal straight out of FIT to design the Vincenzo Michele line for independent boutiques around the country. Vinnie's current girlfriend was a twenty-year-old model named Tasha whose face appeared in a lipstick ad on the back of several city buses. Vinnie liked showing up with her at Nell's or gallery openings or just to eat Tex-Mex food and drink blue margaritas at his favorite restaurant on Columbus Avenue. He gave her a silver fox coat for her birthday—one bought at cost from a furrier whose wife he let shop in the showroom.

"Wow, it's so beautiful!" Tasha said. "I did a shoot for *Elle* in a coat like this about a month ago. I wanted to take it home."

The next morning, she and Vinnie went walking in Central Park, Tasha wearing only the fox coat and a garter belt with stockings and high heels. She'd attached a waist-length fake ponytail to her auburn hair.

Vinnie continued his affair with Ann Marie, who was now a vice president for her store. He had enough contacts in the fashion industry that he didn't really need her Polaroids anymore, but he relished their semi-annual retreat from the world. Ann Marie was a no-problem relationship, a best friend with whom he also had great sex—better sex, when you came down to it, than he had with the bony models in New York. He and Ann Marie sat in cafés, in beach chairs on Greek islands, in four-star restaurants in the French countryside, and talked about the other parts of their lives as if they were describing a quirky movie they had seen the night before. "Do you know," Vinnie told Ann Marie one night over sea bass in Santorini, "that I started out as an elevator man in a Park Avenue co-op? And I mean the service elevator, Ann Marie, wearing one of those canvas jumpsuits, bowing and scraping to the snobbiest assholes you've ever met in your life."

"Oh, honey." She laughed. "I always knew you were total bullshit. But you're such a great bullshit artist—you're the greatest!" She toasted him with her wineglass. "I adore you."

He adored her, too, and he loved being able to talk like this with her, being able to say anything. He felt he could trust her—she'd never judge him, never tell. Anyway, she had to keep her mouth shut about him, since she was the one carrying on the extramarital affair. As well as leaking out all of her supplier's designs to someone who knocked them off faster than they could shoot their ad campaigns.

That summer Vinnie and Michael rented a house out in Quogue. They'd each take a bedroom and then lease the other two out to girls. They would lease only half-shares—two girls sharing each bedroom every other weekend, alternating with four other girls. That way none of the girls would bring back guys they'd met, and if Vinnie and Michael got involved with any of them, they would still be free during the off weekends. They ran an ad in the *Times* real estate section and posted a sign on the bulletin board of the Vertical Club, where they both worked out. They agreed to meet any prospective renter together to make sure she was pretty, clean and wasn't bulimic or strung out on coke.

A girl named Robin called, and they invited her to Vinnie's apartment for a glass of wine. When she arrived in his doorway, Vinnie noticed her shiny black hair cropped at her chin line, intelligent-looking brown eyes and slim figure. She was wearing a Basile blazer, the original of a design the showroom had knocked off for the department stores that spring. A quilted leather Chanel purse hung from her shoulder. "Hi." She held out her hand to shake his. A gold Buccellati bracelet dangled around her wrist. "I'm Robin Horowitz." Vinnie knew exactly who she was.

Would she recognize him, he wondered, now in his cashmere sweater, with his hair longer, pulled back into the little ponytail he was beginning to grow? Would she place someone like him in a luxury condo with olive-green leather couches and the Missoni rug on the floor? He was years older, didn't have that boy face anymore, wasn't wearing the stupid uniform. "I'm Vincenzo," he said, putting on the slightest Italian accent. "This is my business partner, Michael." He poured her a glass of wine. "White okay?"

"Yes, fantastic."

Vinnie felt too warm, uneasy and distracted. All he could picture was hailing taxis for Robin Horowitz, opening the door for Robin Horowitz, Robin Horowitz in his elevator making that snide, unconscious remark to her school friend about bridge-and-tunnel guys. A little knot of fury that had been stored all these years in some tiny tightness of a muscle, some raw nerve cell, started to expand. He took a deep breath. He didn't want to get into any of that with her. His only goal was to make it through the interview without her recognizing him and get her back out the door. "Michael, you tell her about the house," he said.

"Okay, Vin." Michael sat on the couch facing her. He thought she was pretty, classy. She had a nice smile, soft-looking hair. "Well, the place is in Quogue. A new house, only about a half-mile walk to the beach . . ."

They chatted while Vinnie stared at the art book on his coffee table, *Treasures of the Uffizi*. They talked about the house, the Hamptons, the alternating weekends. Michael told her about their business, the showroom, the Vincenzo Michele line coming out in the fall. Robin's eyes followed his gestures, and there seemed to be chemistry between the two. Vinnie was getting a stomachache.

"So, Robin, where do you work?" Vinnie asked.

Now she looked a little uneasy. "Well, I'm trained as a graphic artist," she said, "but I'm kind of between gigs right now." She reached for her glass. "I was hoping, actually, that it would be okay for me to spend some of the weekdays out in Quogue, too, you know, when it's quieter there."

"Yeah, that would be great." Michael grinned. "I was thinking of taking off a week or two this summer and staying out there myself." Michael imagined sitting on the beach with her at sunset. He imagined picking basil in the garden he would plant, making pesto for her when the two of them were alone in the house and everyone else was back in the city. He imagined making love to her in the swimming pool.

Vinnie butted into his fantasy. "So how can you afford it if you're not working?" he asked Robin. He knew it was a rude question, and he already knew the answer. But he felt like an animal that had picked up the scent of blood.

She blushed. "Um. I have some savings. And a little bit of inheritance from when my grandfather passed away two years ago." Her eyes darted around as if she were lying.

She has Daddy's credit card, Vinnie thought, and millions in a trust fund. She could buy the whole damn house tomorrow if she wanted to. And look at her squirming—she's embarrassed.

"But don't worry," she said, looking directly at Vinnie now. "I've got the rent. I can write you a check today if you want." She seemed puzzled for a minute. "You know what?" she said. "You look familiar. I mean, I know everyone uses that as a stupid pickup line, but I'm serious. You really look familiar. Have we met before?"

Vinnie's heart pounded. He realized he shouldn't have drawn her attention to him like that just to get in his little jab. He smoothed his hair back with his fingers. "You belong to the Vertical Club?"

"Yeah, I do."

Michael smiled, picturing her among the girls on the aerobics floor, wearing a brightly colored thong leotard over black tights.

"Well, you probably saw me there," Vinnie said.

"I guess so." Robin shrugged.

Vinnie felt relieved, and then he was angry with himself for his relief. He had nothing to be ashamed of, he thought, why was he so ashamed? At least I've worked my way up to where I am now, he told himself. I didn't have everything handed to me by my rich daddy. Look at this girl. She's smart, she's pretty, she's had every door in the world open to her, and it sounds like she hasn't done one fucking thing with her life. She's the one who should be ashamed. He was ready for the meeting to be over.

He stood, took her half-empty glass from the coffee table and carried it into the kitchen. "So, Robin," he said over his shoulder, "we'll get back to you on the room, okay?"

Robin straightened up, startled.

Michael was startled, too. "I don't see any problem with you renting the room," he said.

Vinnie bent his head and spoke out of the pass-through between the kitchen and the dining area. "No, no problem," he said quickly. "We just have an understanding—Michael and I—that we talk things over privately before making any decision. That's how we do it in our business, and so far, it's been working out pretty well."

Michael's voice showed his annoyance. "Okay, Vin." He thought Vinnie was acting ridiculous. Robin was attractive, she was nice, and obviously, she had the money for the rent. She was exactly the sort of girl they had wanted. He didn't understand why Vinnie had to be so weird about this—what if she committed to another place before they got back to her?

Robin rose to leave. She slipped her chain-and-leather

pocketbook strap over her shoulder. "It was nice meeting both of you."

"Yeah, you, too," Vinnie called from the kitchen.

Michael walked her to the door. He placed a hand on her shoulder. "I'll call you back right away," he promised. "I'm sure it'll all work out fine."

Vinnie stalled for a minute, washing and rewashing the wineglass, long enough for Robin to walk down the hallway and catch the elevator. Then he came out of the kitchen and said, "Look, I'm having none of this girl."

"What the hell?"

"You can tell she's a nut," Vinnie said. "She's spoiled and she's insecure. I bet she's never worked a day in her life. She's probably the type who'll eat health food and leave her dishes in the sink for someone else to clean up."

"I didn't get that impression at all. I thought she seemed pretty great."

"Michael, I know you did, but you're thinking with your dick. Listen. This is just one of those times you have to trust me. Like we do in the showroom when a buyer comes in and no matter how good they look, I can tell they're the one who will send everything back, not pay the bill. You know I have that sixth sense about people—I get it from my grandmother—it's like I can smell trouble. And this Robin Horowitz," Vinnie said, having nearly convinced himself that what he was saying was true, "I can tell she's going to be a bad bet." He grabbed the slip of paper where she'd written down her number. He tore it into small pieces and stuffed it in his pocket.

Michael was stunned and angry. He got up and put on his leather jacket. "Well, since you're such a psychic, I think maybe you'd better meet these girls first. If any of them get your stamp of approval, then call me in. I'm not going to waste any more time." He went to the door.

What could Vinnie say to make things better? "Okay, Mike, I will. Don't worry. I'll do the legwork, and when you show up, I'll present you with a harem of beautiful, agreeable women who will all fall in love with you. I promise, okay?" He felt awful.

Michael rolled his eyes and sighed. "Sure." He closed the door behind him.

Vinnie sat on his couch and opened a copy of *Money* magazine. He couldn't focus on the page. He knew he'd done wrong—he'd wronged both Robin and, worse, his best friend. But he couldn't imagine handling it any other way. The girl made him too uncomfortable. She reminded him of feelings that he just didn't need to feel anymore. He couldn't see having her around all summer, living through what it would be like when she remembered who he was and how he used to carry her Saks and Bergdorf Goodman shopping bags from the curb.

Anyway, it was over. New York was teeming with gorgeous single women all dying to meet a man. He'd fill the house up with models, investment bankers, advertising executives. He'd give Michael first dibs before coming on to any of them. This would all blow over, and everything would be fine. Really, he told himself, it would be.

Still Life with Poodles

— 1988 —

It's ten minutes before midnight, and the Horowitz party in apartment 7B is over. At least that's what Bob and Mimi Horowitz and their grown daughter, Robin, all think. Bob loosens his tie, unbuttons his collar and leans back into the den couch. Bob is one of those men who has become more handsome as he's aged. Robin remembers how he used to look—skinny, with a beaky nose, nervous eyes and unruly black hair that he tried to tame with pomades and gels. Now that he's sixty-two, his trim face and figure make him seem vibrant compared to some of his puffier contemporaries, and his hair, which turned an even shade of charcoal gray several years ago, is cropped short, each strand standing up neatly, the way movie stars are starting to style their hair. Of course, Bob's looks have benefited from his success on Wall Street. He's been a multimillionaire for over half his life. He sits on the board of Columbia University and several prominent Jewish organizations. His vigilant eyes have settled down; his big nose looks dignified. "Well, that was a lovely evening," he says to Robin. "Are you happy with it?"

Mimi, who has not fared as well over time but has coped using perms and hair color, an eye-lift and collagen, blinks and smiles at her daughter. She has put out her best effort, dinner for fifty—family, old friends, new acquaintances. Everyone gathered in the flower-filled apartment to wish Robin happy birthday.

Robin smiles back at her parents. "I'm as happy as I could possibly be," she says, "considering I've just turned thirty and have neither husband nor children nor career."

"Oh, honey!" Mimi's face turns hurt and dewy. Still, Robin can't imagine that Mimi has any idea how it feels to wind up with your mother and father at the end of the evening. To look forward to Hanukkah with them and Christmas with them and New Year's Eve with no one.

Bob has that puzzled look, and Robin knows exactly where his thoughts are going. *You're so beautiful,* he would say, *smart, funny. Any guy in the world would want to marry you.* Then his practical mind would start thrashing around for a solution. *Why don't you come up to Quaker Ridge and take some golf lessons? I see lots of young men on the course every weekend. Some are single, some divorced . . .*

Robin and her father have had this conversation many times. What Robin can't explain to her father is that if she did marry one of those Quaker Ridge men, then she'd be stuck spending the rest of the weekends of her life at a golf club in Westchester, and that, she is sure, is grounds for divorce.

Anyway—surprise!—the party isn't really over. All three Horowitzes start when they hear the door to Mimi's bathroom open and Maximilian Auerbach emerges from the master-suite hallway. Robin figures he must have spent the past fifteen minutes in her mother's bathroom while her family was returning coats and saying good-bye to the last elevatorload of guests.

Robin doesn't know Max well. She met him recently at a presentation given by a Smith Barney broker about corporate responsibility and socially screened investment portfolios. Robin and Max have a few friends in common. She invited him to her party because he is a moderately attractive, wealthy single man with liberal political views, and because she is desperate to find the love of her life. Not that she's super-impressed with Max Auerbach, but at thirty years old, she's learned not to leave stones unturned.

Mimi tips the caterers, and Robin expects Max to say, *I'd better be heading out*, and ask for his coat. Instead, he saunters into the den, sprawls on the couch next to Bob and grins. Robin detects the scent of marijuana as he passes her chair. His maroon sport jacket, strawberry-blond hair, ruddy complexion and bloodshot eyes combine to create an impression of great energy, belied by his present slouch. Robin usually considers her father an imposing figure from the perspective of a potential suitor, but Max slaps Bob on the knee and says,

"We were speaking of dogs. Well, Bob, if you're allergic, a poodle is the only way to go."

"No, I don't like poodles," Bob grumbles. "Little snappy, yappy things."

"Not small poodles. No, of course not. Big ones. A standard poodle." Max sits up and points his finger in the air. "Did you know that the poodle is the most intelligent breed?"

Robin can just hear her father saying, *Who needs an intelligent dog?* But because he is even more desperate than Mimi and Robin put together for his daughter to be suitably married—whatever that means to each of them—he nods, considering. Mimi feigns interest, too. She widens her eyes and puffs up the back of her short auburn hair with her fingers, though she is obviously exhausted from hostessing, and Robin knows she has been dead set against this dog thing for years. Robin slips off her shoes and curls her legs under her in the leather armchair, trying to look charming, or at least as if she is awake. Actually, she's so tired she's decided to sleep over in her childhood bedroom—now redecorated in chintz for the occasional houseguest—rather than pack up all her birthday presents and get a cab crosstown to her own apartment on West Eighty-sixth Street. Max continues to praise poodles.

Robin thinks about her last four blind dates and how futile each one was. She knows by now that passion and fulfillment are not coming her way from some nice Jewish boy who belongs to her aunt Myra's country club or works with her best friend, Alicia, in the marketing department at American Express. Yet she doesn't know where else to look. She can't help it if most of the men she meets are brokers and bankers, unconscious automatons, proud of their rank in some economic machine that, well, among other things, is destroying the natural world. She doesn't have anything to say to these guys, and what they say to her is usually pretty dull, often idiotic, despite their degrees from Princeton or Cornell. She hasn't kissed anyone in over a year.

Lonely as she is, she's not convinced that her problems are even about finding a man. Secretly, she's been collecting course catalogs from faraway schools, eco-travel brochures and New Age workshop schedules. She often fantasizes about some program where, in exchange for tuition, hard work and cheerful participation, she will be granted a life. She reads the Sunday *Times* education section each week, wishing that, as the advertisements promise, a night-school MBA might open up *her* world. She peruses the job classifieds and imagines working as an administrative assistant in a busy downtown office. She knows it sounds absurd, and she doesn't admit it to anyone, but sometimes Robin envies people who don't have trust funds.

In the meantime, Max has a great idea. He jumps to his feet and waves his big red hands as he speaks. His own two standard poodles are downstairs in his car. He'll bring them up so Bob can meet them. The whole family will get to meet them: Isaac and Sybil.

Mimi laughs. "Like Isaac and Sybil Freiburg."

"You know who they are?" Max asks.

Mimi says she's just finished reading the book about the

Freiburgs, bankers and jewelers in Germany and Holland, one of the oldest Jewish families in New York.

"Well, my middle name is Freiburg," Max says, beaming and combing his hair back with his fingers. "I can sign your book if you want. Isaac and Sybil were my great-grandparents." He rushes out to fetch their canine namesakes.

Mimi Horowitz perks up like she's just received a shot of B12. "He's descended from the Freiburgs?"

Bob glows. "He seems to like you a lot," he tells Robin, looking at her like she's the stock certificate of a company that just received a federal contract.

Robin rolls her eyes. Sometimes, she thinks, the less she says, the better she gets along with her parents. Recently, she made the mistake of showing Mimi an article she'd clipped from a human-rights magazine. The story contrasted an overcrowded Alabama orphanage full of black babies to a New York adoption agency with a six-year waiting list for white newborns. "You want me to have kids," Robin said. "How about a black one?"

"Oh, God," Mimi said. "Like Charles Payne's daughter. Her black son is now turning into a black teenager. They hardly ever visit her parents anymore, and when they do, I can't imagine what it's like. You know that her mother has been diagnosed with cancer?

"Really," she added. "Adopting a black child would hardly be fair to anyone."

"You mean to you?" Robin asked.

"No, to you, honey," Mimi insisted. "It would just be so difficult and eventually disappointing. And it would be unfair to the child, who, after all, needs its own community."

"What, a slum in Montgomery? Fine, I'll adopt two—they'll have each other."

"Great, darling, your own gang."

Tonight Robin reminds herself not to mention that the most attractive man at the party was a Puerto Rican catering assistant.

Suddenly, Max is back, and there are dogs in the den, curly-haired poodles the colors of red and white wine. They sniff, they lick, they turn, they wag with the same extroverted personality as their master. Mimi pats them with one hand, and with the other she deftly whisks a crystal candy dish from the coffee table. Robin can tell from the set of her mother's jaw that she is breathing through her mouth to avoid their smell, which is considerable. In fact, they stink, but no one mentions it. Robin, Mimi and Bob take turns caressing Isaac and Sybil's heads. Bob grabs his camera from a desk drawer and takes pictures. The poodles pose with Mimi and Bob, then with Max and Robin together. Bob clicks away, dreaming of grandchildren named Auerbach.

There is a lull in the conversation, and Robin hopes Max will find it a good time to leave. But Mimi is treacherous, and she asks him if he would like some tea or perhaps a glass of juice.

Max has tea *and* juice, some chocolate-covered strawberries and a few slices of leftover filet that he shares with the dogs. He licks chocolate off his fingers, wipes them on his corduroys, then tousles one of the poodles between its ears. He tells everyone about his country house in the Hamptons and about how adorable the poodles are, bounding playfully in the tall grass. They were just there today. Robin thinks she feels fleas burrowing into her velvet skirt and reminds herself to check for deer ticks before bed. If that moment ever comes.

Max disappears down the hallway into Mimi's bathroom for another ten minutes, and Robin imagines his progress. First he might actually do the legitimate thing—unzip his pants and, with rosy penis in hand, take a loud piss into her mother's pink toilet. Then, nine chances out of ten, he leans over the marble vanity, careful not to displace the perfume bottles or enameled dish of bobby pins, and cracks the window. Robin pictures him sitting down on the Lucite vanity stool to roll a joint. He smokes it slowly, while his free hand opens the beveled mirrored medicine chest, and he scans the labels of Mimi's prescriptions.

The poodles settle down on Robin's shoes, and her parents take advantage of Max's absence to yawn, stretch and rub their eyes. "He's very enthusiastic," Mimi whispers. Bob cracks his knuckles. The skin under his eyes has turned the same shade of charcoal gray as his hair. Robin doesn't think she's ever seen her father this patient—certainly not at one-thirty in the morning—and she feels sorry for him.

Max returns, followed by a pungent smell of smoke. He does most of the talking. "Bob, I heard you're on the board of the East Side Jewish Cultural Center. That's great. You know, my family put the JCC on the map." He wraps his arm around

Bob's shoulders, and Bob forces a smile. Max elaborates upon his ancestors' accomplishments. At one point he says that his family put Israel on the map.

It is the dogs who finally bark, because they need to be walked. The Horowitzes send Max, Isaac and Sybil Freiburg Auerbach off with hugs, his cashmere coat, leashes and a blue Tiffany bag full of steak and pâté.

Back in the den, Mimi replaces the crystal dish and opens a window to let out the dog smell. "Well, Bob, I'm still not sold on dogs of our own, but perhaps we could have some grand-poodles." She winks at Robin.

Robin is stony, silent at first. "Mom," she says at last, "I'd take the dogs before the man."

"Why?" her parents ask in unison.

"For Christ's sake, he's pompous and obnoxious, ridiculous and practically delusional! And by the way, did you notice his eyes? He was smoking dope in your bathroom."

"Oh well," Mimi says. "That's what the kids did at your sweet sixteen. I was shooing them out of the bathrooms the whole night. You know. Boys will be boys."

"But Max is forty-two."

"Yes," she glares at her daughter, "and now *you're* thirty."

Robin thinks how, five years from now, if nothing in her life changes, she'll be blowing out her thirty-five candles in the same Chippendale-furnished dining room, surrounded by the same group of pitying cousins, encouraging friends, stray Jewish bachelors and desperate parents. An untimely death is starting to sound attractive, and her mind casts about for less dramatic options. She will take a boat around the world, buy a house in a small New England town, teach literacy to welfare mothers, join an ashram in India. In any case, she vows, this is her last year of suffering empty luxury.

Robin does spend Hanukkah and Christmas with her parents, and the holidays are as depressing as she imagined. Then Max Auerbach calls and invites her to a series of parties for New Year's Eve. With no viable alternative, she graciously accepts. On December 29, Mimi takes her to the Gianni Versace boutique to purchase a slinky silk dress for the occasion. But on the afternoon of the thirty-first, when Robin should be catching a cab to the hair salon, she calls Max's answering machine and cancels. She doesn't even tell her parents, who would be too worried on her behalf to enjoy their theater benefit, but she ends up spending New Year's Eve in her bathrobe, alone in her apartment. She eats scrambled eggs for supper and leafs through her files of catalogs and clippings for hours. At midnight she hears the muffled popping sound of fireworks in the distance and looks out the window. A light snow has begun to fall, and she turns off her bedroom lamp to watch the swirl of white flakes around the streetlight below. Robin presses her nose against the cold glass, and as she sees the crosstown bus roll by, she fingers the article about the orphans in Alabama.

Lucia Sanchez: Angelita *y* Rafael II

– 1981–1989 –

Let me tell you what happened to Angelita and Rafael.

They married in June 1981 at the Meadow Club in Southampton. The wedding was huge and, of course, spectacular. They invited five hundred friends, plus Rafael brought his whole family up from Medellín, and Somoza and Sacasa aunts and cousins assembled from all over the United States and Europe. All the young nieces were put into beautiful pink silk dresses and the nephews into miniature tuxedos, and the children scattered flower petals down the aisle in the clubhouse for Angelita to walk upon. She was a knockout, stunning in a column of cream-colored raw silk that she had imported from Thailand and given to a brilliant old Russian seamstress on Lexington Avenue. The dress was sexy for a bride; it had a high side slit that showed off Angelita's long legs. She wore her hair in braids wrapped around her head, laced with the same white orchid blossoms that had appeared in the photograph where Rafael first saw her and fell in love. It looked like she was wearing a white crown or a halo. Carlos and I sat up close, and as Angelita walked down the aisle toward her groom, we smiled, relishing the look on his face—like Saint Francis receiving the stigmata.

The reception was a raucous fiesta that started at eight and didn't end until five o'clock the next morning. The band was fantastic—a salsa and merengue recording star from Santo Domingo, with twelve members of his Latin orchestra. New York society came dressed to the nines. We were seated at one of the family tables next to Rafael's brother, Andres, a nice enough guy, a typical Colombian provincial who was happy to drink champagne, rub shoulders with European titles and feel like a big shot for the weekend. "I tell you," he confided to Carlos and me, "if I had ten million dollars and I could really be someone in this town, I'd move to New York in a minute."

"My dear," I said. "If you had ten million dollars here, you'd be middle class."

Children ran around the tables screaming with glee. On the dance floor, and out on the clubhouse terraces, Meadow Club members and their starchy wives got drunk and wiggled around to the music until it looked like their stiff asses might splinter apart. Carlos danced with a gringa named Beverly Coddington who lived in Angelita's building. "Oh, how agile you people are!" she shrieked, laughing, throwing her arms up and down like a can opener.

I spoke for a few minutes with her husband. He was sunburned and plump, looked like a standing rib roast. He'd just been down to Washington to visit the new president. "Normally, I don't associate with those actor types," he said, grinning. "But I guess you have to make exceptions sometimes." Thank God, Clara Sacasa grabbed me, and she pulled me into a conga line that snaked out onto the eighteenth green, everybody kicking off their shoes along the way. The night of the wedding was like Carnival in June, with more than one liaison initiated in some member's cabana or on a chaise longue by the pool. A few of the paler guests threw up from the authentic paella and other spicy foods.

Angelita and Rafael honeymooned in Cap d'Antibes at the Eden Roc. When they returned to New York, he moved his things into her apartment, and they rented a small house overlooking Mecox Bay for the rest of the summer. Carlos and I spent a weekend out there at the end of July. The two of them behaved like typical newlyweds, telling intimate little stories of each other's strange habits—how Rafael sent out even his underwear to be dry-cleaned and pressed, how Angelita woke up and required one Godiva chocolate truffle before she could even bear a sip of coffee.

A few months later, they were thrilled to announce that Angelita was pregnant, and they took it as a good omen when Angelita gave birth to Rafaelito on the exact date of their first anniversary. Three years after that, in the fall, they had Marisela, a gorgeous baby who inherited all of her mother's finer features but not her funny eyes. Even as a newborn, she had long, delicate fingers, like the cherubs in mannerist paintings, and from the beginning, we all knew that Marisela Somoza Echevarrí was destined to become a great beauty.

Rafael's businesses grew exponentially in the early 1980s, and pretty soon Greek shipbuilders and other tycoon types started showing up at their more intimate dinner parties. The lovely thing was that even with their extraordinary financial and social success, neither one ever became a snob. They included Carlos and me in all their gatherings, Rafael introducing us to senators and other superheroes as "the friends to whom I owe all my happiness." Their life was like a beautiful dream. Everything went swimmingly until Angelita started hiring the Guatemalan maids.

I first heard about it from our housekeeper, Lorena. Lorena is a very fine person from Buenos Aires, and she spends two days a week in our apartment, keeping it immaculate, grocery-shopping for me and taking care of our laundry. The rest of the week she works for Patricia Montaldo, whose husband runs the American branch of the Banco Santander. Patricia and I are good friends, and naturally, we trade days when one of us is entertaining or needs Lorena for some special job. Anyway, it was Lorena who told me that Angelita had let go of her maid, Elvira, quite suddenly, with little explanation other than it was nothing personal and that excellent references would be provided. Did I know anyone who needed help? I promised Lorena I'd ask around, but before I could, Elvira was snatched up by the Comtesse de Clàve. Maids of Elvira's caliber don't stay unemployed for long.

I didn't think about it again for several months. The couple of times Carlos and I were at Angelita and Rafael's apartment were both catered affairs. Nothing unusual caught my eye until one day when I went to lunch with Angelita at Bice. Afterward, she asked me to come over and see a painting they were "trying out," considering buying for their living room.

Angelita had recently redecorated the whole apartment in a traditional style—lots of patterned fabrics and velvets, a needlepoint carpet, color everywhere. The painting hung over her fireplace. It was by a Hudson River School artist, Jasper Cropsey, I believe—a luminous, innocuous landscape that gave the room a kind of American dignity. "Well, it's not the garden at Argenteuil," I said, "but I thoroughly approve."

"But don't you think Monet would be a little too light for this room?" she asked me, dead serious.

I laughed. I was still not used to how rich she had become. "Oh yes, a Monet would be terrible here."

I drew closer to the landscape to examine it. What I noticed was the dust. Not on the painting, of course—that was a new arrival. But atop the mantelpiece and all the objects on it. Her Second Empire clock covered in dust. Two Ming Dynasty porcelain dogs, dusty from tail to tongue. Crystal candlesticks all dusty, with dusty candles in them. I wondered when was the last time anyone had cleaned. "The painting is lovely," I said. "You should buy it."

While Angelita went into the bar to get us some Perrier, I looked around the room. In all the corners were big hairy balls of dust, like tumbleweeds on the Pampas. The rug did not look vacuumed. I walked over to the window and noticed its sill covered in a layer of fine black soot. Angelita returned. I said, "Your new draperies are beautiful." Each dirty window was decked out in about seven hundred yards of Cowtan and Tout chintz.

A door slammed, there was some squealing in the kitchen, and then Rafaelito charged into the living room, his face looking like he'd eaten chocolate ice cream from a trough. Marisela toddled in after him, hands covered with the same brown smear. "My little darlings! What a mess." Angelita grabbed a couple of cocktail napkins as the two small beasts ran toward her. "No, no. Don't touch Mama's dress. Here, hold my hands." I smelled the most awful sort of raw-sewage odor coming from the little girl. Angelita kissed each child and stood. Cuffing each one's wrists with a hand of her own, she led them toward a maid waiting in the foyer. "Maria, please. Take them to their rooms and clean them up. Marisela needs to be changed."

The maid grunted, dragging the children away as one burst into a fit of howling.

"Get all nice and clean, and I'll be right there, my babies," Angelita called after them.

I will never forget how that maid looked standing in the foyer. She was about four feet tall, with a brown face and a thick black braid. She was built like a small bull. Even the peasants from the mountain towns of Colombia are more graceful than this woman, and from a distance, in their traditional costumes, they can look picturesque. Of course, up close, you see their teeth are rotting, and they smell of cornmeal, dirt and sweat. Anyway, this Maria looked about three rungs down the ladder from our Colombian peasants, and I thought about how, in Central America, the peasantry had so much more Indian blood in it. "Where is your new maid from?" I asked Angelita.

"Guatemala."

"Ah. I thought so. From her accent." She probably couldn't even speak Spanish, never mind English.

Over the following year, even the smallest dinner parties in Angelita's home were catered. Carlos and I thought it strange. This *was* her prerogative, being as wealthy as she now was, and having children to manage. Still, we remembered that when Angelita was single, and in the early years of her marriage, she had loved to cook, and she pulled off marvelous parties and delicious food with the help of only Elvira. If it was a really big crowd, my Lorena might come over to lend a hand with serving. Now, if it was just the four of us, and I hadn't invited them to our home, Rafael always took us out to eat. One time when Le Bernardin was crowded and we had to wait for a table, he and Angelita got into an argument. "Why the hell can't we ever eat at home?" he demanded.

"Ay, Rafael, with the children and everything. It's so difficult to shop, cook, put a dinner together."

"You can put a dinner together with your eyes closed. The problem is those crazy maids. They can't cook. They can't serve. Nothing!"

"Hush, please, my love." Angelita looked embarrassed. "You are not thinking of our priorities—Rafaelito, Marisela." She smiled at us apologetically. "Now that we're an old married couple, you'll have to forgive our domestic disputes. What Rafael is not considering is how wonderful these women are with our children. They treat them as if they were their own."

"Yes." Rafael rolled his eyes. "I'm surprised they don't vacuum the house with the children strapped to their backs, like the women on a coffee plantation."

I guess Rafael hadn't noticed that they didn't vacuum at all. "How many maids do you have now?" I asked Angelita.

"Usually two." She changed the subject, and soon our table was ready.

Something was fishy—aside from the chef at Le Bernardin—but I didn't know what.

Something was going on with Angelita, too, apart from the household. There were times she wasn't around, "busy," she would say, though busy at what no one could imagine. She was absent from major parties even when she was in town, making the excuse that she had to spend time with her children or attend a conference at Rafaelito's school. This seemed a bit implausible. Listen, I have plenty of friends with children who love their children, but the children don't wreck their whole social lives. It wasn't as if Angelita was cold or distant. When we did get together, she was charming, empathic, her usual self. But so often there would be an important luncheon, Margaretha of Bavaria's birthday luncheon at Doubles, for example, and everyone was there except for Angelita. The final straw was when she refused to serve on the committee for the Princess Grace Foundation Gala. It was an incredible opportunity for her, and it would have meant a wonderful time for all of her friends, but she turned down the invitation, handwritten from Caroline of Monaco herself, with no excuse at all.

I met her for lunch at Harry Cipriani, and we had drunk two Bellinis each before I brought up the subject. "So, who is your lover?"

"What!" Angelita's eyes flashed wide open. She looked at me like I was crazy.

"Come on, my dear: We have all noticed your absence. And Rafaelito can't have that many school conferences—he's not learning calculus."

We were silent for a moment while the waiter brought squid-ink risotto. The minute he turned away, I continued, "You needn't be afraid to tell me. I am friends with Rafael, but loyalty to a man only goes so far. I am also friends with Jaime Hernandez, but I was perfectly willing to receive Monica's love letters at my address when she was screwing that Venezuelan sculptor. And don't think I am impervious to temptation myself." I winked at her, thinking about the delicious fun I had with my friend Laura's brother, sneaking around the hallways of their mother's house in Cartagena at midnight.

Angelita burst out laughing. "I can't believe you think I'm having an affair! I would never betray Rafael—I don't even think of those things."

I studied her face as I chewed a purple tentacle. She had an advantage here, with that crooked eye. It made her expression more inscrutable. She laughed, but she didn't talk. I looked around the restaurant. It was a lovely sight. Beautiful women, exquisite young men, the music of different languages in the air—Italian, French, Spanish—glittering jewelry, sparkling flutes of champagne.

"So why did you turn down the Princess Grace Foundation?" I asked. "It was such an honor for you. We all could have had so much fun. What happened?"

"I'm not sure I can take one more gala," she said.

I couldn't believe what she was saying. She was one of the most lively, charming women of New York society. "What is wrong with you?"

"Oh, Lucia, it's a stupid charity. They put on a weekend of parties that cost a million dollars in order to raise what—two hundred thousand, maybe, to give to a few dancers. Who cares?" She looked into her plate and pushed the food around with her fork. "Sometimes all this glamour, all the parties, shopping, dresses . . . Sometimes it feels empty to me. Sometimes I like to focus on other things, things that maybe seem more important."

"Not Marisela's diapers, I hope."

"No, no. Things that matter. You know I really am involved at Rafael's school. A few of the mothers have been putting together a program to introduce the children to the concept of social justice."

"Social justice! Your son is five years old. The only social justice that matters to him is if some older child knocks him over and takes his toy."

"Exactly!" Angelita became animated. "That's exactly where we start. Then we move into lessons about being included or excluded from a group, and later, as the children grow, we will begin to discuss issues like whether boys should be treated differently from girls . . ."

"My God, how boring!" I was worried that perhaps she was slipping back into whatever crazy state of mind had made her marry her first husband. I thought that she might have inherited some kind of existential sorrow from her father, the only son of Anastasio Somoza who did not become president of Nicaragua and now lived a reclusive and rather dissipated life on a ranch in the Spanish countryside. "Angelita!" I lay my hand on her arm. "Come back to the world."

"I would like to think I *am* making a difference in the world," she said. "Working with the children, doing other projects."

"Like what?"

She opened and closed her mouth. She looked about to say something and then stopped herself. "Oh, little things I have up my sleeve." She raised her head and gave me a mischievous smile.

"And you won't tell me a word? I'm your best friend."

"No, no." She giggled. "Let's just say I'm saving humanity."

"You sound crazy. You should see a psychiatrist."

"Actually, I already do."

"Ay, not really? I was only kidding." I took a few sips of Pellegrino water. This could explain her strangeness. Angelita had succumbed to that uniquely American passion for hiring a doctor to convince you that you are miserable in the middle of your charmed and privileged life. Thank God most of our friends were not following that fashion. "Angelita, the psychiatrist must be the problem. You should stop."

She said, "Maybe I will."

We both laughed and ordered tiramisu for dessert.

I was still suspicious about Angelita's maids, and one day when Lorena was at our house, I asked if she still saw Elvira.

"Oh, yes. We go to the same church. Elvira is fine."

"And she is still at her job with the countess?"

"Yes, yes. The job is good." Lorena cocked her head and smiled sadly. "Of course, it's not like working for Señora Somoza. That lady was an angel to her. Señora Clàve is, well, an employer—no more, no less."

In Monte Carlo, in fact, the Comtesse de Clàve had been suspected of murdering her first husband, but there was no proof, so charges were dropped. Nina von Hohenlohe once worked with her on the committee for the Red Cross Ball and reported that she was a bitch. "I imagine she can be a bit moody," I said. But Lorena sealed her lips tight and raised her brows. She wore an expression that meant, *If you say so, Señora, but I certainly won't comment on that.* And how could she, in her position? I continued, "It was so strange what happened with Señora Somoza, no? And now she has these weird women from Guatemala in her home."

I had struck a nerve in Lorena, and now it sang. "I know!" She sounded indignant. "My friend Sofia works in the building. In apartment 8A. The Somoza home has become a kind of joke. No one knows what's going on—not the super, the handymen, any of the housekeepers. The Guatemalan maids come and go. First there's one, then her cousin, then a sister, then the first one leaves. They do not wear proper uniforms. They are not proper housekeepers. Sofia says they don't speak Spanish or English. They talk to no one, and unless they are with the children, they never go out.

"No, Señora, they are not proper housekeepers. And do you know what I think?" She was all worked up over the matter— actually, much more than I.

"Tell me, Lorena."

"I don't think they are maids at all. I think they are illegal aliens!" With that, she tossed her head back, and with her nose in the air, she marched off to our bedroom to change the sheets. I laughed to myself, thinking about how many strings Patricia Montaldo and I had pulled to get a visa for *her*, and then finally a green card.

A friendship is not the same with a man who is happily married. He is occupied with his business, his wife, his children and perhaps a mistress tucked away somewhere to balance out all the domesticity. Although Carlos and I saw Angelita and Rafael frequently throughout their marriage, I did not really have the opportunity to see Rafael alone during those years. If anything, he was the one traveling on business, and Carlos and I took Angelita to parties or had her over for dinner. I have to admit that I missed him—missed the sort of freedom I always felt in talking to him, the little bit of sparring we enjoyed, our flirtation. So you can imagine my pleasure when, early in 1989, I was flying down to Bogotá to meet Carlos, and I ran into Rafael at the Avianca ticket counter. He immediately spoke to one of the clerks and had me moved up to first class to sit with him, and we strolled together toward the gate. I actually relished the several-hour flight ahead of us, even though I am terrified of flying, and I am sure I will die one day in a plane crash.

At first, we spoke of ordinary polite things—politics, gossip, how Rafaelito had insulted his first-grade teacher, calling her a fat cow. We talked about how the situation with the oil business had improved in Colombia since the discovery of the Cano Limon oil field; and Rafael was happy for me that Carlos and I were doing better financially. It wasn't until the plane began to taxi on the runway that our old familiarity was ignited.

"You look pale," he said. "Are you frightened?"

"Yes. It's always like this. Just takeoff and landing. Do you mind if I dig my nails into your skin?"

Rafael smiled and took my hand. He kept it in his long after we were aloft and I had relaxed. When the stewardess came out serving drinks, he ordered champagne and orange juice. We mixed mimosas and talked nonstop, greedy for each other's company, aware that our time was limited. We laughed like old lovers. I read him some wonderful passages from *Love in the Time of Cholera,* and we promised that if we were both widowed, we would marry and spend our old age floating around the world on a cruise ship. One hour before we were scheduled to land in Bogotá, Rafael turned serious.

"Lucia. Angelita really loves you, considers you her closest friend, and you know I would never ask you to be disloyal to her unless you were screwing me. But there is something I need to talk to you about. I need your advice here."

"Tell me, my love."

"Well. You're going to laugh—at a man like me concerned with these household issues. But . . . this business with these maids of hers. It has become impossible, unacceptable."

"I have noticed that they aren't the most efficient."

"My God, *you've* noticed, and so has everyone else in the world, I'm sure! Lucia, the house is dirty. The children are dirty. Everything in disorder—I can't find my papers. These women, they sit in the kitchen at dawn, making tortillas by hand. They can't cook an egg. Angelita has to do everything.

"These women don't speak. I don't know if they *can* speak—even among themselves, they are silent. Silent and cold, like rocks. Angelita says they are kind to her, to the children, and maybe that is so, but with me . . . Lucia, I feel like they hate me, the way they stand there and stare. My God, even if they can't talk, they could smile, no?"

I could feel Rafael's relief, the burden of a big secret lifted. I could feel how much he had needed to speak of all this to someone who understood. He talked freely, and he had much more to say. About his embarrassment in his building. About the absurdity of hiring caterers for a dinner for eight when you had two in help. About the turnover—how one maid left and another arrived, how they were all so similar that sometimes he didn't even notice. "They are all called Maria Something-or-other. Maria Gracia, Maria Cristina. They all look the same—short, squat, dirty.

"It's driving me crazy, Lucia. I go away more than I have to just to escape the house. Angelita is complaining about my traveling so much. And I don't like to leave her—I love her, I love my children. But the way she runs our home—this is supposed to be Park Avenue, not some crazy *finca*!"

Rafael is a man with the humor and intelligence to laugh at himself, and by now we were both splitting our sides. He went on, "The other day I caught one of them walking around the house with no shoes. Can you imagine, these square little brown feet padding down the hallway?"

I wanted to help him, but I was nearly choking. "Did she have all her toes?" I asked.

Rafael threw his head back and hit himself on the forehead. "Ay, Lucia, my life is like some kind of surrealistic movie. Where is Buñuel right now when I need him?"

The stewardess came by, offering a last round of drinks. We were quite drunk already and ordered some mineral water. I sipped from my plastic glass, and I asked him, "I know Angelita likes them, but you are the man of the house. Can you not finally insist that they go? Tell your wife to hire a decent, normal housekeeper and perhaps a nanny for the children?"

Rafael shook his head. "It's the strangest thing. She refuses. In every other way, Angelita is the most agreeable woman I've ever known, but with this one subject, she is adamant."

"Hmn." I'd never seen Angelita "adamant" about anything other than the time she threw that Swede out of my bedroom. But I knew she was off on some weird do-gooding mission, and the maids had to be a part of it. I didn't like to crush my dear friend's enthusiasms, but clearly, she had chosen an eccentric path, and I remembered what that sort of decision had meant for her in the past. Besides, poor Rafael needed his home back. "Would you like *me* to try to get rid of those Guatemalan maids?"

"I don't see how you will convince Angelita."

"I'm not asking for her permission," I said. "I'm asking for yours."

Rafael nodded, looking serious. "Very well." Perhaps he assumed I was going to kill them, and he had decided that any solution would do.

I shot him a flirty look. "Will you buy me another watch?"

He laughed. "I will buy you a diamond crown."

Suddenly, the plane bumped and seemed to drop ten thousand feet out of the sky. I crossed myself and clutched Rafael's wrist. He took my hand and held it in both of his until we landed and the seat-belt sign went off.

There are people in this world who seem to hold unimportant jobs or positions in life but can hold the key to certain access or convenience that is at times essential. I am a practical woman, and as much as I enjoy socializing with all sorts of whoop-de-do characters—the princes, counts and thieves I run into around New York—I never forget to send a Christmas gift to my doctor's secretary or even have the occasional cup of coffee with my account manager at the bank. I find that, unlike some of my more socially discriminating friends, I am always able to get a prescription for antibiotics if I call distressed from the coast of Maine, and my checks don't bounce no matter how dry my cash flow has run. In the same way, I have always seen the value of maintaining a sincere friendship with a very ordinary Cuban woman who lives in Queens and works as an administrative assistant for the Immigration and Naturalization Service downtown. Since I make time to have lunch with her at least two or three times a year, and I call her once in a while to say how are you—a kind of good habit, like flossing my teeth—Rita Garcia was not in any way disturbed or surprised when I asked if she could meet me for a bite the week after I returned from my trip to Colombia.

"I will be perfectly honest with you," I told her over tongue sandwiches in one of those noisy, crowded delicatessens where the waiters are so rude and the food is so good. "This is not one of our ordinary lunches."

She looked at me with interest, a tiny dab of mustard on the edge of her mouth. "No?"

I lowered my voice. "Rita, I am very, very concerned. About something that may be happening to a dear friend of mine."

I told her about the chain of Guatemalans who seemed to be passing through my friend's apartment on their way to somewhere else. "My friend," I told her, "is from a very important family. She has been sheltered and even spoiled all of her life. She is an incredibly kind person—tolerant, patient and perhaps overly naive." I was careful to paint a picture of Angelita's complete lack of involvement with whatever those maids were doing. "She has an unblemished reputation in society, and she would be absolutely mortified if she thought some Mickey Mouse funny business was going on right under her nose in her own home. But Rita," I continued, with a look on my face expressing the gravity of the issue at hand, "I am afraid that my friend is being duped and used. And who knows what harm those people might do to her."

Rita clucked in sympathy. "I see that you need one of our agents. And someone very discreet." I nodded. "Don't worry, Lucia, you can trust me. I know who to talk to. There's a guy on the third floor named McKnight. He's the best one to use for this kind of delicate situation."

"Ah, I knew I could turn to you!"

Rita smiled, lowering her gaze to her french fries.

"And I know you will understand the significance of this problem when I tell you her name."

Rita looked up, her mouth full.

"She is Angelita Somoza."

Rita gasped. "My God!"

Rita was the daughter of a middle-class Cuban restaurant owner who packed up his family and fled to the United States when Castro came into power. She had no sympathy in her bones for any sort of revolutionary after George Washington, and I knew she would take the abuse of lawmakers like the Somozas as a personal affront. "Don't worry, my friend," she assured me in a commanding tone that sounded determined to seek justice. "These people will be gone from Mrs. Somoza's apartment, and not even a dust ruffle will have been disturbed."

"Thank you." I reached across the table and squeezed her hand. I left that lunch knowing things would be handled—though I had no inkling of just how handled they would be.

Rita was the one who called me first, a week after the day we'd had lunch. "I'm so aggravated, I swear, I'm going to quit my job!"

"My dear, what's wrong?"

"We caught five of them. Five—can you believe? Five illegals hiding out in the maid's room of your friend's apartment. That must be some apartment."

"Yes, it's quite nice. But five maids? I knew there were two . . ." This was all a little stranger than I had expected.

"No, five. Four women and a man. McKnight went in with his best guys last weekend when your friends were in the country—you know, I promised you we wouldn't bother them. Anyway, there they were, five Guatemalan Indians sitting on the floor on blankets, one next to the other like they were still riding in the back of the truck, coming across the border into Texas."

This was truly amazing. Face it, I'd known Angelita was up to something in employing those maids—getting some poor Indians into the United States, maybe. But Rita went on to tell me that these Indians were actually outlaws in their own country, part of a tribe of rebels making their way over to Paris, where a communist group, of all things, was receiving them, working with them to build the resistance against the government in Guatemala City.

"Anyway," Rita went on, "the thing that really, really burns me up is that here we are, in the thick of cracking down on a whole ring of immigration violators, when suddenly, we are ordered from somewhere on high to drop the charges, to drop our whole investigation. All we're told is that these communists are 'important witnesses,' and off they go, escorted by a pair of hotshot lawyers and some bigwig from the FBI.

"I swear, Lucia, you can't do your job in this place!"

"Witnesses to what, do you know?" I had no clue what was up, but I had a sickly feeling in my stomach. Was Angelita in trouble?

"It's outrageous. They don't tell us a thing."

"Yes," I said. "That must be very frustrating." I wanted to get off the phone and call Angelita, but I was stuck listening to Rita complain about her job. She went on for a while.

"By the way," Rita said, "your friend was quite upset."

"I can imagine. She is such an innocent kind of person. Compassionate and warmhearted. This all must have hit her as a terrible shock."

"Oh, she was in shock, all right. She even came down to see us. She was sobbing, saying crazy things like her maids were innocent people, that she was the one helping them to get out of Guatemala, that if we were going to punish anyone, it should be her.

"McKnight gave her some tranquilizers and told her to go home. She must have been really stressed. I mean, who would ever believe that a member of the Somoza family would be involved with communists?"

My heart was pounding. Thank God they hadn't checked her background too thoroughly, learned of her first marriage to that socialist nut in Cambridge. "Well, no one in the world! Obviously, Angelita was out of her mind with distress."

"Obviously."

"And also," my brain was working as fast as it could, "perhaps she was frightened when she found out a man had been among them in her home. Maybe she feared he would seek revenge upon her."

"Ohhh. I hadn't thought of that. Yes, you're right. I'll bet she was scared."

"Well, I'd better call her right now." I finally managed to end the conversation.

I dialed Angelita's number. "Hello, my darling, how are you?" Remember, I was supposed to know nothing.

"Hi. I can't talk now." Her voice sounded flat, like a gringo voice. She said, "I'll come to your house as soon as I can." She hung up.

I can't tell you how I worried. I was dying to talk to Carlos about these strange developments, but he was still down in Colombia, trying to negotiate more army protection for the pipeline after another guerrilla attack. I didn't dare mention any of Angelita's problems to him over the phone.

Angelita didn't show up that night, and the next day, when I went out to meet Monica Hernandez for lunch at Lutèce, I left instructions with my doorman to let Angelita in should she come while I was gone. I asked Monica if she'd talked to Angelita lately, but she hadn't since the cocktail party we'd all been to at the Italian Trade Commission the previous week.

"Why?" Monica asked. She hated to think I might know some intimate detail about Angelita before she did.

"Nothing, really." I shook my head. "I was just a little concerned about her. I think she mentioned having some difficulties with her help."

Monica rolled her eyes and stubbed out her cigarette. "My God, Lucia, she's been having that for ages!"

After lunch I went down to Seventh Avenue to shop at the

showroom of a friend who imports Italian sportswear. When I got home, I asked if Angelita had come, but the doorman said no.

I always stayed up those weeks until eleven o'clock, because that was when Carlos called me from Bogotá. When the buzzer rang at fifteen minutes past midnight, it jarred me out of a deep sleep. It was Angelita, downstairs—could she come up? I sleep with a frozen-orange-juice can on top of my head with my hair wrapped around it, to keep my hair smooth in between visits to the beauty parlor. I whipped the can out of my hair, and I jumped out of my cotton T-shirt into silk pajamas and a matching robe. I didn't want Angelita to see me looking like a monster.

Even though it was the middle of the night, she was wearing a Chanel suit. She looked terrible. Her face was drawn and her eyes were red. She started to cry the minute she walked into my apartment. "My love, what is wrong?" I asked her, though I thought I already knew.

"They've taken him away," she sobbed. I supposed she meant that Guatemalan man. I led her to the couch, sat her down and brought her a glass of ice water from the kitchen. She seemed like someone who had been holding herself together for several days, and I let her cry for a good long time before asking any questions. She leaned her head on the back of the sofa, and tears ran down the sides of her face. I dipped a folded tissue in the water and patted her cheeks and forehead. She shook and sobbed. Finally, she sat up and was still, though tears continued to well up in her eyes. In a voice that sounded like she'd been to visit the dead, she said, "I can't believe they've taken Rafael away."

"Rafael!" Suddenly, my lungs were burning, and I felt like smoldering lumps of coal lay next to my heart. "Who took Rafael away?" Angelita shook her head as if in shock. "Angelita, talk to me!"

"The FBI. The DEA. The New York police. And I don't know who else—all of them!" She became hysterical again and cried for another five minutes. I wept, too. As you know, I love Rafael almost as much as my own husband, and on some days even more.

Angelita gasped out her story, and I pretended to know nothing. The crux of it was this: Those stupid son-of-a-bitch communist peasants weren't as stupid as they looked. They spoke and read Spanish and English, and they were starting to learn French. The moment they found themselves in trouble with Immigration, they called a friend who was working in an apartment at Fifth Avenue and Eighty-seventh Street. That friend called the FBI. Those bastards secured their release by providing documents showing that Rafael was laundering money out of his Miami office. Rafael himself was being extradited right now. The government would try him in Florida.

Angelita had been questioned intensely for the past two days—all this after the surprise of losing her maids and dealing with Immigration. She'd tried to subvert the FBI's interest in Rafael by confessing to her participation in a kind of "underground railroad," as she put it, helping political victims get out of Guatemala over to safety in Paris.

"Political victims!" I said. "Aren't those people common bandits, low-class mafiosos supported by Castro and other communists?"

"No." She shook her head in sadness. "Not at all. They are poor Indian peasants, raped and abused by their own government, which is trying to swindle them out of the little bit of land they have to live on. The government gives it instead to rich agriculturalists who prop up the regime.

"Maria Cristina—the one who was so good with Rafaelito when he had the chicken pox? She saw her own son cut up alive by the army, piece by piece, finger by finger, because her husband dared to protest at the Spanish embassy in Guatemala City . . ."

I remembered hearing some years ago about the peasant occupation of the Spanish Embassy, and to me it had sounded like more than a simple protest. But tonight was no night to argue politics with an absurdly guilty Somoza. "How the hell did you get into all this?" I asked her.

"At the school," she sighed. "Horace Mann. One of the mothers from Rafaelito's class is a journalist, really a brilliant woman. We got talking one day about Central America. She told me of this project with Guatemala—which, you know, is just as bad as Nicaragua ever was—and of course I said I'd help."

Jesus Christ, I thought. So this was the "social justice" curriculum she was so crazy about. Her plot to save the world. What a lunatic! It was hard to contain my anger. "So you helped these crappy Guatemalans," I said. "And what about your own family? Look at what happened to Rafael!"

"Well, how was I supposed to know he's a criminal? Do you go around suspecting that Carlos is a criminal?"

"No, he's too poor."

"I didn't know anything about Rafael." She sat up straight and faced me, her eyes big, red and crooked. "Did *you* know anything about Rafael?"

"Me? No, of course not." I needed to be more careful, not get so emotional. "But what makes you believe he really is one? Money laundering—that's not such a big deal. Maybe those documents are false and in fact he's not guilty?"

Angelita hung her head. I had always thought of her as a young woman, but I realized now that she was nearly forty. "His lawyer says the case against him is 'pretty strong.'" She made quotation marks with her fingers. "I had dinner with the lawyer this evening, once all the investigators were through with me."

"My poor darling."

She began to cry again.

"Do you still love Rafael?" I asked.

"Of course. Really, I'm much more afraid that now he hates me." With that, she collapsed into my arms, and I rocked her like a baby.

"Don't worry," I said. "I'm sorry that Rafael has turned out to be a crook, but I am one hundred percent sure that he is not the kind of crook who kills his wife."

Angelita and I stayed up all that night, talking, crying and putting together a list of the people we knew who might be able to twist some arms. We could count on the Colombian ambassador in Washington to help Rafael. Diego Santiago was a wealthy Mexican industrialist who owned a Mediterranean-style palace on Indian Creek Island in Miami. He and his wife, Juanita, were friends with the governor of Florida, as well as just about anyone else who liked rich people and lavish parties. Casey Eisenhower was the best bet if it came to Angelita needing to get through to some of the Bush administration heavies.

Over the following few months, Angelita traveled constantly among New York, Miami and Washington, working on her husband's case. She had been right about Rafael's anger—when she visited him, he was cold and impersonal, and several times he mentioned his willingness to set her free according to whatever terms she wished. "He doesn't understand," she wept on the phone to me one night. "I'm not planning to divorce him."

Rafael refused to let his children see him in jail, so Angelita sent them to Spain to stay with her father and his mistress, with the explanation that Papa was having some troubles with his business and Mama needed to help him. The problem with his case, his lawyers had explained, was that the U.S. government believed he had important information about Pablo Escobar, and they were hoping to squeeze it out of him in exchange for a lighter sentence or perhaps no jail time at all.

Rafael, on the other hand, was not suicidal, and he certainly wasn't going to cave in to their absurd proposition. For a while there was a standoff between the FBI and Rafael. He was held under tight conditions, and since only Angelita and his lawyers were allowed to see him, Carlos and I couldn't go down to visit. Eventually, though, one of Casey's friends must have come through, because out of the blue the Justice Department got interested in a petty drug dealer from Cali whom Rafael was able to lead them to with little fear for his own hide. The case went quickly to trial, and he was sentenced to one year in a minimum-security prison in western Florida, to be reduced to six months if he behaved himself. The three months he'd already spent in federal custody would count as part of his time, so there was no reason he shouldn't be out by September, in time for his son to start the second grade.

Angelita returned briefly to New York after the verdict to check up on the apartment—by the way, she had found a lovely lady from Chile to be her new housekeeper—and gather the things she would need to spend the summer in Florida. She would rent a furnished home in Naples, the closest town to the prison that was decent, and visit Rafael every day until he got out. I bought a ticket to go down there and see them a couple of weeks later. While Angelita was in town, the Hernandezes and Carlos and I gave her a surprise party, everyone toasting her and Rafael. Somebody made a videotape of all of us, carrying on, for her to take to him. She was thrilled and relieved, and she drank champagne and cried with joy.

Four days later, she was back in New York. During her first

visit to the new prison, Rafael had apologized for his transgressions, thanked her for her support and told her to go home and take care of their children. Then he served her with papers for a divorce.

I flew down to Naples to see Rafael in July. Florida that time of year was gray, hot and stickier than the Amazon jungle. I stayed at the new Ritz-Carlton on the coast, but the humidity was still unbearable, and even when it rained, there was no relief. My hair was a disaster; I had to wear it pulled back tight and pinned up in a bun.

I do not drive, so I hired a car to take me to the prison, about forty-five minutes from the hotel. I had never seen an American jail except in the movies and on television, and I expected some horrible place. Instead, the prison looked like a fine retirement home, even a resort. There was a high stucco wall around the whole property, landscaped with palm trees and bougainvillea. The painted metal gates and armed guards at the entrance only added to the compound's air of exclusivity. Believe me, I have been through much tighter security on my way into embassy parties in Europe.

I had also feared I might be visiting Rafael from one side of a thick glass wall, talking through telephones, like we were in some kind of super-modern confessional. I thought he might wear a uniform. But he met me in a large air-conditioned lounge, sporting a beautiful tropical-weight linen suit, looking fit, healthy and happy to see me. He kissed me on both cheeks and led me to a nice little area with a sofa, a coffee table and some wicker chairs. He went over to a counter and brought back a tray with a plastic pitcher of iced tea and some glasses. Other small groups were visiting in there—I noticed an exceptionally beautiful blond woman with a tan guy who had thick white hair and a full mustache. A couple of guards sat quietly on stools by the doors, as if their job were to serve but not hover, like good waiters in a fine restaurant. From the windows, I saw manicured grounds, a couple of tennis courts and a pool with some men swimming laps. Walking paths led to other low-rise buildings beyond. If I hadn't known where I was, I might have imagined myself in the lobby of a Florida hotel.

"Well, your pride may have suffered," I said, "and maybe your bank account, but at least I am not worried for your material comfort. This is sort of posh, no?"

Rafael smiled. "I am fine here. And aside from the fact that we are all men, the company is good. I've met a fascinating man from Cambridge, an art dealer, who got into trouble buying stolen pre-Columbian pottery. It turns out he knows one of my old classmates from the London School of Economics. We've had some wonderful talks, and he's a good tennis player, too. And surely you know Fernando Delbanco?"

"Certainly." He was a Colombian senator whose uncle had been president. I wondered if he'd been caught for something.

"His son and nephew are here. A problem of some cocaine on a yacht. They are lively young men with great senses of humor. The Delbanco cousins, my English friend and I take dinner together. We've made arrangements with a catering company in Naples, so we eat quite decently, though we can't always manage to get the wine. It depends on who's guarding."

I laughed. I was glad to see Rafael's spirit unbroken. "Well, you have a charming jail. I suppose you have to be special to get in."

"Not always." Rafael pointed his finger in the air. "America is sometimes democratic." He told me about three Mexicans who were staying in cells near his. Three rinky-dink guys, peasants from the Yucatán. They were found by the Coast Guard in a rowboat, a couple of miles off the Florida Keys. They had run out of water, they were unconscious, and there were ten kilos of marijuana in the boat. In custody, all three swore they had no idea how the marijuana got there. The government didn't know what to do with them, so they stuck them in the prison for two years. One of them followed Rafael around, doing small services like shining his shoes or cleaning his tennis racket in exchange for tips, chocolate and liquor. "You'd think he'd died and gone to heaven," Rafael said. "Every day he tells me, 'My God, three meals a day! Air-conditioning! A swimming pool! The only thing I miss is a woman.' This is the best he's ever had it in his life."

I squeezed his arm. "Ay, Rafael. It's so good to see you. And as much as you are enjoying yourself here, I can't wait to have you back with us. Just two more months."

He became serious. "Lucia, you and Carlos will always be my friends, and we will always visit each other. But I am not coming back to live in New York."

"Why not?" This sounded like part of his crazy divorce plan. "What are you doing to your life?"

He was planning to move to Monte Carlo. He had friends there, business contacts. He could work from there. "Here," he looked around, "well, things will be a little tight for a while."

"But you don't need to work! Ay, Rafael, come on." I lowered my voice. "You still have money, no?" He nodded. "So forget about working and come home."

He shook his head. "No," he said, his voice firm. "It is not in my nature to stop working. I am not the type of man to sit around the house in the morning, thinking about what to eat for lunch. That would be impossible, like curling up to die. Even from here, I do plenty of business."

I looked at the lines that had formed on his brow, his curved nose, the razor-sharp intelligence that shone in his eyes. I had known Rafael for a long time. He was always completely, exactly himself, and he wasn't going to change now. "Okay," I said. "Monte Carlo is probably a wise idea, and Carlos and I won't mind yachting with you. But what is this business about leaving Angelita? Do you think you're doing this for her sake? She loves you, you know. I'm sure she would go with you to any corner of the world, and Monaco is not that unpleasant a corner."

"I know." His face showed a sadness not yet revealed. His eyes grew big and unfocused. Empty.

"Do you not love her anymore?" That idea had never occurred to me.

"I love her," he said. "I love her more than any other person on earth." He touched the corner of his eye with his fingertip.

"So . . ."

"Lucia. Look at the impulsive things she does. Those maids. The crazy people at the school. Her psychiatrist. All that guilt she carries around, like it's her responsibility to straighten out the world. She's not a realistic person. Living with her—well, it's like being married to an alcoholic or something. You never know what is going to happen."

"Yes, but she is so sweet . . ."

"Sweet, okay, but Lucia, look what I went through. I can't live beside someone like that. *She* is abnormal, and she expects *me* to change.

"No, no. I can't stay with her. It's too risky. Like being married to a bomb. In the end, a women like Angelita, she is too dangerous."

I took his hand and didn't try to sway his opinion. I knew he was right. I also knew he was a man with enough power over his emotions to do whatever was necessary.

I left the prison that day thinking how strange the whole story had been. I felt sorry for Rafael, and I felt sorry for Angelita. And though they are both my close friends to this day, I felt a secret relief that their lives were not my own, that Carlos and I lived together, however simply, in relative peace. It struck me as ironic, the way things turned out for Angelita and Rafael. The word "dangerous"—it rang in my head. Really, I always thought that he would have been the dangerous one for her.

Marley

— 1994 —

We all knew. And each of the three of us knew that the other two knew. But as my mother and I sat at my grandfather's big dark dining room table, eating veal cutlets with lemon and capers, we sure as hell were not going to talk about it.

What we knew was that my mother had just had her tubes tied. What we knew was that she was an only child, I was her only son and, therefore, I was the only grandchild Charles Payne would ever have. What we all knew was that for the past seventeen years, my grandfather had been hoping and hoping and hoping for his daughter to bear another child, preferably while she was married to someone like a husband, and preferably a child who was not lanky, brown-skinned and fuzzy-haired, like me.

Not that I'm bad-looking. I'm tall and fit, and I wear my hair in short dreadlocks that flop around my head when I walk. I look like Jean-Michel Basquiat, or at least like the actor who played him in the movie. Girls seem to like me, and think I'm fairly handsome, so long as you're not expecting me to be white. But this evening it was starting to occur to my grandfather that the bulk of his fortune might eventually find its way into the hands of what he and my dead grandmother Peggy had always referred to as a "mulatto"—something that sounded to me like a small donkey, or maybe a designer coffee drink, as in "I'll have a double mulatto to go, two packets of Equal."

Anyway, at the table, my mother started picking a fight with my grandfather about golf. She called it "a bunch of red-faced white men plotting world domination while chasing a little ball over chemically poisoned fields."

"Sandra, it's a sport." My grandfather shook his head. His pale gray hair matched his gray suit. "I wasn't plotting world domination down at the Cloisters. I mostly listened to Bud Ritter gripe about his tendinitis. Once or twice in the afternoon, we played croquet. I was enjoying myself. Relaxing. It was my first vacation since your mother passed away. Don't you think I have a right to relax for a few days?"

"At whose expense?" My mother looked like she might jump out of her chair. "You give no thought to the social costs of what you do, what you buy, where you go." Her voice was getting higher. She was waving her fork around; I thought it might catch in her blond hair. "I mean, look at where you live!" My grandfather sat calmly, waiting for her to spit out whatever was coming. He looked as if, in his mind, he were slowly counting backward from ten. "Here you are, still in this stuffy old building. A building where my son—your own grandson—would not be permitted to purchase an apartment. Because of the color of his skin!"

"Oh, enough of this." My grandfather folded his linen napkin and placed it on the table. "Come on. Let's go to the den. We'll have dessert in there."

Though I'd never liked him much, I could see that my grandfather and I were like Stalin and Roosevelt. Different ideologies, common enemy.

My mom and I lived downtown in a loft on West Broadway. She taught ashtanga yoga and volunteered for Bread Not Bombs. Since kindergarten, I'd gone to the Little Brick Village School, where families and teachers expressed gratitude daily for finding themselves together in a nurturing community in the middle of New York City. Of course, the tuition cost around twenty-five grand a year, everyone was rich, and as seniors, my class was taking calculus and AP history and applying to the Ivy Leagues. But we played at simplicity—the way Marie Antoinette had played shepherdess in her *hameaux* at Versailles. There were only two other "minority" students in my grade: one completely black girl on scholarship who took the train down from the Bronx, and a Puerto Rican guy who lived in the projects on Avenue D. The lower grades were now loaded with what the school proudly called "diversity"—Chinese girls adopted by wealthy white parents.

While I was growing up, my mother didn't talk much to her

parents. She used to tell me she didn't get along with them; they saw things too differently. We visited them once in a while—grudgingly, on my mother's part. We spent Thanksgiving and Christmas with friends; artists, designers and political activists who also lived downtown. My mother always got wrapped up in an argument with one of the other guests over U.S. foreign policy or the corporate-sponsored media. We attended benefits for causes like gun control and Greenpeace. My mother joined committees but eventually quit them because she didn't like the way they were run. Sometimes she had a boyfriend; invariably, they'd break up after some big blowout. As far as I could tell, she wasn't able to get along with anyone, so I didn't really understand why she discriminated against my grandparents. But I guessed that the problem had something to do with me—my illegitimacy, my dark skin.

Things had changed the previous summer, when my grandmother Peggy died after a sudden recurrence of breast cancer. I was away on an Outward Bound trip in the Rockies, and my mother was on retreat at Thich Nhat Hanh's Plum Village in France. Charles had been unable to reach us in time, and neither of us made it to the funeral. I think my mother felt guilty, though she wasn't the sort of person to admit it. She didn't become any less combative—she still had the victory-in-defeat personality of Saddam Hussein—but we started visiting my grandfather on a regular basis. At first he treated me like some kind of alien, asking questions like what foods did I eat. It took him awhile to get it that I was civilized and I'd generally eat whatever was served. It took me awhile to understand that my grandfather was relieved to have me there at the table. Even if I wasn't the grandson of his dreams, I was a good buffer between him and my mother.

My dad didn't exist for any of us. My mother once told me the story of how she'd slept with some Jamaican exchange student when she was seventeen. It had been a one-night thing right before he left to go back home, like he sowed some seed and then—floof!—flew away. In honor of my Jamaican heritage, my mother named me Marley, after Bob Marley. And gave me her own last name, Payne. It was a pretty weird combination—Marley Payne—like I was destined from birth to assume the presidency of the First Rastafarian Bank of New York. Now the only times my mother ever mentioned my father were when she stuffed condoms into my pockets before I went to a party. She'd lecture me about AIDS or knocking up some girl. Like the concept of my dad was useful only for sex ed.

Even though everyone associated with my school was a Democrat, at least, if not outright Green Party, many of my classmates lived in buildings like my grandfather's: snooty uptown co-ops on Fifth, Park or Central Park West. When I was fifteen, I accidentally invented one of my favorite games, Goof the Doorman—Mortify the Liberals. It started when I went to dinner at Chris Whitter's place in the San Remo. I arrived at the front door carrying a package of biscotti from Dean & Deluca that my mother had told me to bring. The doorman asked if he could help me, so I said "I'm going to the Whitters'."

"That package for the Whitters?" he said. I nodded. "Service entrance is around the side, on Seventy-fourth Street."

I went around the corner and was buzzed up as a delivery boy. I rode the service elevator and rang the back door.

"They sent you up the back!" Chris Whitter's mom looked like she'd run over a kitten. She was writhing in spasms of rich white guilt. "Jesus Christ, Marley, I'm so sorry. Those ignorant fools! And you, such a sweetheart, bringing us cookies." She hugged me. Then she held me away from her with her hands on my upper arms, and she looked me in the eyes. "Marley, I will speak to everyone who works in this building, and I promise you, this will never happen here again!"

I thought the whole thing was so funny that I brought flowers or cookies every time I went to a new building. The scene always played out the same way.

One day I played Goof the Doorman in my grandfather's building. I hadn't planned to; it just happened. I had come home from school that afternoon, knowing we were supposed to have dinner with him that night. My mother had a bad cold. "Marley, I'm staying in," she said, "but I told Dad you'd be there by six-thirty."

"You what!"

"I said you'd go. You're not sick."

"I'm not going there alone. What do I need to see him for? Shit, old Pink-face doesn't want to see me!" I walked into my room.

My mother followed me in. "Look. Stop fucking with me when I'm sick. Your grandfather is expecting you. And he does so want to see you. He said the other day that he likes you, and believe me, coming from him that's a miracle. He told me he's glad when you show up with me. So stop giving me a hard time and get your ass uptown tonight!"

"You know why he likes me there?" I glared at my mother. "You know why?"

She glared back at me, her nose red and her icy blue eyes flashing like the lights on a cop car.

"He likes to have me there so he doesn't have to be alone with you!" I charged past her and slammed the door on my way out of the loft.

I was so mad I caught the train uptown right then. When I arrived at Eighty-sixth Street, I walked down to my grandfather's building but stopped on the east side of Park Avenue. I realized I was about two hours early. I saw the doorman come out to the curb and hail someone a cab. He was a new guy. I walked back to Lexington and bought a bunch of flowers. I'd decided to play Goof the Doorman, but I had to find a new angle. My arriving on the service elevator wouldn't enrage Charles Payne one bit. He'd probably only shake his head over the terrible, irreparable error of judgment that my mother had made seventeen years earlier.

My mother had once spoken about a French baroness who lived in the penthouse. She said my grandmother was always kissing the baroness's ass, desperate to become her friend, but no matter what, she'd never been invited to her apartment.

I decided to see if I could get in.

I didn't even know the baroness's name. I held the flowers up to my chest. "I am going to the baroness in the penthouse," I told the doorman.

He hardly looked at me. "Service entrance on Eighty-third Street."

A handyman in gray coveralls took me up to the penthouse in the service elevator. He waited on the landing as a maid answered the back door.

"I have flowers for the baroness," I said. The maid held out her hand to receive them. "With a message I need to convey personally."

She looked at me with suspicion. So did the handyman. "One moment," she said, closing the door in my face.

When it opened again, a white-haired lady with turquoise-blue eyes stood next to the maid in the doorway, leaning on a carved wooden cane. She was old, about eighty. She wore an aqua cardigan open over an aqua turtleneck and a black-white-and-aqua-plaid skirt. "May I help you?" she said in a clear voice with no foreign accent.

I started, "These flowers are from Peggy Payne. Now, I know Peggy Payne has gone from us. But her spirit lives on in these flowers." I would babble nonsense until something happened. Maybe the handyman would grab me and throw me out of the building. Maybe they'd call the police. "In her mortal guise, Peggy always spoke of you, Baroness. She always wished to know you, to be welcome in your home. She never managed to win your favor, but perhaps in her spirit form—"

"Oh, I know who you are!" the baroness said. "The grand-child. Come in. Come in!"

The maid and the handyman exchanged a look. I flashed them each a big white-toothed smile.

The baroness led me through the pantry and the kitchen, out through the dining room, across a foyer with a black-and-white marble floor and into her living room. It was already late in the afternoon, but the windows were tall, and light flooded the apartment. Beyond the windows, a brick terrace planted with evergreens surrounded the penthouse. I could see a little stone fountain through the French doors. The living room itself was bright and colorful. There were rugs with swirly de-signs in pink, aqua and gold, curvy sofas covered in gold-and-white-striped silk, a white marble coffee table with a gold base. Flowers everywhere, blooming in pots and in vases. The room was so brilliant that I almost forgot what an idiot I'd just made of myself.

I was still holding the bouquet. "I, um, I guess you didn't need any more flowers."

"Don't be silly, young man. Can't you tell? Flowers are my favorite things in the world." She took the bouquet. My flowers were garbage compared to the roses and orchids all over her room. But she sniffed them as if I had brought her something rare and precious. "How lovely they are. Marie!" she called to the maid who had followed us to the entrance of the living room and stood watching me, still suspicious that I might be the reincarnation of Robespierre. "Marie, please. Take these flowers our young guest brought and put them in a vase of warm water. Perhaps stir in a teaspoon of the rose food that's under the pantry sink." Marie snatched the bouquet and turned away in a silent huff. "Don't mind her," the baroness whispered. "She's French."

"Um. I thought *you* were French"

"French! I'm from Fairfield, Ohio. My maiden name was Idabell Smith—that doesn't sound very continental, does it?" She laughed.

"But aren't you a baroness?" I couldn't believe I was speaking to her this way, directly, like some old friend of the family who had been expecting me.

"Good Lord, I am no such thing." She sat down on one of the sofas and motioned for me to sit opposite her. The maid came back with my bouquet in a green glass vase. "Right here on the table, Marie. That's perfect. My dear, shall we have some tea?"

"Uh, sure. Thank you."

"Tea for us, please, Marie." She smiled at me.

"So, if you're not a baroness . . ."

"Well, it's not an entirely unfounded rumor." She told me how her first husband had worked as legal counsel for the American embassy in Paris between the world wars. He caught pneumonia during the blizzard of 1933 and died later that winter. She had stayed on in Paris, teaching English to diplomats. She fell in love with a young French socialist, and they married in 1935. "His parents were terrible snobs because they had a title. Of course, Claude was the black sheep of the family.

"When the war broke out with Germany, Claude and I came to New York. That's when we bought this apartment. Some silly journalist found out about Claude's ancestry, and our names suddenly turned up in all the society columns. Can you imagine how we laughed when we saw it in print: Baroness Idabell Smith d'Alençon? What an absurd name!

"You must forgive me, my dear, but I'm ninety-one years old, and I've forgotten your name . . ."

"Well, mine is pretty absurd, too."

We talked and laughed and drank tea. I couldn't believe what a good time I was having with this old lady, but Idabell had more going for her than most of my friends. She told me stories about living in Europe and in New York during the war, her friendship with Mrs. Roosevelt and later with the Kennedys. I told her about living in SoHo. The sun went down, and she switched on crystal lamps around the room. A couple of times I got up to leave—I didn't want to overstay my welcome, especially considering the way I'd come in—but she insisted I visit with her until I had to go down to my grandfather's for dinner.

I admitted that I wasn't exactly looking forward to dinner with him. That I felt he didn't like me. "It's not even personal," I said. "We hardly know each other."

"Marley, your grandfather's always been conservative—very conservative. Not to assassinate his character, but among gossipers, the word 'fascist' has been used. You must realize, given his background and the beliefs he's held all his life, what an extraordinary leap it's been for him to accept a grandson who is half"—she hesitated—"half African-American."

"Black, Idabell. You can say black. I'm not anything African at all. If anything, I'm Jamaican-American. But face it, nobody cares about nationality here. We're talking skin color."

"Well, you're right about that." Idabell leaned forward, poured more tea for herself and topped off my cup.

"In addition to the question of race," she continued, "which we both know was enough to send your grandfather over the edge, there was the class issue. We can't do much more than speculate, but perhaps Charles would have been more accepting had your father been someone like the son of the Nigerian ambassador to the UN. But that Charles Payne's grandson was fathered by his own chauffeur . . . There were questions of race *and* class *and* trust . . ."

"Say what?"

"Excuse me?"

"What about 'Charles Payne's own chauffeur'? I mean, is this some kind of Richard Wright sequel?"

Idabell looked puzzled. Her mouth became soft. Her eyes cast about the room, from flower to flower like a pair of bees, landing here on a white orchid, there on a deep purple African violet. She put her veined, spotted hand over her lips and dropped her head. "Oh dear," she said, gazing at her skirt. "I'm afraid I've gone somewhere I don't belong."

I mumbled, "I'm the one who barged into your house today."

I sat still, with my hands folded. I kept opening my mouth, starting to say something. Nothing came out but soft grunts. I waited for Idabell to speak. She knew about my father. Knew things that I didn't know—things that no one was ever planning to reveal. Her brow wrinkled deeply. She knew I wanted to hear about it. She looked as if she was deciding. She raised her pale eyebrows and opened her blue-green eyes wide. "Do you mean to say they never told you?" she finally said, and I knew I would get the whole story.

"I was under the impression my father was a music student? A violinist?"

"A Jamaican violinist?" Idabell looked like she was trying not to laugh. We stared at each other. Maybe we were just nervous, but we both cracked up. "A Jamaican violinist!" she nearly shrieked, like it was the funniest thing she had ever heard.

As quickly as we had started laughing, we both got quiet again. She rubbed one hand with another. She looked me in the eyes and spoke clearly. "Your father was Charles's driver for many years. His name was Simon. He drove Charles to and from his office, and he drove your grandmother and your mother when they shopped or had appointments. He knew your mother from the time she was a child. In Charles's view, she was still a child when you were conceived. I don't know how the events unfolded, but I do know that Simon was fired quite suddenly one day, and about six months later, your mother came home with a coffee-colored baby.

"There was a great deal of gossip among the maids and the handymen. Some said your grandfather planned to press charges against his chauffeur. Others were sure Simon had already left the country. Everything I know I learned from my old butler Jean-Pierre. I didn't speak about this with any of my neighbors, though I'd wager many here thought it a scandal."

Idabell smiled. "I do remember meeting you once in the elevator. You were squalling and screaming like the world was coming to an end, and your mother bounced you in her arms. Instead of seeming harried, as most young mothers would, she had a mischievous smile on her face, like you were a little bomb and she was proud of all the ruckus you could make."

"That would be her." I shook my head, the way cats do when you mess with their ears, and my dreads flapped against my face. "So my father was the family chauffeur."

I sat and thought for a minute. Then I asked her, "Why do you think they didn't tell me? I mean, I understand that Charles wouldn't, but what about my mother—why did she go in for all that B.S. about the talented Jamaican music student? You know she said it was a one-night fling? She knew him one night and never even found out his last name?"

"I don't know," Idabell said. "I don't know what deal she had to cut with her parents—remember, she lived here with you for at least a year before she was able to move out on her own. I don't know what was going on in her heart. Perhaps she wanted you to feel that you belonged unequivocally to this social class and this environment. That if you thought of your father as a talented musician, you might have more self-regard."

"So really my father is some kind of slob?"

"No." Idabell was firm. "No. He wasn't a slob at all. He was very kind. More than once I came downstairs looking for a cab, and there were none to be found. The doorman Peter said

Simon wasn't expecting Mrs. Payne for an hour or more, and he'd be happy to give me a lift. Your father was handsome and polite. When I tried to pay him, he refused to take my money. 'No, miss,' he would say to me in a Jamaican accent, 'I have a good job. I don't care to take advantage.' He always jumped out and held the door for me. He was quite tall, like you."

"So why did my mother have to cover it all up? Okay, at first I understand. But why is she lying about it still?" It was weird that she was lying at all. "You know, my mother is the kind of person who will say anything to anyone. She'll tell you if she doesn't like your face—in fact, she won't be able not to tell you, if that's what she thinks." I leaned forward in my seat with my feet apart. I rested my elbows on my knees.

Idabell tipped her head to the side and brushed a stray hair from her cheek. "We don't know what she felt, Marley. But you need to remember something. Your mother knew Simon for a long, long time. When he left, how might she have felt? Perhaps she didn't want to discuss him with the people around her. Perhaps it hurt her to speak of him, or to hear what others would say. Perhaps with time, the whole subject of your father froze up inside her. Have you ever thought, Marley, that perhaps she loved him?"

"Oh." I slowly bent my head toward my hands. When my cheeks met my palms, I felt tears.

Idabell was quiet for a few moments. Then she said, "This is all very big news for you, my dear. You will have a lot to think about. Maybe you'll want to ask your grandfather some questions tonight, since your mother won't be around. You may be surprised to find that there are things he'd like to discuss with you one on one. You never know."

"Boy, that's for sure!" I looked around her beautiful, ornate living room with my mouth hanging open. "Jesus Christ!"

Idabell laughed, and we began to speak of other things. She said she didn't think much of Clinton. "He's no better than a Goldwater Republican. Of course, this is the opinion of an old mink-coat socialist."

When it was time to go downstairs, she walked me to the front door and waited until the elevator arrived. "Please come to see me again. You know, my best friend died of lymphoma last year. She was only sixty-four. I think it quite unfair that a woman my age should lose a friend twenty-seven years her junior. These days I'm lonely." I promised I'd stop by the following week before dinner at my grandfather's.

I was pumped by the time I sat down with my grandfather in his wood-paneled den. Usually, that room intimidated me—the marble fireplace with its brass screen, the dark green leather armchairs, all those crystal decanters of rare Scotches and other amber-colored liquors. But tonight I felt at home, like I could say whatever I wanted. No fewer than three sentences into our conversation, which had been heading in the same direction as always, about my schoolwork and where I wanted to go to college, I asked my grandfather why people called him a fascist.

"Oh, for Christ's sake, Marley. Who says that, your mother?" I didn't correct him. "You shouldn't listen to your mother. Well, you should when it comes to things like homework and curfews, but you mustn't take on her opinions, her judgments.

"I grew up in different times from yours, Marley. I grew up during the Depression, saw a lot of suffering in this country. Then came the war. Those were real fascists. Your mother's so spoiled. She's never felt threatened, never had to fight just to live or go about her daily business. She loves to criticize me for making money—she says I'm superficial, materialistic. We didn't see it like that in my day. After the war, my group of friends, we all worked hard. We wanted to feel secure, to provide a safe, comfortable life for our families, to provide our children with opportunities, education. The way your mother views it, you'd think Peggy and I tried to destroy her."

My grandfather crossed one leg over the other. I noticed he was wearing charcoal-gray socks printed with navy and purple paisley. "I'm not a fascist, Marley," he continued. "I'm a bond trader. Each morning I get up early, go downtown to my office in the Trade Center. I work up on the hundred and third floor, where the boys from Cantor Fitzgerald are kind enough to rent out some space to an old geezer like me. I try to make a little money for myself and for others, and if I'm lucky, I succeed.

"I don't know why your mother despises me. She certainly doesn't despise the fruits of my labors, the trust fund she's lived on quite comfortably since she turned twenty-one. But she's always had it in for me, Marley. Honestly, I don't understand why she bestows the pleasure of her company on me so often now."

Today was a day for honesty. So I told him the truth. "She says she feels sorry for you."

"Hmmph!" My grandfather straightened up in his chair. "Then I shall pity her back!" His blue eyes twinkled. I would even say—and this is a stretch—that in his outrage, Charles Payne looked merry.

Now was the time to ask him. It was hard to control myself. An image of my father, Simon, floated in my mind, as if he were downstairs right now, waiting by the curb. I wanted to know his last name, where he was from.

I took a deep breath. These were not questions for Charles Payne. Soon enough my mother would tell me everything. I noticed I was tapping my foot, and I made it stop.

"Charles," I began. "Grandfather." It was always hard to know what to call him. "There's something I'd like to talk to you about."

"Shoot."

"You know, I agree with you that a lot of what my mother says is kind of hotheaded. And most of the time I don't pay much attention to her ranting. But one thing she said the other night, it stung, because it was true." My grandfather looked right at me, his eyes steady. I imagined he was like this when he did business. I felt nervous, but I went on. "The thing about me never being able to buy an apartment in this building. Or in any other building like this, no matter how much money I had. I mean, you don't see many brown-skinned people buying apartments in buildings like this, do you?"

"No." He shook his head. "One doesn't."

"Well, what I'm asking—and I hope you don't see this as any ill intent. I hope you understand I want you to stay healthy and live for a long time. But what I'm asking is, well, when you do go, that you would consider leaving this apartment to me. My mother doesn't want it, you know, and I—I guess I just like it here."

I didn't mean to, but I broke into a smile. I felt embarrassed. My grandfather's cheeks reddened, and he half smiled, too. We were both surprised, though I didn't know exactly why, I'd known what I was going to say. I think the weirdest thing was that my grandfather and I were sitting in his den smiling at each other. I shrugged and turned my palms up. I felt even younger than I was.

My grandfather looked around the room, at his books, the fireplace, the heavy drapes on the windows. He looked out past the wooden double doors into the living room, at the Oriental rug and the puffy maroon sofas. He seemed to be assessing the value of the transaction. Or maybe trying to picture me someday living here in his home.

It was at least a minute before he curled his hands around the armrests of his chair and looked me in the eye again. "Yes, Marley," he said. "I see your point. I'll call my lawyer in the morning, and the apartment will be left to you." He slowly nodded, approving the plan.

I felt like shouting. Or crying. Or jumping across the room to hug him, though I'd never hugged an old white man before. But my grandfather remained composed. I did, too. After a moment he said, "Well, now that our business is complete, shall we have a drink?"

Dick Sapphire's Tsuris

— 1999 —

Never wake a sleeping person. His mother, Ethel, used to tell him that. Why not? he asked the darkness of his bedroom. *You could give them a heart attack.* Even with her dead these five years, there was no lack of conversation between Dick and Ethel Sapphire. Dick wished he could wake up Shel—Sidney, he caught himself, Sidney, Sidney. He'd never get accustomed to that name. It was more professional, she'd said the day she told him she was changing it. "Professional!" Dick had been disgusted. "It's not a woman's name. It's a goddamned city in Australia!" They'd had such an argument.

He listened to his wife breathing in her sleep. He'd settle for an argument with her now. How he missed the way they used to stay up late and talk, argue, laugh, gossip, until one or two in the morning. Now she went to bed at nine, got up at four-thirty. By six o'clock she was on the air saying, "Good morning, this is Sidney Sapphire for *The A.M. Show,* here to start

the day with you. Visiting with us today in our studio is . . ."
And on it went for the next three hours, Dick watching her on
TV, eating his bran cereal and berries alone—*alone like a dog,*
Ethel would have said.

Sidney was happy. Her ratings were high, she had earned
over three million dollars last year, and she was up for a new
contract. Dick thought, Who needs a wife who makes three
million dollars? It was eleven o'clock, and he felt restless. On
top of everything, his chiropractor had advised him to sleep
on his back to avoid compressing his shoulders. How could
anyone sleep on his back? He felt too vulnerable lying with his
throat exposed, so someone might come along and slit it or
strangle him—impossible to sleep like that. His doctor had offered to write him a prescription. "I don't want pills," Dick had
said. "So you sleep, but it doesn't matter, because in the morning you're hungover and you feel like hell anyway. You might
as well stay up and save the call to Madison Chemists."

He wasn't going to sleep tonight. He slid his legs out from
the covers, bobbed his foot around on the rug until he located
his slippers, then stood up and straightened his nightshirt. He
crept off to the bathroom for his robe and padded down the
master hallway. He groped in the air and found the doorknob,
unlatched it and silently latched it behind him. What had happened to the days when he would rustle around in bed and
Shelley—she was still Shelley then—would wake up saying,
"Honey, what's on your mind?"

A banana and a glass of milk sometimes relaxed him. Dick
carried them from the kitchen back to the upstairs den and

lounged on the couch in front of the Weather Channel, a chenille afghan draped over his legs. He watched amorphous green patches of low pressure dance across a map of the continental United States. He liked the music; it was soothing. The screen said it was Tuesday, October 12, 1999, 11:13 P.M. EST. Tomorrow there would be thunderstorms in the Ohio Valley, a chance of scattered showers in northern New England.

Christ, that was some board meeting, Dick thought, the first one since all the uproar in the co-op had settled. Since Marvin Adler finally finished renovating the penthouse into a palatial monstrosity of Italian marble worthy of Mussolini. Since he moved in his circus troupe of a family. Dick could have shot Beverly Coddington tonight for the look on her face. That woman should hire a plastic surgeon to permanently raise one of her eyebrows and spare herself the effort. He couldn't believe the way things turned out, after all he had done to get that damned Adler into the building. He could hear Ethel's Brooklyn accent, *No good deed goes unpunished, Richard.*

It had started a year earlier, the day he ran into Bob Horowitz in the elevator. "Dick, good morning, I was thinking of you," Bob said as he stepped in on the seventh floor. "I was going to call you at the office today."

"Here I am."

"Any chance you could meet me for a drink at the club this week? I've got something on my mind. I'd like your input."

"Yeah, sure." The elevator stopped at the lobby. "Thanks,"

Dick said to the attendant. He and Bob walked past the door-man Peter, who held open the front door. They chatted on the sidewalk, midway between their two cars—Dick's black Lexus, Bob's gray BMW—each manned by a driver. There was a crisp fall breeze on Park Avenue. "How about Thursday afternoon?" Dick said. "I'll meet you at four in the bar."

"Four it is." Bob gave him a swift pat on the back and disappeared into his car.

The Harmonie Club bar had green plaid carpeting, oak-paneled walls and brown leather chairs. Dick found Bob at a table near the window. "Sorry," Dick said. "I had a client on the phone from Los Angeles. They have a different sense of time there."

Dick ordered Scotch and water, Bob a vodka martini. They spent a few minutes catching up. Mimi Horowitz had turned an ankle in Quebec City during their Silversea cruise, but she was healing up fine. "You can't imagine the money I've saved," Bob said, laughing, "keeping her off Madison Avenue for two weeks." His daughter, Robin, had married at last, some mountain biker who sold sporting equipment in Durango, Colorado. "Don't ask me. The guy seems nice enough, and she was thirty-nine years old. She says she's happy, so if she's happy, that's what matters, right?"

"Yeah, listen, I've still got Madeline floundering around single. Ritchie, thank God, bought out his partner's practice, and he's affiliated with Columbia-Presbyterian. His wife's a doll, the girls go to Spence, everything's normal." Dick rapped his knuckles on the side of the glass-covered oak table. "My wife, meanwhile, is taking over the world. People come up to us in restaurants and ask for her autograph. Do you know someone actually congratulated me in Aquavit the other night? For being her husband?"

Bob shook his head. "Mr. Sidney Sapphire, huh?"

"Christ, Bob, you don't know what it's like. You and Mimi take a cruise of the Saint Lawrence. You leave for Boca after Thanksgiving. Sidney saves her vacation time for dermabrasion and redoing her teeth. This wasn't how I'd planned my old age. We haven't been to Europe in two years."

The matter Bob wanted to discuss was the penthouse. The baroness's estate, now in the hands of her daughter and a couple of nephews, had put the apartment on the market the previous spring. There had been a good contract that summer, but it fell through. "I heard about it from my friend Chas Greenberg. He'd written a letter of reference for the buyer, Danny Tchartikoff—you've heard of him, right?"

"Didn't he use to be chairman of Associated Stores?"

"That's him," Bob said. "Chas told me Danny sold out his shares two years ago for forty million dollars. He had what he already had, plus a house in Palm Beach, one in Easthampton and whatever he got for his old apartment on Fifth—I'd say Tchartikoff was solvent. Member of the City Athletic Club, no criminal record, same wife for twenty years, two nice kids, teenagers. The board turned him down."

"Our board?"

"Yeah. Coddington. Payne. The accountant upstairs with no lips—that group."

"What was their reason?"

"They said his assets were spread too thin. Too many households. Alimony to the first wife."

"On forty million dollars?"

"Exactly." Bob signaled the waiter and ordered another drink. "You want one?" Dick shook his head. "Anyway, Danny's found another place on top of the Beresford, but Chas got curious. He asked around and heard there had been a previous turndown last May. It was a movie executive from California. Lots of money, nice family, solid references. Same excuse from the board."

Dick asked, "So what do you think is going on?"

Bob stirred the olive around in his drink and then bit into it. He laid the toothpick in the ashtray. "Well, the studio executive's name is Ivan Reynolds, but he grew up in Woodmere, Long Island, under the name Irving Resnick."

"I smell a rat."

"I'm thinking that old French baroness was the only reason any of us Israelites ever got to buy in to Nine-eighty Park."

"Strange," Dick said. "The French are such anti-Semites."

Bob chuckled. "Listen. Have you ever heard of Marvin Adler?"

Bob Horowitz had heard of everyone, Dick thought. He and Sidney had seen him recently at a UJA benefit. He was hopping from table to table, shaking hands and kissing old ladies like he was running for president of the United States. In private, they called him King of the Jews. "I don't know Marvin Adler," Dick said.

Bob told him about the entrepreneur from Kansas City, only forty-five years old, who had started out in the supermarket business and recently become the majority shareholder of a midwestern telephone company. "You know the type," Bob said. "Like a Trump or Carl Icahn. Pretty blond wife, Learjet flying him around. But the bottom line is he seems like a nice guy. He's down-to-earth, not a big boaster, doesn't come off as a maniac or a backstabber. He just happens to be very successful and obscenely wealthy."

"Define 'obscene' for me here."

"Oh, I don't know, Dick. The guy's probably a billionaire or close to it. As far as I'm concerned, someone obscenely wealthy has more money than I could ever dream of, and he's thirty years younger than me to boot. Will that do?"

"Absolutely."

"The problem is this. Adler's wife has her heart set on our penthouse, and Marvin made a very solid offer to the baroness's daughter, who by now is ready to unload her mother's damn apartment, stop paying seven thousand a month maintenance, and redecorate her villa in Saint-Tropez, buy a yacht, whatever. Marvin got my name from a mutual friend on the board of the UJA and invited me to lunch. He asked if I'd write him a reference, figuring a letter from a neighbor would seal the deal. He also, by the way, made a five-million-dollar pledge to the UJA, so I should have taken *him* to lunch. Of course I'll write the reference. But I don't want him getting turned down, especially over the shape of his nose."

"No kidding." Dick swallowed the last sip of his drink and thought a minute. "I've got a good real estate guy in my firm," he said. "I'll have him look over our shareholder's agreement and the co-op bylaws. I'll let you know what he says."

Dick had always supported Jewish organizations, helped out Jewish friends, sent money to plant trees in Israel. But he had never taken on a cause, and he wasn't sure now was a good time to start. And this cause—anti-Semitism on Park Avenue—it didn't feel like a winner. Not that he didn't hate discrimination; of course it was an outrage that a guy like Danny Tchartikoff couldn't buy whatever the hell he wanted with his forty million dollars. But Dick had lived with it all his life, like a kind of background noise he barely heard anymore. Sure, there were clubs he couldn't join, communities where he wasn't welcome, clients he was not asked to represent. His religion and the way it was received by the world had affected his whole life, his whole way of thinking, the choices he'd made in his education, career, hell, even marriage—wasn't it a kind of racy privilege he'd exercised, marrying two gentile women, the privilege of the handsome American Jew who had made it pretty big? And he appreciated being a Jew in America as compared to, say, Germany or Poland or Russia. God, did he appreciate it. "Life, Liberty and the Pursuit of Happiness"—

didn't he have those? So what if he couldn't join Apawamis in Rye. He was a member of Old Oaks. The point was to play golf with his friends, and his friends were all at Old Oaks.

In general, the social segregation in which he had lived his entire life didn't bother him much. In this particular instance, however, the bigotry of his neighbors—because that's what it was, in all its plain ugliness, bigotry—well, it couldn't be accepted. He wasn't going to live in a restricted building, not in the year 1998. What had always been background noise was now a big brass trumpet blaring in his ear. He thought, What a pain in the ass.

Dick explained to his associate that this wasn't the kind of situation where anybody wanted to sue anyone. Neither Ivan Reynolds nor Danny Tchartikoff was about to take the stand in an antidiscrimination suit. "But think of the publicity!" the young lawyer said. "They'd be heroes."

"Nobody wants publicity around the fact that they were turned down by a Park Avenue co-op board. We just need to find a way so it won't happen again."

His associate came back the next day with an idea. The election of the board of directors was coming up. There was a clause in a footnote to the co-op bylaws that could, theoretically, allow a shareholder to pool his votes and cast them all for one director. "In other words," he explained, "on the next ballot, instead of casting one vote for each of the seven nominees, you would give all seven of your votes to one candidate.

And your neighbor Bob Horowitz could cast all of his votes for the same candidate. What you'd have to do, given the number of apartments in your building, is find two more shareholders to team up with, then decide which of you would run. You'd get a man on the board, and one witness should be enough to keep them from pulling any more tricks."

Dick could count on the baroness's estate to vote with him and Bob. But who would be the fourth ally?

The Sapphires invited Bob and Mimi up for an early dinner the following week to discuss the problem. Dick outlined his plan. "We need to find another conspirator. Do you think that's possible?"

Sidney giggled. "Can you believe what we're reduced to? Boy, if my producers ever got a whiff of this story. Mimi, have some more wine—the walls of Rome are burning."

"I think I will, thank you." Mimi wore a new Vincenzo Ferretti suit, a Cartier watch and about six rings stacked up on her two ring fingers, diamonds twisted this way and that. "Now, what about Charles Payne? I see his black grandson here pretty often. Blacks, Jews . . . maybe he's not so anti-Semitic as we think."

"Nah." Bob shook his gray head. "He's been on the board for years."

"But doesn't he have his office down at Cantor Fitzgerald? They're all Jewish. Maybe if you called him, he'd be sympathetic."

"Sorry, Mimi," Dick said, "he may do business with our kind, but he doesn't socialize."

"Forget it, honey. *Schvartze* grandson, Jewish associates or no—the man's a Nazi."

"He's right," Sidney said. "Payne's a fascist. Our housekeeper, Irina, tells me how he treats his maid. And he's the worst tipper in the building—like Ebenezer Scrooge with the doormen at Christmas."

"Yeah, forget about Payne."

"Okay, okay." Mimi waved a hand in the air—her ring finger drooping from the weight of her jewelry—as if to banish Charles Payne from the room. "Though, really, if anyone has an honest reason to gripe about his help, it's him." Everyone roared with laughter. "I mean, imagine if that had been our Robin."

They tossed around the names of some neighbors. "What about Mrs. Bailey?" Dick suggested. "She's always seemed like a nice lady."

Sidney jumped in. "Oh, no, darling, she's a slumlord. You were away, but do you two remember that day all those blacks and Puerto Ricans came down from Harlem?"

"It was dreadful," Mimi said. "They were her tenants. It was February, and they'd gone a whole week with no heat or hot water. They came down here and picketed our building with signs calling her a racist and all other kinds of names. I read later in the paper that she evicted them all."

"Scratch Mrs. Bailey," said Dick.

"I wouldn't want to," Bob joked.

Sidney rang a crystal bell, and Irina emerged from the kitchen to clear the dinner plates. She whispered something in Sidney's ear, and Sidney rose. "Excuse me for a moment."

Dick watched his wife walk by, then he glanced over at Mimi Horowitz. Sidney looked at least ten years younger— well, she probably was ten years younger than Mimi. But hell, she looked twenty years younger, tall, blond and beautiful. She was up there with any woman: gorgeous, smart and classy. He smiled to himself. He didn't always think of it this way, but tonight he was proud of her. He made a mental note to tell her later.

Sidney came back with a puzzled expression, carrying a silver coffeepot. "What is it?" Dick asked, but she shook her head and chatted up Mimi about her ankle and her orthopedist while Irina passed around fruit salad and a tray of biscotti.

When Irina left the room, Sidney spoke in a low voice. "I swear, the maids know everything we do."

"They could write a gossip column," Mimi said.

"Irina just called me into the kitchen to mention that Angela Somoza has a new fiancé."

"Congratulations to her," Bob said. "After they shot Pablo Escobar, I wondered who she could date."

Sidney smiled. "No, listen. Angela Somoza's intended is the vice director of the Anti-Defamation League."

"He's got to be *meshuga*," Dick said. "What's a nice boy like him doing with a third-world dictator?"

"Whatever he's doing, he's been doing it for a while. And keeping it under wraps, because he's still getting divorced."

"Imagine finding out that I was leaving you for a Somoza," Bob said to Mimi. "You'd give me the apartment and be happy to get out with your life."

"Can't the poor woman change her name?" Mimi asked. "If I were her, I'd call myself Angela Smith. I mean, she's actually a very attractive girl."

"She scares me to death," Dick said. "Something about her eyes. And that accent. She reminds me of a character in a cartoon the kids used to watch—*Rocky and Bullwinkle,* remember? Who was that dark-haired villainess?"

"Natasha," Mimi said.

"I always thought Natasha was kind of sexy," Bob said. "Didn't you find her sexy?" he asked Dick.

"I don't know, Bob. It depends what you're into. But Angela Somoza scares me to death."

"Angela Somoza is our fourth shareholder for the election," Sidney said.

"And you're calling Charles Payne a fascist?"

"Think about it, Dick. The vice director of the Anti-Defamation League is going to be her husband. He'll probably move into the building. Angela Somoza is our fourth."

"She's right," Mimi said.

The two men nodded. Sidney was right. Angela Somoza was their best bet for infiltrating the board. Dick turned his palm up. "Okay. Well, Bob, I guess you should call her."

"No, you call her, Dick."

"No, you."

"Christ, *I* will," said Sidney. "You two big old cowards."

When Sidney went to bed that night, Dick was watching *Larry King Live,* and he forgot to tell her about feeling proud of her. The next day Mimi sent up a box of chocolates, thanking Sidney for a lovely evening.

A week later, Sidney had lunch with Angela Somoza at Paper Moon. "She's a very remarkable woman," Sidney told Dick that evening.

"Oh, I'm sure you're right there."

"No, really. She's intelligent, thoughtful—she has a wonderful sense of humor. Did you know that she works part-time for the ACLU? That's how she met her fiancé. At a conference about hate crimes and the First Amendment. Believe me, she's got a lot more going for her than Mimi Horowitz."

"Yeah, anyone does."

Mimi Horowitz was the near-fate that Dick had twice escaped. The "nice Jewish girl" his mother had wanted him to marry. Most of his friends had married that type of woman. The "nice Jewish girls" came from Brooklyn, Long Island and the Boston area, as well as Manhattan. They had accents, nasal voices, a passion for shopping. Ethel had been furious when Dick announced his engagement to Lauren. "An Irish *shiksa* is stealing the prince of the family!" she had shrieked. She threatened to die, spontaneously. When instead, ten years later, Lauren was the one to die, Ethel had actually said, "Well, Richard, what did you expect?" She spent the next few years collecting single Jewish women for her son. She and her sister, Dick's aunt Edythe, even followed an attractive woman out of Temple Emmanuel one Saturday morning. The two ladies in hats stalked her up Madison Avenue into Gristede's, and when she finished shopping, they wheedled her name and address out of the manager. Ethel couldn't understand why Dick refused to call her. "That suicidal *shiksa* destroyed your spirit," she said.

Of course, when Dick met Shelley at Mike and Vicki Peltz's anniversary party and, soon after, married her, Lauren became some kind of saint in Ethel's mind, or at least in her comments to his new wife. "The mother of your children" was the phrase she used to get under Shelley's skin, even though Shelley converted to Judaism and Lauren had not.

"She's an old lady," Dick used to tell Shelley. "She's fixed in her opinions. Have patience—she's got heart trouble. She could die any day."

In fact, Ethel Sapphire lived twenty years into their marriage. When Shelley landed her first job in television and changed her name, Ethel told her over dinner in their home, "Your husband's a good sport." Sidney had said that night she wanted to clop her mother-in-law over the head with a lamb shank.

But he *was* a good sport, Dick thought. If he'd married a nice Jewish girl, he would be taking cruises now, buying a house down in Florida or maybe out in Arizona at the Boulders. Then again, he'd be sharing that house with someone who looked and thought and sounded like Mimi Horowitz. Dick didn't know what to think of himself. At heart, he was probably more anti-Semitic than all the stuffy members of the

980 board put together. And now here he was, championing the Jewish cause.

Sidney reported that Angela was "one hundred percent sympathetic" to their complaint against the board. She would certainly vote with the Sapphires and the Horowitzes, and if they didn't mind, she would pursue the matter in her own way, too.

Angela, it seemed, was on some kind of social terms with Beverly Coddington: Both were members of the Colony and the Meadow Club, though Angela alluded to a certain chilliness Beverly had shown her since the arrest of her ex-husband. But through mutual friends, Angela managed to convey the message to Beverly that an eighth candidate was likely to seek election to the 980 Park board of directors, and if he did run, he had the votes to oust an incumbent. Out of nowhere, Angela reported to Sidney, Beverly called her, regretting that it had been ages since they'd gone to lunch. Could they meet perhaps this Wednesday at the Colony Club for a bite?

"I would love to see you on Wednesday," Angela replied, "but I do have a plan with another friend—well, you know her, Sidney Sapphire from our building. Perhaps the three of us could all get together?"

"I was hoping for some time with you alone."

"Ay, Beverly, that would be marvelous, but unfortunately, Wednesday is my only day free. I am leaving for Madrid a few days later and won't be back for two weeks. If you like, we could postpone it until November."

"No, no, that's quite all right." Angela knew it would have to be all right. The board meeting was October 30, and that was the deadline for fixing the nominations. "I suppose I'll just have to have the pleasure of closer acquaintance with your friend Mrs. Sapphire." Beverly's tone of voice made her distress clear.

Dick chuckled as Sidney described her luncheon with Angela Somoza and Beverly Coddington.

"First of all," Sidney said, "the Colony dining room is one of the dreariest of all these dreary clubs. The waiters look like something out of *Remains of the Day,* and the food is what we made in my home economics class in high school. Beverly ordered creamed chicken fricassee over rice."

They had chatted pleasantries for nearly an hour. Beverly couldn't have been more curious about Angela's children or Sidney's lineup of interviews. There came a point when Sidney wondered if Beverly would bring up anything about the building at all. They were halfway through dessert—a dry, crumbly almond cake and tea—and still no mention of the board. Finally, Angela nudged Sidney's foot under the table and said, "I hear Peter our doorman is retiring."

"Yes, I've heard that, too," Beverly said. "He's the most dependable man. I will miss him so."

"Me, too," Angela said. "A lot of changes seem to be happening all at once in our building, no?" Sidney noticed a gleam in her eye.

The subject could not be avoided further. "Yes," Beverly said, looking thoughtful. "I'm a bit concerned. There seems to be some ruckus brewing—some nonsense going on among the men in our building."

Angela said, "Men like Sidney's husband, perhaps?"

Beverly wrinkled her face into a tight little prune of a smile and reached over to squeeze Sidney's hand. "Your husband, my husband. Men! They're just so competitive all the time, I don't quite know what to do with them.

"One hears the psychologists saying that men compete, women cooperate. Can't you imagine how much better off the whole world would be if the women took over? Though I don't know who would balance the checkbooks." Beverly laughed, and Sidney and Angela laughed, too, though not *with* Beverly.

"Anyway," Beverly went on, "I was hoping to call upon you girls to discourage anyone who might want to upset the neighborly atmosphere we enjoy. I think we've all gotten along splendidly in our building. And though we've had *elections* every few years," she looked at Sidney, "there's never actually been a *contest*." She said the word "contest" as if it were a vulgar thing.

It was true, Sidney thought. There had never been any choices on the ballot. The board put up their slate of nominees, and the shareholders all checked the "for" box without questioning.

"Yes, I know about elections of that type," Angela said forcefully. "I think my grandfather invented them. His sons were fond of them, too, though I suppose it was just that sort of election that got Uncle Tachito assassinated."

Beverly made another face, this one as if she'd discovered a cockroach in her cake. She quickly reached for her teacup. Sidney bit her lip to keep from laughing out loud. She couldn't look at either of her two companions.

"Dick, my God, I had tears welling up in my eyes," she told him that night.

"Ha! The Dictator took down old White Bread. So what's the upshot of all this?"

Beverly was going to discuss the matter with the other members of the board. "She asked that we give her a week to try to come up with a friendly solution. I think the idea that any of her cronies might *lose* an election is too much for her."

Dick said, "The ball's in their court now."

It took under a week for the letter to arrive.

In order to welcome some new talent and insight to our deliberations, without depriving ourselves of the expertise of its current members, the Board of Directors of 980 Park Avenue has voted to expand, adding two new seats. After much consideration of the many worthy residents in our building, the Board has nominated Mr. Richard Sapphire of apartment 12A and Ms. Angela Somoza of 4B. We sincerely hope they will agree to join our slate and serve our building.

The letter was signed by Charles Payne.

The election went off without a hitch. In early December, the new board of nine members convened in the Coddington dining room to interview Marvin Adler and consider his application to purchase the penthouse.

Marvin Adler was not at all what Dick had expected. Though his financial statements were awe-inspiring and his personal references glowing, the man himself was a kind of slob. He was fat, with long, greasy-looking gray hair and a shadow of a beard. He wore a herringbone sport jacket and a crooked tie over jeans and green lizard cowboy boots. The least he could have done, Dick thought, was put on a suit. Marvin also showed up without his wife, Giselle, who, he said, was chairing a benefit down in SoHo that she couldn't escape. Dick found Adler's stance before the board disrespectful. Aside from his absurd dress and lack of a wife for an occasion that was surely her duty, the man seemed smug, lawless, too sure of the entitlement his money would buy. He spoke to the board members in a tone that was overly familiar, laughed too loud, slouched in his chair and dominated the interview. Dick felt embarrassed for Adler and for himself. This was the man for whom everyone else in the room believed he had lobbied?

Dick tried to read Angela Somoza's expression, but her eyes were strange, not exactly calibrated with each other, and he couldn't get a sense of her. Though by now she and Sidney were great pals, he didn't know her at all, had no idea what her assessment of a man like Marvin Adler might be. Who knew—she dressed beautifully, carrying herself like a foreign princess. Then again, her ex-husband had gone to jail. Maybe she liked outlaws. She certainly had been raised by them.

At the end of the interview, everyone shook Marvin Adler's huge, fleshy hand, and Beverly Coddington saw him to the door. "Well," Charles Payne said. "He's an unconventional-looking fellow, but there's no question about his fiscal stability. And," his blue eyes bored right into Dick's face, "there seems to be a desire for some fresh blood in this place—am I not correct?"

There was a long silence in the room. Dick noticed many pairs of eyes on him, and he strained not to redden. He was surprised, he was embarrassed, but most of all, he was angry. He was angry with Marvin Adler for flouting the dignity of the board interview. He was angry with Bob Horowitz for putting him up to this—for the sake of a contribution to the UJA that was none of Dick's business. He was furious at all the blue eyes in the room twinkling at him, delighting in his humiliation. Above all, he was disgusted with himself, ruffled with indignations that he could hardly sort out.

He was more disgusted when he realized that the board was waiting for *him* to make the motion to accept Adler's application. He would be the one to go on record in the minutes as the man who had led this crass cowboy to the 980 penthouse. The board had lost its battle, but Dick would be responsible for the results of the fray. He had never felt so alone in his life.

"Excuse me," Angela Somoza's accent broke the silence. "I am not yet familiar with your procedures. What exactly do we do now?"

Beverly Coddington cleared her throat. "Normally, we discuss the applicant until someone makes a motion to accept or decline his offer to purchase."

"Ah," Angela said. "Well, he can afford it, and he has excellent references, so what's to discuss? I motion we accept him." She held her head high and looked into the face of each person around the table in turn.

Dick smiled when his eyes met hers. She was a fine woman—brave, elegant and just, like a figure of Liberty leading the People. And she had just saved his ass. "Second," he said.

Charles Payne asked, "Everyone in favor?"

Marvin Adler was approved unanimously. The formal meeting concluded, the board members adjourned to the living room, and Beverly's maid passed around cocktails and hors d'oeuvres. Miniature hot dogs wrapped in pastry dough. Squares of mild cheddar cheese on Wheat Thins. Harold Coddington emerged from "banishment," as he called it, in his den. "Actually, I was watching the most interesting show on the Discovery Channel," he boomed, "about meerkats. Though they don't look much like cats at all."

Dick approached Angela, who stood by a sentimental oil portrait of Beverly and her two daughters, painted against a hideous yellow-and-gray-streaked background. "You're a compassionate woman," he said.

Angela laughed. "As they used to say all the time on that English comedy show, 'I wasn't expecting the Spanish Inquisition.'"

Dick laughed, too, but a shiver registered between his shoulder blades. The Spanish Inquisition didn't seem so far removed from Angela Somoza's world.

Marvin Adler closed on the apartment in January 1999, and through the rest of the winter, a team of architects and designers rushed in and out of the lobby with their sketches and blueprints. The new board met three times to review plans for Adler's ostentatious project. At each meeting Dick felt the sting of the old board members' silent reproach. He took it upon himself to find every possible rule of the shareholders' agreement that might curb Adler's designs. A planned two-story glass atrium on the terrace was reduced to a modest meditation pavilion. "Meditation?" Beverly Coddington had asked. Adler would not be permitted to treat the exterior walls with stucco and sheep's urine to create the antique Mediterranean effect his head architect had proposed, and additional fountains would not be allowed. The mosaic floor in the foyer was approved. "There's nothing we can do about that one," Dick said in defeat. All spring, carpenters, masons, plumbers, even marble workers flown in from Carrara tormented the building's residents with the banging and scraping, and the service elevator was permanently occupied. Peter, the old doorman, retired in May. "I seem to be getting out just in time," he said to Dick on his last day. Dick cringed.

The presence of the Adler family was far worse than the contractors. Giselle Adler turned out to be a devout Buddhist, and her home was always open to traveling monks. "Jesus Christ," Dick said to Sidney one evening in September. "I came in tonight, and there must have been two dozen men with shaved heads and bright orange robes, sitting in the lobby on huge suitcases, waiting for Giselle to come home. What the hell do they have in those suitcases? They wear the same orange robes all the time."

"Sand, Dick," Sidney said. "They're doing a Tibetan sand mandala down at Rockefeller Center tomorrow morning."

"A what?" He shook his head. "Forget it, I don't want to know."

There was a teenage son who was disturbed. In late September two stocky attendants in white jackets carried him out through the lobby, bound and cursing, to a wilderness rehabilitation program in the Adirondacks. "Your friends the Adlers have a rather colorful life," Beverly said to Dick the next morning in the elevator. Dick wished he had a sign to wear on his chest: *They are not my friends.*

A conversation with Madeline was the one consolation in his year. She came by for dinner on a Wednesday night, and—this was unusual—she stayed to keep her father company for a while after Sidney went to bed. They sat in the library downstairs, drinking decaf and talking. Dick resisted the temptation to ask her, *Honey, you're thirty-seven now—what are you planning to do with your life?* He wouldn't push those buttons; he'd stay out of that never-ending argument. When he felt the urge, he clamped his jaws shut, took three deep breaths through his nose, then brought up what had been in the news that morning. "So, our randy president got all weepy at his prayer breakfast yesterday. Choked up over the nation's forgiveness."

Madeline laughed. "That man needs Yom Kippur. Though 'the nation' has no business condemning or forgiving him. Hillary, on the other hand, should throw him out."

She was right; Clinton was a boob. On the other hand, Dick wished he could say something to Madeline about not holding a grudge against all the men in the world because she'd had a couple of lousy boyfriends. He took a deep breath. "Hillary wants to be our senator."

"Oh, please. Who's she kidding?"

"At least they bought in Chappaqua, thank God. All we needed at Old Oaks were Bill, his buddy Vernon and the Secret Service guys tying up the golf course. Joe Segal said they had jitters at Quaker Ridge, too. All over Westchester, it became a kind of NIMBY thing."

"Oh," Madeline said. "You'll never believe who I ran into at a gallery opening last week."

"Who?"

"Claudia. Claudia Bloom. I wouldn't have recognized her. She dyed her hair red. She told me *I* looked exactly the same."

Dick smiled. She did look the same—soft, rosy cheeks with dimples, her mother's blue eyes, long, wavy light brown hair that even that Swiss nanny never could tame. Madeline was not beautiful in the way that fashionable women were today—tall, sleek and stick-thin. But she was lovely like a girl in an old master painting. Why couldn't some nice guy see that in her? Or maybe they did, but *she* was too prickly. "So did you speak to her?"

"Speak, my God, we fell into each other's arms. We talked all through the opening, and then she sent her husband home so we could go out for dinner alone. We talked until midnight, until we were hoarse.

"It was great, just great. She's an architect. They live in Chelsea."

"Does she have kids?"

"No. She never wanted them."

Even if Dick detected a hint of defensiveness in her voice, he wasn't going to press it. *Stop cross-examining your daughter,* he remembered Sidney saying. He would try to stay on neutral ground. "So, what does her husband do? I don't mean that in a sexist way—I'm just curious. Is he a nice guy?"

"Yeah, he seems really nice. He's an architect, too." A strange expression formed on Madeline's face. "You wanna know something funny? I didn't think of it at the time, but he looks a lot like *you.*"

"That is funny. I hope he looks younger." Dick also couldn't help hoping that Claudia's husband had some single friends to introduce to Madeline. And he couldn't help asking after Claudia's mother, though he knew the conversation could take a quick, ugly turn and Madeline might leave in a huff. But dammit, he thought, Rosalind had been one of his and Lauren's closest friends—he had a right to inquire about her after so many years. "And Rosalind?" He sat tense, watching his daughter's face.

She smiled, and he tried not to show his relief. "She's fine. She's a photographer. Actually, she's gotten kind of famous— she just had a one-woman show in a big gallery in Amsterdam. I'm sure you remember how artistic she always was."

Dick did not remember that about her, but this was the last thing he would admit to now. Had Rosalind married? That was what he wanted to know. Forget it. He wouldn't push Madeline any further. Already this was the most intimate, peaceful exchange with his daughter that he could remember.

"But Dad," she went on, "something pretty interesting came out." She pulled her legs up on the couch and sat Indian-style. "You know, I always thought that you and Claudia's mother were"—she searched for the right word—"involved when Mom died."

"Really?" Everyone had thought so.

"Claudia told me Rosalind swore up and down that she never slept with you."

"No, we never did." Dick's name had been dragged through the mud, the subject of endless whispering among his friends' wives, and he wasn't even getting laid. Unlike Bill Clinton.

Madeline shook her head. "The worst thing about it all is I've been angry and fucked up all these years over nothing."

Dick sighed. He wanted to take her in his arms and hold her to his chest the way he used to when she was a little baby. He would have to settle for words. "I don't think it's over nothing, sweetheart. I think it was enough that you had a mother who took her own life. I think it was enough that our marriage had been sour for years, that she'd lost all her zest and sparkle and I'd fallen out of love with her. And no, even though I wasn't having an affair with Rosalind Bloom, given my druthers, I would have. At that time Rosalind had everything Lauren had lost—she was funny, warmhearted and kooky. She was alive. Madeline, your mother died years before she really died. I watched every minute of it, and I still can't tell you why it happened." Or what he could have done, Dick thought. That question plagued him to this day.

But what mattered now was Madeline. "I'll tell you what, Snookie," he said. "I'd give anything in the world to see you getting some fun out of life. Is there anything I can do for you—find you a therapist, send you on a trip, buy you some new clothes?"

"No, Daddy." She smiled at him, her eyes moist. "I think it's an inside job." She brushed her hair back from her shoulder. "Anyway, I'm glad to talk this all out with you—finally.

"And I'm glad to know Claudia again. I didn't realize how much I'd missed her all these years."

"I know how that is," he said. "There are guys I talk to every week—in business, at the club—but even though he's lived in San Francisco since 1960, and I only see him once or twice a year, there's no one I have more laughs with than Ray Mazur. I've known him since kindergarten. You know, he's the one who taught me to pee standing up after I was beaten by some bullies at school who caught me in the boys' room peeing like a girl."

"But hadn't your dad . . . ?"

"My father thought childrearing was women's work."

"And Nanna?"

"My mother didn't talk about those things."

"Christ, with your mother, it's amazing you haven't spent your life hiding under the kitchen sink."

"Who had the option?"

Dick had slept well that night, long and soundly—no bolting awake at two A.M., no dreams of tooth extractions. He had slept like a man who had carried a heavy load over a hard trek and at long last delivered it to the place it belonged. He had slept in that perfect, restful way—in the way he had no hopes of sleeping after tonight's horrible board meeting.

In addition to the old guard's digs and daggers, which Dick accepted like Saint Sebastian shot through with arrows, Angela Somoza had announced that she was resigning from the board. Not only resigning, but she was moving out of 980 Park altogether, putting her apartment on the market and starting to look for a brownstone. "Bruce and I will marry in December," she told the board with joy. "And as much as I love it here, we've decided it's best to start our new life on neutral ground, best both for us and for the children. You know, we have four of them between us."

Everyone wished her the greatest happiness. Dick could picture the calculations ticking behind Charles Payne's bright eyes—*Two birds with one stone, how convenient. No more South American mafia. No more Jewish resistance.* Dick would serve out the remaining two years of his term, then, boom, the board would oust him and go back to business as usual.

If only he could resign, too, Dick thought, watching the local forecast, partly cloudy in Central Park, winds from the southwest at ten to fifteen miles per hour. But he wouldn't resign, he would hold up his head and stick it out. Didn't he always?

The world felt upside down. His wife was a television celebrity, his daughter pushing forty and unmarried. The market was off its high, and some said it might fall even more. All the computers were supposed to crash on New Year's Eve. Al Gore, that arrogant stick-in-the-mud, would become the next president. And Dick himself had been responsible for letting a Trojan horse full of orange-robed monks and a deranged, screaming teenager into his building.

Forty-five minutes into a countdown of the century's worst hurricanes, Dick began to nod off on the couch. *What a mess, Richard,* Ethel said from the afterlife as he dozed. *What a tummel—not one thing normal like it used to be.* She made him feel like everything was his fault—that was her genius—but it worked on him. And what could he have done differently, he wondered. He'd studied hard, gone to law school, made partner. He'd done the best he could with Lauren, he was good to Sidney, he took care of his kids. He gave money to charity and tried to live according to his principles. Where had he gone wrong?

I had lunch at the club with Helen Applebaum, Ethel said. *She has the perfect son—he never married.* He's a fag, Mom, Dick tried to reply, but she went on. *He still lives with Helen in Palm Beach. He eats breakfast with her every morning, takes her to brunch at the club on Sunday. He never ignores her, escorts her to all the parties, and each night he comes home to her saying, "Mother, I love you. Come here. I want to kiss your teeth."*

Beverly Coddington:
Better Homes and Husbands

— 2000 —

It was most disconcerting, upsetting, in fact. I was walking up Madison Avenue that May morning, during the first spring of the new millennium. I was searching for a cushion. Harold's doctor had said he could use more back support, and I thought something embroidered with a few dogs or a hunting scene and then some fringe around the edges would look perfect in the den. I was, I suppose, distracted, and just as I was passing the Carlyle, I collided with a tall man in a lovely gray trench coat. He held my arm rather firmly, and I believed he had lost his balance. "Oh dear, I am dreadfully sorry!" I said.

I looked up at his face. He was Negro, which surprised me, but so well dressed that it never occurred to me to be afraid. I felt something hard against my breastbone, and he whispered, "Just give me your purse and nothing bad will happen."

It required a moment for me to register that he was holding a gun—yes, a large, black man was holding a gun to my chest in broad daylight, right in front of the Carlyle Hotel, as if this were the most normal thing in the world. I yielded my bag, my Gucci one with the bamboo handle. The fellow said, "Don't make a sound." Then he was gone.

I don't know how much time elapsed while I stood and watched people pass through the revolving door of the hotel, hail taxis and emerge with packages from the shops across the street. It wasn't until a bus roared by, emitting a noxious cloud of exhaust, that I was jarred from my paralysis. I hurried up the block, not knowing where I was hurrying to. I spotted the canopy of Madison Chemists. Harold and I have been using them for years, and they all know me. Automatically, I turned inside and made my way past the cosmetics and hair ornaments to the pharmacist's counter, where the druggist who has been serving me since our girls were children was on duty.

"Good morning, Mrs. Coddington," he said, "what can I do for you today?"

I tried to respond, but I was still all muddled. "Good morning, Mr. Rosen, I'm not quite sure. It seems . . ." My hands shook, and I felt dizzy. "Oh dear," I continued. "It seems that I have just been . . . held up," and with those words, I began to tremble all over and feel flushed. I reached for a tissue before I was conscious that I no longer had my purse. That realization—tangible proof that what I had just experienced had indeed happened—caused me to shake even harder. Truly, I believed I might faint cold, right there before the eyes of my poor startled pharmacist.

Fortunately, Mr. Rosen has always been a kindly man. I recall how he used to send over cherry-flavored cough drops when the girls had their colds and flus, and how graciously he had thanked me for our condolence card when his wife passed away from lung cancer ten years ago. Now Mr. Rosen raised a section of the countertop, gently took my arm and ushered me into a private office at the back of the pharmacy. "Willis, take over the counter," he called out and closed the door behind us. He lowered me into a green vinyl armchair and pulled the desk chair over. He sat beside me, patting my shoulder. When he asked if I'd been injured, I could only shake my head no.

I could still feel the metal of the gun against my chest. I conjured up visions of gun blasts and blood seeping through my yellow suit. Then I remembered Mother's voice saying, *Don't let bad thoughts live rent-free in your head.* I struggled to push away the terrifying images. I rested my forehead in my hands while tiny spots of light fizzed in my mind's eye. Mr. Rosen stayed close to me with his hand on my shoulder, saying over and over again, "That's all right, Mrs. Coddington, you're safe now."

When I could speak clearly, I explained the details of my misadventure. Mr. Rosen was outraged. He called our local police precinct, but they were not particularly impressed by the story, having more urgent matters to attend to. Frankly, I was relieved not to make a big to-do. Mr. Rosen phoned

American Express, and though I did not know my account number, he managed to convince them to void my card and send out a new one by overnight post. He was concerned that the thief might have my apartment key, but I explained that between the doorman and elevator man, our building was like a fortress. Harold and I never locked our door, and I didn't carry a key.

Mr. Rosen was a calming, attentive presence, and my nerves slowly settled. I was positive I looked frayed from the burst of emotion, so he had one of the stockboys bring me a pressed-powder compact with which I could straighten myself up a bit. Then Mr. Rosen offered his arm and escorted me through the aisles of the shop as if he were leading me into a gala dinner. "Come, Mrs. Coddington," he said. "The first thing you need is a handbag. We have some pretty items up front." I chose a woven straw clutch trimmed in navy, yellow and white grosgrain ribbon that Mr. Rosen said matched my suit quite well—not a serious bag, but the sort of thing that would be fine at the beach club in July. He dropped a small packet of facial tissues into the new purse and asked me what else I might need. I protested that he was overly considerate. I could manage with a pair of magnifying glasses until my optometrist replaced my prescription ones. "Nonsense," he said. "I will not let you out of my sight until you are fully equipped. Now, do you use eye shadow?"

I laughed and felt myself start to relax. Together we tracked down my Misty Rose lipstick and the pale gray eyebrow pencil I always carried. I hesitated before requesting my favorite under-eye concealer. "I don't believe I've ever discussed the contents of my pocketbook with a man," I said. "Really, this is rather intimate knowledge!"

The skin around the corners of Mr. Rosen's eyes wrinkled up, and he said that to stay in business, a pharmacist must always be discreet. I looked for the large round sunglass shape I adored, but Mr. Rosen encouraged me to select a narrower pair. "If you don't mind my saying so, Mrs. Coddington, I find these more flattering for your face." He extracted a twenty-dollar bill from his wallet and asked if it would be enough for the afternoon. I didn't need any money—I was on foot and planned to go straight home—but he insisted and tucked the bill into a change purse that he took from a display stand.

"Well, thank you," I said by the door of the shop. "You have been more of a help and a comfort than you can know." I asked if he'd made a note of my purchases to charge to our account, but he smiled at me and said everything was on the house. He wouldn't listen to a word of my arguments.

"After all, Mrs. Coddington, you and your family have been loyal clients of Madison Chemists for—"

"Oh, please, don't say how long!" Then we both had a laugh. I thanked him again and left.

My mood was so restored by my hour in the pharmacy that I took myself out for a datenut-and-cream-cheese sandwich at the Lexington Luncheonette and even visited Mother in the hospital on the way home. Not that seeing her involves much conversation—she is ninety-four years old, and the coma seems permanent since her last stroke. Her doctor says it's only a matter of time before the rest of her systems fail, but I do like to stop in every couple of days to put fresh flowers by her bedside and change her television channel to CNN from those Spanish melodramas her nurse always watches. God knows, if Mother did ever come to, she'd want to hear immediately what had happened in the world during her absence.

Harold was distressed to see me still in my suit when he came home. With all the drama of the morning, I had forgotten about the opera-board dinner he was to chair. I rushed into my powder-blue chiffon gown and somehow managed to put up my hair. In the car crosstown, Harold asked how my day had been, but I didn't mention the holdup. He was preoccupied with the speech he would give, and I thought it unkind to upset him any more than I already had.

Naturally, Harold performed marvelously at the podium. He thanked the major donors, throwing in witty yet flattering remarks to each one, and he brought us all to tears eulogizing a former board chairman who had passed away during the winter. He looked so distinguished in his dress clothes, white hair combed back from his temples. The spotlight shone on his broad forehead, and I felt proud of him. Dear Harry, I thought. I certainly have been lucky in the husband department. Forty-seven years together, and never in our home, never once, have we raised our voices to each other. You have always been hard-working and generous, even relatively faithful.

I smiled and remembered how I'd gone weeping to Mother when I first became suspicious. She had assured me that some degree of alley-catting about was perfectly normal—something to be expected with a man of Harold Coddington's stature. She advised me to feign complete ignorance, wait it out and devote myself in the meantime to some other activity that might absorb and improve me. I took up bridge lessons with the current national champion until my playing became quite strong, stronger even than Harold's. In the end, I believe he was more vexed about my superiority at bridge than I had been over his little adventures. Anyway, I thought, as I watched Harold and Beverly Sills present a plaque to the widow of the former chairman, that sort of funny business has been over for a long, long time. I left the party that night a happy woman.

The next day I spent half an hour with Oscar Biddle, our attorney, to be sure that my living will was shipshape. "No tubes, Oc," I told him, "no IV, no respirator. If I can't play golf, or if I fail to enchant you with my conversation, then it's time to bury me, do you understand?" He notarized my signature and asked when we would be moving to the beach. I was unsure, with Mother so ill. "We'll come out on weekends, and perhaps Harold will stay the weeks in July and August, but oh, I don't know, he's so helpless without me, I hate leaving him alone."

I returned to the hospital and found Mother with her hair combed in a strange frothy coif that, had she known of it, would have scandalized her. There were also some three-dimensional optical-illusion cards picturing the Ascent of the Virgin and other Roman magic taped to her headboard. I decided to confront the little Spanish-speaking nurse. She was dreadfully kind and took great care of Mother, always washing her and massaging her limbs. I did not want to offend her. But her religious practice was primitive; I often had to unlace a particular string of enameled rosary beads from Mother's folded white fingers. Not that Mother wasn't a devout woman—she had continued to attend church in the summers long after Daddy gave up God for yacht racing. But she was Episcopalian, for heaven's sake! I delicately explained to the girl that her decorations were not of Mother's own creed and might frighten or disorient her if she ever did awaken. Then I slipped down the hall to phone Monsieur Michel and make a hair appointment for Mother, though I warned him to be tactful. "The girl has been so attentive, Michel, even if *santeria* is her forte and not hairdressing."

I left the neurological unit and stopped off at the Lexington Luncheonette for a cup of coffee. Oddly enough, Mr. Rosen was sitting alone in a booth by the window. I had planned to perch on a stool at the counter, but he waved me over. "Please, Mrs. Coddington, won't you join me?" It would have been uncivilized to refuse, given his gallantry of the day before. To tell the truth, I was not unhappy to see him. The visit to Mother had left me feeling a bit low, and any lively company was welcome. Mr. Rosen stood and extended a hand to help me into the seat across from him. I ordered my coffee, and he asked, "Won't you have anything at all to eat?"

"No thanks, Mr. Rosen, I have just come from the hospital, and anyway, now that we are going to the country on weekends and wearing summer things, my figure cannot take another extra ounce."

He smiled and said something charming about my silhouette. Perhaps from someone else in his position the statement might have seemed rude, but I was so disarmed by this gentle man that I laughed like a young girl and began to feel the whole spell of the dreary hospital—and it is the best one in the city—lifting away from me. I looked at Mr. Rosen's face, for I've always looked people straight in the eye, and I noticed how soft his brown eyes appeared under his bifocals and how the creases around his eyelids, though not ordinarily a mark of handsomeness, gave him an expression of calm wisdom and goodwill. And I remarked to myself, What a shame he was widowed so early. Really, he was not the type to become a cranky old man, and a wife could be comfortable with him well into her elder years.

The following week I was walking home from the florist where I had ordered the arrangements for Thursday night's dinner party. As I passed the luncheonette, I saw Mr. Rosen sitting in the same booth by the window, and he tapped his fingers on the glass and motioned me to come in. I chatted with him about my day and my plans for the week. He inquired about Mother's health and asked unusual questions, like what sort of flowers I had ordered and which ones were my favorites. We got into a long discussion about gardening, and he surprised me with his knowledge of heirloom roses.

After the first two encounters, which were entirely by chance, meeting up with Mr. Rosen became a habit. He took his daily break in the luncheonette at three o'clock exactly, and I would drop in on my way back from the hospital or my errands once or possibly twice a week. Soon it didn't feel odd anymore to sit in the window booth for an hour, drinking coffee with my pharmacist. It was something cheerful to do after my visits with Mother. And Mr. Rosen, well, he was a comfort. Not that Harold wasn't. It was always a pleasure when he came home in the evening, but with Mr. Rosen I felt different, not as if I were with a man at all. Surely, I was always aware that he was a man. He was not effeminate, and he behaved in a gentlemanly way toward me. But—how can I say it—I experienced a certain ease in his presence. It was more like sitting with an old friend. Except I'd never had a friendship that felt this way. Maybe it was how I thought being with a dear old friend ought to feel.

The weeks were quiet as the middle of July approached. Our circle had moved out to the country, and Harold and I lived a full social life only on the weekends when we were there also. I was torn, reluctant to deprive him of the best part of the season—those long mornings of golf and the afternoon bridge game at our cabana—yet I felt compelled to stay close to Mother, at least Monday through Thursday. Harold was a sport about our plight. During the days, he went to the office, the poor old dear—I couldn't remember a summer he had actually worked since we were in our thirties—and he took advantage of our isolation in the evenings by rereading all of the Durants' *Story of Civilization*. I did my best to keep him amused at dinner. I had our cook try out new recipes, and I told him funny stories about the various characters who worked at the hospital. I never spoke of my meetings with Mr. Rosen. There was absolutely nothing to hide, but it did not seem possible to explain this unusual friendship to Harold, especially since I had never told him of my holdup in the first place, and by now it would be awkward to mention.

I was beginning to notice things about Mr. Rosen, notice and remember them. Images of him floated into my mind at unlikely moments: standing at the counter in Payard while I ordered a tart for dessert, or as I rode the elevator up to Mother's room. I pictured how he held the tinny coffee-shop fork. It seemed so small in his hand, which was tan with liver spots and tufts of black hair across the top. I had learned the exact pattern of creases around his eyes, crosshatched into squares and rectangles that made a tiny mosaic of skin under his glasses. One Tuesday morning I woke up startled. I had been dreaming of the methodical way in which he cut his piece of pie, and the impression was so vivid that it seemed more real than my own surroundings. I felt as if these images had intruded upon me without my permission—somehow they had become a part of me, part of my mind and my person. More than mere thoughts, they were imprints, and I experienced them like unwelcome caresses. I shuddered, chiding myself for my silliness. Mother once said that any mental distraction could be cured by a good play or exhibit, so I marched straight over to the Metropolitan to see the Chardin show and fill my mind with art and culture rather than visions of my pharmacist's wrinkles.

There was no reason I should have wept that afternoon. Mother was the same as she always was—unconscious but probably comfortable in her bed. I changed the water in her vase and arranged for her to have fresh air. I was quite merry later on, as I sat in the booth at the luncheonette and recounted to Mr. Rosen the events of my past few days: how Betsy Sumner's engagement party for her daughter had come off beautifully on Saturday night; how I'd picked up Coco from the groomer's and within an hour, our cook spilled tomato juice all over the dog's fluffy white coat; how I'd done battle with the floor supervisor on the neurological unit in order to have the window guards unlocked in Mother's room. "She is in a coma, for God's sake," I had told him. "It's not likely that she'll jump from the window!"

Mr. Rosen laughed and agreed that yes, bureaucrats can be so stupidly rigid. Then he looked at me with his kind, velvety eyes and said, "My dear Mrs. Coddington. You are a strong woman. You take all this strain wonderfully well, admirably well." He removed his glasses and pulled a felt cloth from his pants pocket, which he used to wipe the lenses. "Sometimes," he continued, "I'm afraid you take it too well."

I asked what he could possibly mean by that.

"I mean that you are always going around caring for people, looking after them. Who looks after you?"

It was the strangest comment, and at first it made me angry. "Excuse me, Mr. Rosen. I am a fully grown woman. I'm in perfect health. I have two beautiful homes, a lovely family and many friends." It was as if I had to defend myself, which was ridiculous. "Why on earth would I require anyone to look after me?" I stared straight at him. Then I began to weep. "Oh dear," I said. "I think that after my trip to the hospital, your questioning has unnerved me."

He handed me a paper napkin from the dispenser on our table. "I'm sorry," he said softly. "I didn't mean to upset you."

I couldn't stop crying. And I couldn't stop thinking of Mother, alone in that awful hospital bed. "She looks so small," I said.

Mr. Rosen reached across the table and took my hand. He held it between both of his, which were warm and a bit rough. "There, there." He patted my wrist. "There, there, Mrs. Coddington."

We sat that way for a good long time, while I wept and sniffled, dabbing my eyes with the napkin. Eventually, I calmed down, but I did not feel I had regained my composure. I felt like a naughty child who had thrown a tantrum and become still, but only because she was exhausted. Then I said, "What rough hands you have, Mr. Rosen! Rough like a laborer's."

He grinned, patted my wrist one final time, released it and stirred his coffee. "At home I like to build things. I've been refitting my family room with bookshelves, putting together a library. I can't get my car in the garage anymore. It's become a carpentry shop."

"Carpentry! Oh dear, what a funny hobby!"

He laughed, and I laughed, and then he convinced me to

taste his apple pie. It was gluey and oversweet, but I allowed that it was delicious so as not to insult him. He beamed at me with the openness of a happy little boy. Then I felt a strange pang in my stomach, as if I were with someone dangerous. I left the luncheonette as soon as it was polite to excuse myself.

In the morning I went directly to Madison Chemists. "Hello, Mrs. Coddington." Mr. Rosen leaned over the counter with his weight on his palms, like an amorous young man in an old movie. "How can I help you?"

I could not look at his face. I was afraid that if I so much as peeked into his eyes, I would not have the courage to say what needed to be said.

"Oh, Mr. Rosen." I fussed with some tins of black-currant pastilles that sat by the cash register. "I am here to pick up the refills of my prescriptions and two bottles of my husband's hair tonic. I am leaving this afternoon for the country and will not be in town for a while, unless, of course, the situation with Mother becomes grave. I've decided, you see, that my dear Harold needs a vacation more than Mother requires my presence at the hospital. He has been working awfully hard, and lately, I've not attended to him the way that I usually do—we have both been so busy . . ." My voice felt weak.

"I see."

I glanced up and noticed that Mr. Rosen was not smiling anymore. He took his glasses from his nose and polished them. I could hardly bear the discomfort, and I made some trivial comment about the new digital thermometers on display. "I will have your things in a minute," he said and turned back to his shelves.

I told him our driver would fetch them later. "Have a pleasant summer, Mr. Rosen."

"You, too, Mrs. Coddington."

The August days were long and lovely by the seashore. It was a joy to see Harold relax and gain a healthy pink glow about his face. I relished strolling by the edge of the surf or reading a magazine in the shade of our cabana, while children splashed in the pool under the careful watch of their nannies. I co-chaired the ladies' bridge tournament with Puddie Van Cleef, and all of our friends were delighted that Harold and I had rejoined them for the dinner parties and club dances that gobbled up one warm summer evening after the next. For those first few weeks, life felt fresh, soothing and perfect.

I called the hospital every morning to check up on Mother. I didn't trouble with the resident doctors, who could be so arrogant and intentionally obscure; I spoke instead to Mother's nurse when she came on her daily shift. "I just bathed Mrs. Winthrop," she would inform me, or "Mrs. Winthrop is breathing gently today." I made sure I picked out a gift for the girl at the Red Cross auction. And one for Monsieur Michel, who had promised to stop in weekly to do Mother's hair and also remove any holy objects that might have accumulated.

A terrific heat wave set in about the twentieth of August, and even near the beach, it was sultry and humid. We all remained inside the clubhouse and played bridge. Reports came over the television set describing hundred-degree days in the city: Buses and trains were breaking down regularly, and the crime rate had soared. I suddenly found myself thinking of Mr. Rosen again. How was he faring in the heat? Was his home air-conditioned? Where did he even live—certainly not in Manhattan. We had spent so much time together, yet I knew little of his life beyond the pharmacy. Obsession is perhaps too strong a word, but it became a preoccupation of mine to imagine his home and how he spent his evenings. I wondered how his garden was surviving the temperature, which books filled his new shelves and what people he might see—surely such a kind man had friends. I wondered if he continued to walk over to the luncheonette during this oppressive heat, and if perhaps he now drank his coffee iced.

I thought a great deal about Mother and became concerned for her, too. The nurse assured me that Mother's room was well air-conditioned, but honestly, I was not convinced by her report. Who knew which tropical island she came from; her standards could not have been the same as Mother's. My nerves were taut, and my bridge game suffered. Harold observed me fidgeting with my napkin one day over luncheon at the Van Cleefs'. He stopped Puddie in the middle of a sentence to ask if I was not slightly distracted.

I said, "Darling Harry, you are the original sensitive man. Yes, I am a bit out of sorts, thinking of Mother all alone during this dreadful weather. If you don't mind, I think I might take the car into town tomorrow morning, just to peek in on her." My plan surprised even me, and I wondered what I was up to. Harold offered to accompany me, but I refused. "Don't make me worry about you dropping from heat stroke on top of everything else!" Puddie graciously volunteered herself and George as Harold's baby-sitters for the duration of my trip.

The climate in the city was insufferable, but Mother's room was cool and comfortable, as the girl had said. Still, I was glad to have come. This was the first time in all of Mother's long years that she was not spending the summer in Newport. Silly thought, but I wished somehow to console her, even if all I did was bring fresh roses that she could not see. Perhaps she might at least smell them.

After the hospital, I had the car drop me off at Madison Chemists, and I dismissed the driver. I picked out a new toiletries bag at the front of the store, an eye-pencil sharpener in the cosmetics department, and one of those terry-cloth-lined shower caps. Slowly, I made my way back to the pharmacy. As usual, Mr. Rosen was there, looking very tanned against his white pharmacist's coat and the white counter and shelves surrounding him. He smiled at me with his mouth closed, in a way that looked reserved or formal. "Good morning, Mrs. Coddington. I'm surprised to see you in this weather—I hope nothing has turned for the worse with your mother."

I shook my head. "Oh no, she is the same." My voice cracked, and I believe I even blushed, if a woman my age can still do that. "I was just concerned," I continued, "for her comfort during this awful heat. Concerned, and possibly guilty, being so far away. Not that she knows whether I am here with her or in Timbuktu on a camel, and perhaps it is snowing wherever Mother's mind has drifted today." As I spoke this nonsense, I saw Mr. Rosen's shoulders relax and the muscles of his face ease. It even looked as if he might be trying to repress a grin. This infuriated me but made me bold. "Anyway," I said with more poise, "I abandoned my husband in Southampton and came into town because I felt compelled to check up on her," I looked straight into Mr. Rosen's brown eyes, "and on everyone."

Now a strange ruddy color rose in his cheeks, and we stood planted face-to-face, obviously burning up. Abruptly, we both began to laugh, hard, like silly children—silly *old* children, outraged to find ourselves subject to absurd emotions in a Manhattan pharmacy at eleven-thirty in the morning, on a day when the temperature had already reached ninety-seven degrees Fahrenheit.

At last I stopped laughing. "Oh dear." I set my purchases on the counter. I didn't know what else to say. "Would you be kind enough to charge these to my account and have them delivered?"

He looked at me with—how can I say it—tenderness, I believe. "No, Mrs. Coddington. I will not send these. But they will be in my care when I go to the luncheonette this afternoon." And then he smiled so warmly, with his tanned face crinkling all about, that I felt like sobbing.

"Very well." I laid my hand, for a moment, lightly upon his. I turned and left the shop.

The oppressive heat made further errands impossible, yet I did not wish to go home. I returned to the hospital, bought a sandwich and an iced tea in the cafeteria and took my lunch up to Mother's room. There was a 3-D card of the *Pietà* on Mother's nightstand, and reflexively, I went to remove it. But then I thought, *If this is all it takes to bring happiness to the nurse's life, so be it.* I asked her to leave me alone with Mother; I would ring if we needed anything.

I pulled a chair close to Mother's bedside and watched the news while I ate. Then I switched off the television. I took Mother's thin hand in my own, and I wept, tears dropping onto my skirt. Though I knew I would visit the hospital many more times, it felt like this was the day to say farewell. She and I were both leaving the same world, yet we were to travel in different directions. Silently, I apologized for all the ways in which I had disappointed her and all the ways I might fail her still. We sat together in the quiet, Mother and I, in the cool shelter of her room. I stared at the empty television screen as if I expected some new show to come on, and for the first time in my life, I absolutely did not know what would happen next.